Clements R. Markham, Pedro de Cieza de León

The Second Part of the Chronicle of Peru

Clements R. Markham, Pedro de Cieza de León

The Second Part of the Chronicle of Peru

ISBN/EAN: 9783337383244

Printed in Europe, USA, Canada, Australia, Japan

Cover: Foto ©Andreas Hilbeck / pixelio.de

More available books at **www.hansebooks.com**

THE
SECOND PART
OF THE
CHRONICLE OF PERU.

BY

PEDRO DE CIEZA DE LEON.

TRANSLATED AND EDITED,

With Notes and an Introduction,

BY

CLEMENTS R. MARKHAM, C.B., F.R.S.

LONDON:
PRINTED FOR THE HAKLUYT SOCIETY.

MDCCCLXXXIII.

LONDON:

WHITING AND COMPANY, LIMITED, SARDINIA STREET, LINCOLN'S-INN-FIELDS.

COUNCIL

OF

THE HAKLUYT SOCIETY.

TABLE OF CONTENTS.

INDEX.

[In the Index, "i" refers to the volume containing the First Part of the Chronicle of Cieza de Leon; and "ii", to the present volume.]

DEDICATION.

TO

ANDRES AVELINO CACERES

(General of Brigade in the Peruvian Army),

And to his gallant companions in arms, now heroically defending their native country against fearful odds, I dedicate this edition of the narrative of that scholarly soldier, Pedro de Cieza de Leon, who warmly sympathised with the people of the land of the Yncas, advocated their cause, and denounced their wrongs.

The natives of the valley of Xauxa, descendants of the Huancas mentioned by Cieza de Leon, have suffered most cruelly from the inroads of the Chilian soldiery, and on this classic ground the brave Caceres and his little army have striven to protect these people from robbery and outrage. Cieza de Leon mentions a fact relating to the Huancas of the Xauxa valley, which gives us a high estimate of their civilization. The cruelties and robberies of the Spanish conquerors, whose deeds are now outdone by their Chilian imitators, would have led to the complete destruction of the natives if it had not been for the excellent order and concert of their polity. They made an agreement among themselves that if an army of Spaniards passed through any of their districts, and did such damage as would be caused by the destruction of growing crops, by the sacking of houses, and other mischief of still worse kinds, the accountants should keep careful records of the injury done. The accounts were then examined and checked : and if one district had lost more than another, those which had suffered less made up part of the difference; so that the burden was shared equally by all.[1]

It is among the descendants of these Huancas that the Chilians are now committing havoc. With the Peruvians, with the men who are fighting in the noblest of all causes—the defence of their Fatherland—with General Caceres and his companions in arms, must be the hearty sympathies and best wishes of all who hate wrong and love patriotic devotion. Through that devotion, through the sacrifices and self-denials entailed upon the unfortunate people of the land of the Yncas, may be seen those rays of light which break the black cloud now hanging over the country and the race described by Cieza de Leon in the following pages.

May his narrative excite the interest of many readers, and so enlist sympathy for the descendants of that people whose story he tells so well.

[1] See p. 34.

June 1883.

INTRODUCTION.

THE present volume, which has been selected for issue by the Hakluyt Society, contains the Second Part of the *Chronicle of Peru*, by Pedro de Cieza de Leon. The First Part formed one of the Society's volumes for 1864, having been translated from the Antwerp edition of 1554.

When I translated and edited the First Part, no other had been printed. I then had reason to believe that the author completed the second and third parts of his Chronicle, and that one of these parts had come into the possession of Mr. Lenox of New York, in manuscript. I lamented the disappearance of the Second Part, and referred to it as one of the greatest losses that had been sustained by South American literature.[1]

It has now been discovered that the manuscript narrative which Mr. Prescott frequently refers to, in his *History of the Conquest of Peru*, as "*Sarmiento*", and which he considered to be one of the most valuable of his authorities, is in reality the Second Part of the work of Cieza de Leon. Mr. Prescott quotes the title in his critical notice.[2] "*para el Illmo Señor Dn. Juan Sarmiento, Presidente del Consejo Rl. de Indias*", and assumes that this Don Juan Sarmiento

---

[1] Introduction, p. xviii. [2] *History*, i, p. 161.

was the author, who, after having travelled in all parts of Peru and diligently collected information from the Ynca nobles, subsequently became President of the Council of the Indies. In reality, the word *para* means "for", and not "by", and the manuscript is simply addressed to Dr. Sarmiento, who never crossed the Atlantic in his life, and who only held the post of President of the Council of the Indies for twenty months.[1]

Mr. Prescott made much use of both parts, and considered them to be works of great merit. If what he says in praise of the author he supposed to be Sarmiento,[2] is added to what he says of Cieza de Leon,[3] it will at once be seen that the latter, really the only author, is a very important authority indeed.

It is with a feeling of reverential regret that the present editor refers to any mistake, even one so slight as this, of the illustrious American historian. Some of my brightest and happiest memories are of the ten days I spent at Pepperell with Mr. Prescott, when I was on the eve of commencing my studies in the land of the Yncas. He it was who encouraged me to undertake my Peruvian investigations, and to

---

[1] The Spanish editor accounts for Mr. Prescott's mistake by supposing that the person employed to copy the manuscript had written *por* (by) instead of *para* (for). But this is not so, as Mr. Prescott himself quotes the word *para* (i, p. 161). The Spanish editor refers to a life of Sarmiento in the *Historia del Colejio Viejo de San Bartolomé Mayor de la celebre Universidad de Salamanca*, 2d edicion, Primera Parte, p. 336.

[2] *Conquest of Peru*, i, 160-62.   [3] *Ibid.*, ii, 297-99.

persevere in them. To his kindly advice and assistance I owe more than I can say, and to him is due, in no small degree, the value of anything I have since been able to do in furtherance of Peruvian research.

The evidence that the work attributed by Prescott to Sarmiento is in reality the Second Part of the *Chronicle* of Cieza de Leon is quite conclusive. There are no less than ten occasions on which the author of the Second Part (Prescott's " Sarmiento") refers to passages in his First Part, which occur in the First Part of Cieza de Leon.[1] In one place there is a reference in the Second Part to the actual number of the chapter in the First Part.[2] In the Second Part, the author mentions having gone to Toledo to present the First Part of his *Chronicle* to the Prince Don Felipe ;[3] and this statement is equivalent to having signed his name. For only one First Part of a chronicle relating to the Indies was dedicated to the Prince, namely that of Cieza de Leon. The author of the Second Part also mentions having been to Bahaire, near Cartagena, and to the province of Arma—places visited by Cieza de Leon, and mentioned in his First Part.

The manuscript of the Second Part was preserved in the library of the Escurial,[4] in a bad copy dating

---

[1] *Cronica*, ii, pp. 25, 44, 45, 51, 131, 160, 173, 180, 193, 212.

[2] *Ibid.*, ii, p. 212, reference to chapter liii (liv in the incorrectly numbered Antwerp edition) of the First Part. See my Translation, p. 192.   [3] Page 84.

[4] *Biblioteca de Escorial*, códice L, j, 5 from folio 1 to 130 inclusive.

from the middle, or end, of the 16th century. The
first sheet is missing, and the second begins in the
middle of a sentence towards the end of the third
chapter. Thus the two opening chapters and part
of the third are lost.

The text of the Escurial manuscript has been
printed by two accomplished scholars—the Peruvian
Dr. Manuel Gonzalez de la Rosa in 1873 ; and the
Spaniard Don Marcos Jimenez de la Espada at
Madrid in 1880. Both, independently, detected the
mistake of Prescott as soon as they began to examine the text critically. The text was reprinted
by Dr. de la Rosa with scrupulous care; the spelling,
imperfect punctuation, and capricious use of capitals
in the manuscript being very carefully preserved.
But instead of retaining the manuscript numbering
of chapters, Dr. de la Rosa omits the fragment of
chapter iii, and calls the fourth chapter, chapter i.
An edition was printed off by Mr. Trübner, but
soon afterwards Dr. de la Rosa left London for Peru,
without completing the editorial work. So that
this edition of the second part of Cieza de Leon
has never been editorially completed or published,
and remains on Mr. Trübner's hands.

Don Marcos Jimenez de la Espada, to whom the
student of Peruvian history is so much indebted for
other precious editorial work, delayed his publication
of the text of the Second Part of Cieza de Leon,
because he had heard from Don Pascual de Gayan-
gos that the learned Peruvian, Dr. de la Rosa, was
engaged upon the same work. It was not until

1880 that the edition of Espada was published at Madrid.[1] The Spanish editor has corrected the spelling and punctuation, and has supplied many useful notes. Five copies appear to have been made of the Escurial manuscript. One, very carelessly executed, is in the Academy of History at Madrid. The second was in the collection of Lord Kingsborough, from which was copied, through Mr. Rich's agency, the one supplied to Mr. Prescott, which is the third. The fourth and fifth are those from which the versions of Rosa and Espada were printed.

In the Prologue to his First Part, Cieza de Leon announced the plan of his great work :—.

PART I.   The divisions and description of the provinces of Peru.
PART II.   The government, great deeds, origin, policy, buildings, and roads of the Yncas.
PART III. Discovery and conquest of Peru by Pizarro, and rebellion of the Indians.
PART IV. *Book I.*   War between Pizarro and Almagro.
Book II.   War of the young Almagro.
Book III. The civil war of Quito.
Book IV. War of Huarina.
Book V. War of Xaquixaguana.
Commentary I. Events from the founding of the Audience to the departure of the President.
Commentary II. Events to the arrival of the Viceroy Mendoza.

PART I of this very complete Chronicle of Peru was published at Seville in folio, by Martin Clement

---

[1] *Biblioteca Hispano-Ultramarina. Segunda Parte de la Crónica del Perú*, que trata del Señorio de los Incas Yupanquis y de sus grandes hechos y gobernacion, éscrita por Pedro de Cieza de Leon. La publica Márcos Jimenez de la Espada. Madrid, Imprenta de Manuel Gines Hernandez, Libertad, 16 duplicado, bajo, 1880. Pp. 279, and xi of Introduction.

in 1553. A second edition, in duodecimo, was printed at Antwerp by Jean Steeltz in 1554 ;[1] and another independent edition, also at Antwerp and in the same year, by Martin Nucio. In 1555 an Italian translation, by Agostino di Gravalis, appeared at Rome, and was reprinted at Venice by Giordano Ziletti, in 1560. A third Italian version was published at Venice in 1566. An English translation by John Stevens came out in London in 1576. The latest Spanish edition forms part of the second volume of the *Historiadores Primitivos de Indias*, in the *Biblioteca de Autores Españoles* (vol. 26), and is edited by Don Enrique de Vedia. It was published at Madrid in 1853. Lastly, the Hakluyt Society issued a translation in English in 1864.[2]

PART II remained in manuscript until 1873, when the Peruvian editor, and in 1880 the Spanish editor, printed their versions. An English translation is now, for the first time, issued by the Hakluyt Society.

PART III, and *Books I and II* of PART IV, are still in manuscript and inaccessible, but Don M. J. de la Espada knows that they exist and where, although he has not seen them.

Book III of PART IV long remained inedited. The manuscript is in the Royal Library at Madrid,

---

[1] This was the edition used by Prescott ; and by me in translating the First Part for the Hakluyt Society.

[2] Don M. J. de la Espada says of the Hakluyt Society's volume :—" Edicion muy bella. Bien anotada en la parte geográfica y de historia natural, en la historica y biografica con los comentarios de Garcilasso y las decadas de Herrera."

and is in handwriting of the middle of the 16th century. It includes the war of Quito, and is divided into 239 chapters. A copy of this manuscript was included in the collection of Don Antonio de Uguina, on whose death it passed into the possession of M. Ternaux-Compans of Paris. Afterwards Mr. Rich obtained it, and sold it in 1849 to Mr. Lenox of New York for £600. At length this *Book III* of Part IV was printed and edited in 1877, with an interesting and very learned introduction by Don Marcos Jimenez de la Espada.[1]

Books IV and V of PART IV, and the two *Commentaries*, are not known to be in existence; but they were written, for Cieza de Leon refers to them in his Prologue as completed.

Mr. Prescott was mistaken in supposing that Cieza de Leon only completed the First Part.[2] He worked so diligently, and with such ability, and sound judgment, that he was able to finish the whole of the grand work he had projected. He is thus the greatest and most illustrious among the historians of Peru. So that his fate has been peculiarly hard. For more than three centuries his First Part only

---

[1] *Biblioteca Hispano-Ultramarina.* Tercero libro de las Guerras Civiles del Peru, el cual se llama la Guerra de Quito, hecho por Pedro de Cieza de Leon, Coronista de las cosas de las Indias. Madrid, 1877. Prólogo por M. J. de la Espada, pp. cxix. La Guerra de Quito, pp. 176. Apendices, pp. 120.

[2] "The First Part, as already noticed, was alone completed. The author died without having covered any portion of the magnificent ground plan which he had confidently laid out."—*Conquest of Peru,* ii, p. 298.

has been credited to him. His most valuable Second Part, though used and highly appreciated by Mr. Prescott, was attributed to an obscure lawyer who never was out of Spain in his life. One book of his Fourth Part has also at length been edited, but all the rest of his work still remains in manuscript. The accomplished Spanish editor, Don Marcos Jimenez de la Espada, was influenced in his labours and researches by a generous zeal to repair, in some degree, the great injustice which has been done to the memory of Cieza de Leon.

In my Introduction to the First Part, I gave some account of the author, all indeed that could be gathered from the part of his work then accessible; and I said that he was supposed to have been born in Seville.[1] This is an error. The Spanish editor has pointed out the authority for believing that the place of his birth was the town of Llerena in Estremadura.[2] In my former Introduction I suggested

---

[1] So says Fray Buenaventura de Salinas y Cordova, in his *Memorial de las Historias dal Nuevo Mundo Piru* (Lima 1630), but without giving any authority.

[2] Herrera gives Llerena as the birthplace of Cieza de Leon (Dec. vi, lib. vi, cap. 4 ; and Dec. vii, lib. ix, cap. 19). In the latter of these two passages, in the first edition, the word is printed *Erena*, an error which is repeated in the editions of Antwerp and of Gonzalez Barcia. Piedrahita (lib. iv, cap. 2) repeats that Cieza de Leon was a native of Llerena. The town of Llerena is nineteen leagues east of Badajos, at the foot of the Sierra de San Miguel. It was taken from the Saracens in 1241 ; and in 1340 Alfonso XI assembled the Cortes at Llerena. Besides Cieza, it produced the Holguins, and Juan de Pozo, the watchmaker who placed the *giralda* on the tower of Seville.

from the dates, and from the company in which we find him immediately on landing in America, that young Cieza de Leon, then a boy between 13 and 15, sailed from his native land in one of the ships which formed the expeditionary fleet of Don Pedro de Heredia, who had obtained a grant of the government of the region between the river Magdalena and the gulf of Darien. This fleet left Cadiz in 1532, and arrived at Cartagena in 1533. But the Spanish editor has shown that there are difficulties in the way of this conclusion, and Cieza himself is slightly contradictory in the matter of dates. He, however, mentions having seen the treasures of Atahualpa at Seville, when they arrived from Caxamarca,[1] which was in 1534. Señor de le Espada, therefore, concludes that our author did not sail for America until 1534, and that he embarked with the ships of Rodrigo Duran, which anchored at Cartagena in November 1534. At all events he was in San Sebastian de Buena Vista in 1537,[2] and was with the first Spaniards who opened a road from the north to the south sea. Thence he accompanied Pedro Vadillo in his expedition up the valley of the Cauca to Cali, and then joined Jorge de Robledo, who established towns in this Cauca valley, and conquered some of the cannibal tribes. It was at this time, in 1541, when at Cartago in the Cauca valley, that our author conceived a strong desire to write an account of the strange things that

---

[1] See my Translation, p. 335.   [2] My Translation, p. 40.

were to be seen in the new world.[1] "Oftentimes when the other soldiers were reposing, I was tiring myself by writing. Neither fatigue, nor the ruggedness of the country, nor the mountains and rivers, nor intolerable hunger and suffering, have ever been sufficient to obstruct my two duties, namely, writing, and following my flag and my captain without fault." In 1547 he joined the President Gasca in his march to Cuzco, and was present at the final rout of Gonzalo Pizarro. After a residence at Cuzco he undertook a journey southwards to Charcas, under the special auspices of Gasca, and with the sole object of learning all that was worthy of notice. Returning to Lima he finished his First Part on September 8th, 1550. He says he was then thirty-two years of age, and had passed seventeen of them in the Indies.

The Second Part was also nearly completed before Cieza de Leon left Peru, because he mentions having shown most of it to two learned judges at Lima, Dr. Bravo de Saravia and the Licentiate Hernando de Santillan. The latter was himself the author of a valuable work on the government of the Yncas,

---

[1] Mr. Robert Blake White, who has travelled in the valley of the Cauca, read an interesting paper on the "Central Provinces of Colombia", at the meeting of the Royal Geographical Society on February 26th, 1883. He afterwards read the First Part of the Chronicle of Cieza de Leon, and was struck by the accuracy with which the soldier-historian described that same region which Mr. Blake White travelled over more than three hundred years afterwards. The English explorer was much interested in the perusal of the work of his Spanish predecessor.

which also long remained in manuscript. It was first printed in Madrid in 1879, having been edited by Don Marcos Jimenez de la Espada. From incidental notices in the Second Part, we learn how diligently young Cieza de Leon collected information respecting the history and government of the Yncas, after he had written his accurate yet picturesque description of the country in his First Part. He often asked the Indians what they knew of their condition before the Yncas became their lords.[1] He carefully examined the temple of Cacha, and inquired into the traditions concerning it, from the intelligent native governor of an adjacent village.[2] In 1550 he went to Cuzco with the object of collecting information, and it was arranged by Juan de Saavedra, the Corregidor of that city, that one of the surviving descendants of the great Ynca Huayna Ccapac, an intelligent and learned native named Cayu Tupac, should confer with him. At the very time when Cieza de Leon was diligently studying the history of the Yncas under the guidance of this Peruvian " Pundit", the young Ynca Garcilasso de la Vega, then eleven years of age, was at school in the same old city of Cuzco, learning Latin under the good Canon Cuellar. The two historians must often have seen each other, the little half-caste boy playing in the streets with his schoolfellows, and the stately young Spanish soldier studying carefully with his noble Ynca friend. Cieza de Leon explains the

[1] Page 2.   [2] Page 7.

plan of his Second Part, which was, first to review the system of government of the Yncas, and then to narrate the events of the reign of each sovereign. He weighs conflicting evidence, and gives the version which appears to him to be nearest the truth, sometimes also adding the grounds of his decision. He spared no pains to obtain the best and most authentic information; and his sympathy with the conquered people, and generous appreciation of their many good and noble qualities, give a special charm to his narrative.

Cieza de Leon is certainly one of the most important authorities on Ynca history and civilization, whether we consider his peculiar advantages in collecting information, or his character as a conscientious historian. His remarks respecting the Ynca roads and system of posts, on the use of the *quipus*, on the system of colonists, and on the ceremonial songs and recitations to preserve the memory of historical events, are of the first importance. He bears striking evidence of the historical faculty possessed by the learned men at the court of the Yncas. After saying that, on the death of a sovereign, the chroniclers related the events of his reign to his successor, he adds:—" They could well do this, for there were among them some men with good memories, sound judgments, and subtle genius, and full of reasoning power, as we can bear witness who have heard them even in these our days."[1]

Students owe much to the labours of Don Marcos

[1] Page 32.

Jimenez de la Espada. He has not only edited the text of the Second Part of Cieza de Leon, and his *War of Quito*, but also the hitherto inedited narratives of Betanzos, Molina, Salcamayhua, Santillan, and an anonymous work, all of great importance with reference to the history and civilization of the Yncas. These additions to our knowledge are sufficient to show us how much there is to learn before anything approaching to a correct appreciation of this interesting subject can be attained. The future historian who will at last achieve this task, must be intimately acquainted with every part of the Yncarial empire, must be a thorough Quichua scholar, must have closely studied all early Spanish writers, and must possess the critical faculty to enable him to assign its proper weight to the varied evidence given by many different authorities. The present useful labour of editing and indexing will prepare the way for the future work. It is the accumulation, sorting, and preparation of the materials with which the noble edifice will some day be built.

The Index of the present volume is classified on the same principle as those in the volumes of Garcilasso de la Vega, Acosta, Molina, Salcamayhua, Avila, and Polo de Ondegardo. The student is thus able to see, without trouble, the Quichua words and the names of places and persons which are mentioned by each author. His studies will in this way be much facilitated, especially if he undertakes the task of weighing the respective value of facts and opinions given by different writers. Such an investigation is one essential step towards the comprehension of the history and civilization of the Yncas. A more important inquiry refers to the assignment of traditions, customs, beliefs, and words to the different races which were comprehended in the Yncarial empire. But this can only be attempted by students of the native languages. It is from Peru itself—from learned and painstaking Peruvian scholars—that we must look for future real progress in this most interesting field of research. Republican Peru has already produced many eminent writers who have devoted their talents to historical studies, and to the elucidation of the archæology and philology of their native land. The names of Rivero, Paz Soldan, Palma, Zegarra, Barranca, Mujica, and others, at once occur to the mind. Peru, in her undeserved misfortunes, has shown that her sons can fight bravely for their beloved fatherland. In literature, many of her sons have shed lustre on their country's history. In no christian land is there warmer family affection; in none is there truer and more cordial hospitality. Those who know Peru best, most deeply regret her misfortunes, and most heartily desire her future welfare.

THE ANCIENT YNCA DRAMA.

THE reference of Cieza de Leon to the songs and
recitations at the court of the Yncas suggests the
question of the existence among the ancient Peruvians of a drama, or system of representing historical and other events by means of dialogues.
This, therefore, seems a suitable opportunity for
examining what light is thrown on the question in
the works which, in a translated form, have been
issued by the Hakluyt Society; and for considering
the most reasonable conclusion to be derived from
the materials now within our reach.

At page 32 of the present volume, Cieza de Leon
says that the most learned among the people were
selected to make known historical events by songs
and recitations, which were handed down from
memory. This is the germ of dramatic representation, which might be expected to attain fuller de-
velopment; and that it did so is clear from the
evidence of other historians. Garcilasso de la Vega
says:—"The *Amautas*, or philosophers, were not
wanting in ability to compose comedies and tragedies,
which were represented before their kings on solemn

festivals. The subject matter of the tragedy always related to military deeds, triumphs, and victories, or to the grandeur of former kings and of other heroic men. The arguments of the comedies were on agriculture and familiar household subjects. All the plays were on decorous and important topics, the sentences being such as befitted the occasion. They understood the composition of long and short verses, with the right number of syllables in each. They did not use rhymes in the verses, but all were blank."[1] The native author, Salcamayhua, also bears witness to the existence of an ancient drama, and even gives the Quichua names of four different kinds of plays. "In the festival they represented plays called *añay sauca*,[2] *hayachuca*,[3] *llama-llama*,[4] and *hañamsi*."[5] That the memory of the old dramatic lore was preserved, and handed down after the Spanish conquest, is proved by the sentence pronounced on the rebels at Cuzco in 1781, by the Judge Areche. It prohibited "the representation of dramas, as well as all other festivals which the Indians celebrated in memory of their Yncas."[6] Dr. Justiniani, a descendant of the Yncas, who was eighty-five when I knew him, in 1853, told me that he could remember having seen, when a very little

---

[1] Vol. i, p. 194.

[2] *Añay*, interjection of praise ; *sauca*, joy, pleasure.

[3] A word referring to some kind of head-dress.

[4] Very brutish. Probably a farce. [5] Tragic.

[6] *Coleccion de obras y documentos por Don Pedro de Angelis*, vol. v (Buenos Ayres, 1836-37).

boy, a Quichua tragedy acted by Indians in the town of Tinta.[1]

The Spanish priests took advantage of this aptitude of the Indians for dramatic representation, and composed religious plays in the Quichua language, in imitation of the *Autos Sacramentales* then in vogue.   Garcilasso says,—"The Jesuits composed comedies for the Indians to act, *because they knew that this was the custom in the time of the Yncas.*" He mentions three such plays,[2] and adds, "the Indian lads repeated the dialogues with so much grace, feeling, and correct action that they gave universal satisfaction and pleasure; and with so much plaintive softness in the songs, that many Spaniards shed tears of joy at seeing their ability and skill.   From that time the Spaniards disabused themselves of the opinion that the Indians were dull, barbarous, and stupid."

Several of these religious plays were written by the Spanish priests in the Quichua language, for the people to perform at great festivals, and they of course bear unmistakeable evidence of their Spanish origin.   I possess two of these plays.   One is by Dr. Lunarejo, a native of Cuzco, and a celebrated Quichua scholar, who flourished in the eighteenth century.   It is entitled *Comedia famosa del pobre mas rico*, and is on the plan of the "Autos" of

---

[1] Padre Francisco Ituri also speaks of the " Quichua dramas transmitted to our day by an unbroken tradition."—*Carta critica sobre " La Historia de America de Juan B. Muñoz"* (Rome, 1797).

[2] Vol. i, pp. 203-204.

Lope de Vega and Calderon. The other is anonymous and appears to be of earlier date. The title is *Usca Paucar, Auto Sacramental el Patrocinio de Maria.*

We thus have evidence that the Yncas cultivated the drama in ancient times; that some of the plays were handed down and were acted as late as 1781; and that the Spanish priests, finding that the Peruvians possessed traditional aptitude for dramatic performances, turned this talent to account in the inculcation of religious dogma. It might, therefore, naturally be expected that one or more of the ancient Ynca plays, as distinguished from the religious "Autos" of Spanish times, would have been preserved. It has long been known that at least one such drama does exist, under the title of *Ollantay*, and Quichua scholars concur in the belief that it is really of ancient origin, and that it dates from pre-Spanish times.

The drama of *Ollantay*, as it now exists, was arranged for representation, divided into scenes, and supplied with stage directions in Spanish times; but competent Quichua students believe that most of the dialogues, speeches, and songs date from a period before the conquest; and that consequently it is an Ynca drama. The manuscript copies are probably numerous, some carelessly made by ignorant scribes, and containing modern words in substitution of what may have been illegible in the originals. But others are older and more correct versions, and these alone should be referred to in discussing the question of the date of this composition. A really critical text has not, however, been hitherto established, from which all modern interpolations have been excluded, and the readings in the most authentic and oldest versions alone retained.

The drama was first brought to notice by Don Manuel Palacios, in the *Museo Erudito*, a periodical published at Cuzco in 1837. The learned Peruvian mineralogist and antiquary, Don Mariano Eduardo de Rivero,[1] in his work entitled *Antiguedades Peruanas*, gave two specimens from it, in Quichua and Spanish. Señor Rivero says that copies of *Ollantay*, written in the sixteenth and seventeenth centuries, are preserved in private libraries at Cuzco.[2] The whole text was first printed by Dr. von Tschudi at the end of his Quichua Grammar, but without a translation, in 1853.[3] The manuscript used by the learned German was copied from one preserved in the Dominican monastery at Cuzco by one of the monks, between 1840 and 1845, for the artist Ruggendas of Munich, who gave it to Dr. von Tschudi, the original being much damaged and in parts illegible.

In April 1853 I had the opportunity of examining and transcribing a version of *Ollantay*, which, I was informed, contained the purest text. It belonged to

---

[1] *Antiguedades Peruanas por Mariano Eduardo de Rivero y Juan Diego de Tschudi* (Viena, 1851), p. 116.

[2] *Ibid.*, pp. 116, 117.

[3] *Die Kechua Sprache*, von J. J. von Tschudi (Wien, 1853), pp. 71-110.

Dr. Don Pablo Justiniani, the aged priest of the village of Laris, in the heart of the eastern Andes.[1] His father, Dr. Justo Pastor Justiniani, had copied it from the original manuscript belonging to Dr. Don Antonio Valdez, the priest of Sicuani in 1780, and the friend of the unfortunate Ynca Tupac Amaru. Dr. Valdez died in the year 1816. He is said to have been the first to reduce the drama to writing, and to arrange it for the stage,[2] but this is clearly an error, as there is a manuscript of 1730, and others dating from the previous century, according to Rivero. The manuscript of Valdez is, however, one of great value, as it preserves all the original forms, and the fame of the owner as a Quichua scholar is

---

[1] He was a son of Dr. Justo Pastor Justiniani, a surgeon, by Doña Manuela Simancas Cataño, a lineal descendant of Hualpa Tupac Ynca Yupanqui, one of whose daughters was the mother of Garcilasso Ynca de la Vega the historian. Dr. Justo Pastor's father was Don Nicolo Ambrosio Justiniani, his grandfather Don Luis Justiniani, his great-grandfather also Don Luis of Seville, whose parents belonged to the Genoese family of Justiniani, descended from the Emperor Justinian. This first Don Luis Justiniani came to Peru and married Doña Catalina Ortiz de Orue, whose father, Don Pedro Ortiz de Orue, a Biscayan, was one of the first conquerors, and whose mother was the Princess Tupac Usca, daughter of the Ynca Manco Ccapac II.

[2] The Quichua drama of *Ollantay* was reviewed in a periodical published at Cuzco in 1837, called the *Museo Erudito*, Nos. 5 to 9. The editor, Don Manuel Palacios, says that the story was handed down by immemorial tradition, but that the drama was written by Dr. Valdez. The editor had inquired of Don Juan Hualpa, a noble Curaca of Belem in Cuzco, and of the Curacas of San Sebastian and San Blas, near Cuzco, who agreed in their account of the tradition, which was that the rebellion of Ollantay arose from the abduction of an *aclla* or virgin of the Sun.

some guarantee for its accuracy. In 1853 it was in the possession of Don Narciso Cuentas of Tinta, the nephew and heir of Dr. Valdez. Another copy taken from the Valdez manuscript, was in possession of Dr. Rosas, the priest of Chinchero near Cuzco. I carefully collated the Justiniani and Rosas copies. In the year 1871 I published the text of my copy of the Justiniani version, with an attempt at a literal English translation.[1] But in three or four passages I adopted the reading of Von Tschudi's version, and in all I was wrong. I should, as I have since convinced myself, have adhered closely to the Justiniani text. In this text, however, there are several additions inserted by a later hand when the drama was arranged for the stage. These. I placed in brackets.

In 1873 the Peruvian scholar, Dr. Don Manuel Gonzalez de la Rosa, informed me that he had in his possession the manuscripts of Dr. Justo Sahuaraura Ynca, Archdeacon of Cuzco, and a descendant of Paullu, the younger son of the great Ynca Huayna Ccapac. Among them is a version of the drama of *Ollantay*, which Dr. de la Rosa considers to be authentic and very accurate. This text has not hitherto been published.

Don José S. Barranca, in 1868, published an ex-

---

[1] *Ollanta, an ancient Ynca Drama*, translated from the original Quichua. By Clements R. Markham, C.B. (Trübner, 1871.) Pp. 128, with introduction and notes. My translation, owing to my imperfect knowledge of the language, contained numerous mistakes, which have been duly pointed out by Zegarra, a native of the country, in his work published subsequently.

cellent Spanish translation, chiefly from the text of Von Tschudi, now called the Dominican text. It is preceded by an interesting introduction, and the author announced that he was preparing for the press a carefully edited Quichuan text, but I am not aware that this has yet seen the light.[1] In 1876 the Peruvian poet, Don Constantino Carrasco, published, in Lima, a version of the drama of *Ollantay* in verse, paraphrased from the translation of Barranca. It is preceded by a critical introduction from the pen of the accomplished Peruvian writer, Don Ricardo Palma, who expressed an opinion that the drama was composed after the Spanish conquest.

In 1874 the enthusiastic Peruvian student of the language of the Yncas, Dr. José Fernandez Nodal, printed the Quichua text with a Spanish translation in parallel columns. This version has several different readings.[2]

In 1875 Dr. von Tschudi published a second text of *Ollantay*, at Vienna, with a translation. His new version, like the first, is mainly from the Dominican

[1] " *Ollanta o' sea la severidad de un Padre y la clemencia de un Rey*, drama dividido en tres actos, traducido del Quichua al Castellano, cos notas diversas, por José S. Barranca." (Lima, 1868.) Pp. 16 and 71.

[2] "*Los vinculos de Ollanta y Cusi Kcuyllor, Drama en Quichua*. Obra compilada y espurgada con la version Castellana al frente de su testo por el Dr. José Fernandez Nodal, Abogado de los tribunales de justicia de la Republica del Peru : bajo los auspicios de La Redentora Sociedad de Filantropos para mejorar la suerte de los Aborijenes Peruanos." (Ayacucho, en el deposito del Autor.) Dr. Nodal commenced, but never completed, an English translation.

text, but partly from another manuscript which bears the date " La Paz, June 18th, 1735".[1] This important date proves that Dr. Valdez was not the author, as supposed by the editor of the *Museo Erudito*, but merely the possessor of one of the best manuscripts.[2]

Don Gavino Pacheco Zegarra published the text of *Ollantay* at Paris, in 1878; his version being taken from a manuscript found among the books of his great-uncle, Don Pedro Zegarra. He added a free translation, and numerous valuable notes. The work of Zegarra is by far the most important that has appeared on this subject; for the accomplished Peruvian has the great advantage of knowing Quichua from his earliest childhood. To this advantage, not possessed by any previous writer, he unites extensive learning, literary ability, and very considerable critical sagacity. He is fully convinced of the antiquity of the drama.[3]

In his *Races Aryennes*, Don Vicente Fidel Lopez

[1] "*Ollanta*. Ein Altperuanisches Drama aus der Kechuasprache. Ubersetzt und commentirt von J. J. von Tschudi." (Wien, 1875.) 4to., pp. 220.

[2] Lopez also tells us that his father was a personal friend of Dr. Valdez, and never heard that the learned Quichua scholar was the author of *Ollantay*. On the contrary, he believed that the drama was very ancient. Mariano Moreno, another intimate friend of Dr. Valdez, bears the same testimony. *Races Aryennes*, p. 325.

[3] *Collection Linguistique Américaine*. Tome iv. " Ollantaï, drama en vers Quechuas du temps des Incas : traduit et commenté." Par Gavino Pacheco Zegarra. Paris : Maisonneuve et Cie., 25, Quai Voltaire, 1878, pp. clxxiv and 265. At the end there is a vocabulary o all the words in the text of *Ollantay*.

refers to the drama of *Ollantay*, and discusses the meaning of the word. The editors and critics to whom I have referred, all being students of the Quichua language, have come to the conclusion that *Ollantay* is an ancient Ynca drama. Some of them, including myself, arrived at this conclusion after long study and much hesitation.[1] The following is the argument of the drama. Ollantay, General of Anti-Suyu, was deeply enamoured of the princess Cusi-Ccoyllur, the chief beauty of the court of the Ynca Pachacutec. In vain the High Priest, Uillac-Umu, endeavoured to dissuade him, and even performed a miracle to divert him from his illegal love. Pachacutec, the Ynca, rejected the suitor for his daughter's hand, and Ollantay rose in rebellion, occupying the great fortress, consisting of colossal ruins, which has ever since been called Ollantay-tampu. Meanwhile, Cusi Ccoyllur gave birth to a child which was named Yma Sumac ("how beautiful"). For this transgression the princess was immured in a dungeon in the Aclla Huasi, or convent of Sacred Virgins, for ten years. Pachacutec died, and the sceptre passed to his son Ynca Yupanqui.

---

[1] In my book, *Cuzco and Lima*, 1853, written when I was twenty-two, immediately after transcribing the Justiniani version, I assumed the antiquity of the drama. But in my later work, *Travels in Peru and India* (1862), I expressed a doubt, and inclined to the opinion that Dr. Valdez was the author (Note, p. 138). A subsequent detailed and critical study of the text obliged me to revert to my former belief that *Ollantay* was, in the main, a composition of Ynca origin, dating from before the conquest. All I have since read has confirmed me in this opinion.

Ollantay was at length conquered by a stratagem. Concealing his army in a neighbouring ravine, the general Rumi-ñaui came to the stronghold of the rebels, and appeared before Ollantay covered with blood. He declared that he had been cruelly treated by the Ynca, and that he desired to join the insurrection. Encouraging the insurgents to celebrate a festival with drunken orgies, he admitted his own troops and captured the whole party, including Ollantay. Next there is a touching dialogue between Yma Sumac and one of the virgins, who allows her to visit her mother in the dungeon. Finally the great rebel is pardoned by the magnanimous Ynca, and the unfortunate princess is restored to the arms of her lover. One of the characters, a facetious servant lad, named Piqui Chaqui, supplies the comic vein which runs through the piece.

There are ample proofs of the antiquity of the tradition, and that the name of Ollantay was known in the days of the Yncas, and was applied to the famous ruins near Cuzco. Father Cristobal de Molina, a very high authority, writing in 1580, mentions Ollantay-tampu in connection with a curious sacrificial ceremony.[1] Salcamayhua, a writer of the seventeenth century, also mentions Ollantay.[2] The name, therefore, was well known before the Spanish conquest.[3] The name of Rumi-ñaui, which means

---

[1] See p. 51.   [2] P. 116.

[3] Don Vicente Lopez suggests the following derivation for the name of Ollantay. The second part, *Antay*, signifies "of the Andes", anything belonging to the Andes. *Oll* would be a cor-

"stone-eye", as that of the general who, by the stratagem of mutilating his face, deceived Ollantay, is not uncommon in Ynca history. A general of Atahualpa had the same name. It is a curious fact, as corroborative of this part of the story, that in 1837 an Indian presented to Don Antonio Maria Alvarez, then Prefect of Cuzco, an ancient earthen drinking vessel, moulded into the shape of a man's head and bust. He said that it had been handed down in his family for generations, as the likeness of Rumi-ñaui. The person represented must have been a general, from the *masccapaycha* or ornament on the forehead, and wounds are cut on the face in accordance with the argument of the drama.

But the chief reasons for assigning a date before the Spanish conquest to the speeches and dialogues of *Ollantay*, have reference to the internal evidence. Throughout the piece there is not the remotest

ruption of *Ull* or *Uill*. The correct form would be *Uill—Antay* or *Uilla Antay*. *Uilla* means a legend, tradition, or history, *The Legend of the Andes*. Several of the manuscripts have *Apu-Ollantay*, *Apu*, meaning chief, *The Legend of the Chief of the Andes*."

Barranca proposes *Ulla* as a derivative of *Ullu*, " the power of love." *Ccahuari-Ullanta*, as an expression of admiration.

Nodal thinks that *Olla* is really *Colla*, the *c* having suffered elision, that the *n* is the pronoun for the third person, and *ta* the accusative. He translates *Ollanta* as " her lover", with reference to Cusi-coyllur.

Dr. de la Rosa says that Lopez is mistaken in his etymology, that the suggestion of Barranca is more plausible ; but that he thinks he has himself hit upon a more rational derivation. He has not, however, yet given it to the world.

Zegarra rejects all these derivations.

allusion to Christianity, an impossible phenomenon if the drama had been written in Spanish times, like the comedy of Dr. Lunarejo and the *Usca-paucar*. It contains songs of indubitable antiquity, and in use among the purest Quichua people. The language is archaic; there are many words which have long disappeared from the spoken Quichua, and are now only found in the earliest vocabularies. The grammatical forms, such as *cca* instead of *pa* for the genitive, are ancient. The state of society represented in the drama is entirely Pagan, without a sign of Spanish contact. The metre is octo-syllabic, like that of the Ynca song preserved by Blas Valera, and is the same as the most ancient verses in the collection of Dr. Justiniani. In the early and pure copies there is not an allusion to anything, or any animal, introduced by Europeans. All arguments must of course be based on the most authentic text, and not on later copies into which many errors have crept, such as the substitution of words like *misi* (a cat), and *asna* (a donkey), corrected in another copy to *llama*, for the original word, in both cases, *atuc* (a fox).

In the final decision of a question of this kind, it is always an advantage to have an able antagonist who will take the trouble to state all that can be said against the generally received opinion. In the present case the "Devil's Advocate" is no less a person than General Don Bartolomé Mitré, the ex-President of the Argentine Republic. General Mitré maintains that the drama of *Ollantay* is entirely of

Spanish origin, and that it was written in modern times.[1] His opinion is not to be despised; for he is evidently a man of extensive reading, and is possessed of critical insight of a high order. But his knowledge of the Quichua language and of the Spanish authors who wrote in the first century after the conquest of Peru is limited, as will presently appear. Nevertheless, the accomplished general and statesman would no doubt have proved his case if it had been possible. The facts, however, are too numerous, and too closely arrayed against him. His attack was well planned and gallantly delivered, but it has utterly failed.[2]

The General's first assault is made upon the evidence of the existence of dramatic compositions among the Yncas. Garcilasso de la Vega is declared to be the sole authority, and he is unceremoniously set aside as unworthy of credit. Cieza de Leon and

---

[1] *Ollantay. Estudio sobre el drama Quechua.* Por Bartolomé Mitré, publicada en la *Nueva Revista* de Buenos Ayres. (Buenos Ayres, 1881.) Pp. 44.

[2] Bartolomé Mitré was born on June 26th, 1821, and in early life was several years in Peru and Chile as an officer and journalist. Returning to Buenos Ayres, he distinguished himself as an orator in the Representative Assembly, and was Minister of War in 1859. In 1860 he was appointed Governor of Buenos Ayres, and was promoted to the rank of General. On September 17th, 1860, he defeated General Urquiza in the battle of Pavon, and soon afterwards signed a treaty with him. On October 5th, 1862, he was elected President of the Argentine Republic, and held that office with credit to himself and benefit to his country for six years. He is an able and enlightened statesman, as well as an accomplished scholar. General Mitré is the author of a *Life of General Belgrano* and other works.

Acosta are then triumphantly referred to as being absolutely silent on the subject. But General Mitré had evidently only read the first part of Cieza de Leon, and was still ignorant of the contents of the present volume. He was equally ignorant of the work of Salcamayhua, where the names of four different kinds of dramatic compositions are given. There is, quite independently of the positive statement of Garcilasso, ample evidence of the existence of a drama of some kind in the time of the Yncas.

His next point is that *Ollantay* is throughout, in general form and minute details, a Christian and cavalieresque play *de capa y espada*, such as those of Lope de Vega and Calderon. Mr. Ticknor says that *comedias de capa y espada* excluded those dramas in which royal personages appear; their main and moving principle is gallantry; the story is almost always involved and intriguing; and accompanied with an underplot and parody on the characters and adventures of the principal parties, formed out of those of the servants and other inferior personages.[1] *Ollantay* is a historical play including royal personages; the main and moving principle is not gallantry of the *capa y espada* type, the story is simple and not intriguing, and it is not accompanied with an underplot. So that the Quichua drama is not only unlike a Spanish *comedia de capa y espada*, but it would be difficult to find two classes of compositions, both being dra-

----

[1] *Ticknor*, ii, p. 167.

matic, which are more completely distinct from each other.

Next, General Mitré objects that the sentiments prevailing in *Ollantay* are pride of caste, conjugal fidelity, military spirit, filial love, humanity to the vanquished, horror of polygamy, royal magnanimity, which are proper to European civilisation, but opposed to all that is known of Ynca social life. Yet pride of caste is described, by nearly all writers on the subject, as a noteworthy characteristic of the Ynca family. There are many touching stories told of conjugal fidelity and filial love among the Peruvians by writers contemporaneous with the conquest; and I am tempted to relate one of these stories at the end of the present critical notice. The military spirit was sedulously cultivated by the Yncas, who were always engaged in new conquests. The exercise of magnanimity and of humanity to the conquered was constantly inculcated, and was a part of the established policy of the Yncas, as we are told by nearly all the early writers. Polygamy is nowhere spoken of with horror in *Ollantay*. All the sentiments enumerated by General Mitré as peculiar to European civilisation, are those which went towards the formation of the best part of the Ynca character, and which would naturally be met with in a Quichua drama.

The next objection is that rebellion is approved in the drama of *Ollantay*, and that such countenance would be impossible at a despotic court like that of the Yncas. The remark applies equally to the court of Spain. It may be admitted that the encouragement of rebellion as a principle would not be tolerated unless it eventually redounded to the credit of the sovereign. Successful rebellion was not unknown in Ynca history, and Yupanqui Pachacutec himself, the sovereign of the play, deposed his brother Urco, according to Cieza de Leon. That story would not be heard with displeasure. Nor would that of *Ollantay*, where the rebel is subdued, and where the magnanimity of the sovereign is celebrated.

The whole of the arguments of the General, based on internal evidence afforded by words and passages in the play, may be set aside, because none of the words upon which he relies as evidence of Spanish origin are to be found in the true version. The true version must be considered as that which excludes all words and passages which are not common to *all* the older manuscripts. On this principle all the words relied upon by the General are corrupt readings which have crept in through the carelessness of copiers.[1]

---

[1] The points raised by General Mitré may, however, be enumerated and disposed of in a foot-note :—

I. He discusses the words *huañuy ychunantin*, or "death with his scythe". The word *ychuna* means an instrument for cutting *ychu* (grass). General Mitré argues that the idea of death with a scythe is exclusively European. But the word does not occur in the Rosas version, although I printed it by mistake in my book. Nodal has *ychuspa*, which is quite a different word.

II. The High Priest performs a miracle by squeezing water out of a flower. Ollantay exclaims it would be easier to squeeze it from a rock. General Mitré says that the idea must have been

General Mitré objects that the High Priest alludes to the broken thread of destiny, which is a strictly Greek image. He misunderstands the passage. The High Priest compares the consequence of the act, which will bring destruction on Ollantay, not with the thread of destiny entangled and severed, but with the wool and frame of a native weaving machine overturned and broken, a natural and indigenous figure suggested by things often before the speaker's own eyes. The remainder of the General's attack is occupied in efforts to find traces of old world ideas in *Ollantay*, most of his analogies being very far-fetched. There is a *yaravi* or song, describing the beauty of the heroine, which the General compares with the Song of Solomon.

suggested by the miracle of Moses making a fountain flow from a rock. It is really a play upon words, involving an essentially Quichuan idea. The word in the Rosas version is not rock, but brick. *Ttica* is a flower, and *tica* a brick. The general could not have hit upon a passage which is more certainly of native origin.

III. General Mitré refers to the words *misi* (cat), *asna* (ass), and *llama* occurring, and considers their appearance as a proof of Spanish origin. But all are the errors of copyists. In the true version the word *atoc* (a fox), takes the place of those words in every instance.

IV. The General further maintains that the interjection *ay !* which occurs fifteen times in the Dominican text, is not Quichuan, but Spanish, and is an indisputable proof of Spanish origin. But another manuscript text has *nay !* and *anay*, which are good Quichuan interjections.

V. There is an allusion to an owl on the roof as a warning of death, which General Mitré considers to be an anachronism. This is not the case. It is alluded to as a popular superstition by the Council of Lima in 1583.

The only resemblance is that both describe personal beauty by comparisons with the beauties of nature, and this is common to nearly all poetry. But General Mitré, by using Zegarra's somewhat free translation, attributes figures to the song which it does not contain, such as a " countenance white and transparent as alabaster, bosoms as white as pieces of ice, cheeks like roses fallen on snow, eyebrows like bows sending forth burning and slaughter - dealing arrows, fingers like bolls of opening cotton." There is nothing of all this in the authentic text. In the real song all the similes are strictly and essentially Quichuan. Her forehead is compared to *Quilla*, the moon ; her eyes, not to arrows, but to two suns ; her eyebrows to rainbows, the insignia of the Yncas. Her tresses are black, mixed with gold, just as the plaited hair of an Ynca princess is represented in an ancient picture at Cuzco. The bloom of her cheek is compared with the *achancaray*, a red flower peculiar to Peru ; her bosoms, not to snow, but to the *utcu* swelling out of the bolls, a simile which is also essentially Peruvian. These figures show that the *yaravi* could not possibly have been composed anywhere but in the land where the *achancaray* and the *utcu* flourish within sight of the snows of the Andes. General Mitré objects to a copper-coloured beauty being praised for her fairness, and to her skin being compared with snow. The Ynca prin-cesses, as we know from some ancient pictures and descriptions, were naturally much fairer than the common people, and this striking difference would as naturally lead to fairness of skin being prized, celebrated, exaggerated, and, by a poetical licence, compared with the fairest thing in the Peruvian landscape.

Still referring to an erroneous reading, General Mitré objects that the Ynca says :—"Take this ring in thy hand, that thou mayest never forget that it is thy duty to show clemency to all. Rise, thou art a hero,"—which, he suggests, must be an idea taken from arming knights in the middle ages. Possibly ; but the Ynca never makes such a speech in the authentic text[1] of *Ollantay*. He says:—"Receive this *head dress*, that thou mayest command my army, and this arrow, that I destine for you." The presentation of a head-dress is a peculiarly Yncarial ceremony, and this passage is one among many which furnish strong internal proofs of the antiquity of the drama.

The critic then proceeds to refer to three more alleged anachronisms. The deceased Ynca is said to be spoken of as buried, when Yncas were always embalmed, and the bodies preserved in the temple ; black is mentioned as the colour for mourning, when the Yncas used grey ; and the city of Cuzco is said to have elected a new Ynca, though the Peruvian monarchy was hereditary. The replies are that the word *pampasacta* from *pampani*, to bury, is used, in the oldest songs, for interments of every kind ; that the word for mourning, in the authentic

---

[1] The word *sipi* (a ring) is a later interpolation, not in the Justiniani text.

version, is not *yana* (black), but *ccica* (grey) ; and that the great men of Cuzco, in the cases of this very Ynca Yupanqui (according to Cieza de Leon) and others, did select the sovereign under special circumstances.

The next objection is that the Ynca, after pardoning Ollantay, appointed him to be his successor and invested him with the fringe; which, it is contended, is historically false, and impossible in ancient Peru. But the Ynca merely invested Ollantay with the insignia of his rank as a great chief (the *yellow* fringe, not the *crimson* fringe peculiar to the sovereign), and appointed him to rule at Cuzco during the sovereign's absence, a very different thing. Such appointments were of constant occurrence, and are recorded over and over again by Cieza de Leon.

Thus General Mitré fails to establish the existence of a single allusion to things of European origin in the drama of *Ollantay.*

Treating of the one comic character in the piece, the servant of Ollantay, and referring to his frequent use of puns and expressions with double meanings, the General contends that his wit is Andalusian, and that it is contrary to the genius of the Quichua language. In reality, the speeches of this servant, Piqui Chaqui, are so thoroughly native and of the soil, his allusions and double meanings are so hidden, that no Spaniard—no one but a native —could have written or even conceived them. In one of the Quichua plays, written by Spanish priests, in my possession, there is a "gracioso" named Quespillo, whose fun is broad and without a sign of *double entendre*. If Quespillo is a Spanish creation, Piqui-chaqui is as certainly of native conception. This is one strong proof that *Ollantay*, differing so completely in all respects from the Quichua religious dramas prepared by Spanish priests, is of pure native origin.

Next, General Mitré compares a simple speech of Urco-huaranca, the general of Ollantay, with an enumeration of forces in Homer; a reference to his services, made by Ollantay, to some speech in the Spanish drama of the Cid Campeador; and the election of Ollantay by his army, to an election by the Prætorian guard described by Tacitus. These allusions are too far-fetched and vague to need special replies; but they require wonderful erudition on the part of General Mitré's imaginary Spanish author. Rumi-ñaui, in order to make Ollantay think that he had been ill-treated by the Ynca, mutilated his face. Zopyrus, in the story told by Herodotus, for a similar purpose, cut off his nose and ears, which Rumi-ñaui did not do. Nevertheless, General Mitré jumps at the conclusion that the idea must have been copied from Herodotus. It will be remembered that the story of the mutilation of Rumi-ñaui is preserved on an ancient piece of Ynca pottery.

General Mitré then quotes a speech of Ollantay, when he receives the Ynca's pardon, from my book, a text which he had all along repudiated, in order to use the Dominican text as better suited to his purpose. His criticism on this speech is sound, but the lines I inserted were evidently interpolated by the person who arranged the drama for acting. I had, consequently, placed them in brackets as doubtful, and noted their omission by Von Tschudi and Barranca, a fact which the General does not mention. The passage is not authentic, and would be omitted in a properly revised version. It is in fact omitted by Zegarra. But this use, by General Mitré, first of one text and then of another, as it happens to suit his purpose, is not conducive to the proper object of criticism, namely, the discovery of truth. It shows also that his critical essay is premature, and that it should not have been attempted until all the versions had been critically examined and collated, and an authoritative text established.

The octo-syllabic metre in which the drama is written was also used by Spanish dramatists, and, consequently, according to General Mitré, the drama of *Ollantay* was written by a Spaniard. But it is also a native Peruvian metre. The ancient song given by Garcilasso de la Vega, though printed in lines of four syllables, is really octo-syllabic. These eight-syllable lines are composed with great facility in many languages, and are natural to the Quichua, most of the ancient songs in the collection of Dr. Justiniani being octo-syllabic. Consequently, though also used in Spanish literature, they do not therefore indicate a Spanish origin.

The greater part of General Mitré's argument amounts to little more than this. There is a river in Macedon, and there is a river in Monmouth, therefore Macedon and Monmouth are the same place. It is a very old argument, but it has never been looked upon as conclusive. The General's theory requires an unknown Spanish author living in the eighteenth century, and writing in the Quichua language, of portentous erudition, who borrowed his ideas from the Pentateuch, the Song of Solomon, Homer, Tacitus, Herodotus, Shakespeare, Lope de Vega, Mrs. Ratcliffe, and the ballads of the Cid; and who yet excluded the most distant allusion to Christianity or to anything Spanish. He could not have been a priest, for we possess Quichua plays composed by Spanish priests, and they are entirely and radically different from *Ollantay*, containing, as was inevitable, constant allusions to Christianity, and none to the classic authors of antiquity. Yet the imaginary author must have known Quichua perfectly, in its earliest and most archaic form, and have been versed in all the plays upon words and double meanings used by initiated natives. It may safely be affirmed that no such prodigy ever existed in the eighteenth century, and, consequently, the General's theory falls to pieces like a house of cards.

At the same time, General Mitré has done good service to literature by the publication of this elaborate criticism. Every argument that the ingenuity of an accomplished scholar could bring forward against the authenticity of *Ollantay* has been adduced. Quichua students now know all that can possibly be said against the antiquity of the play,

and they know that what is not based on incorrect
readings, is far-fetched and fanciful. The former
considerations which led them to the conclusion that
most of the dialogues and songs dated from the
time of the Yncas, remain in full force, unshaken by
anything General Mitré has written. The new
points he has raised, prove to be either based on corrupt readings, or to be of no validity in themselves.

It is gratifying to find that the rich and interesting language of the Yncas continues to be studied
by ardent young Peruvian scholars. Among them
is Dr. Martin Antonio Mujica, a native of Huancave-
lica, who is making Quichua a serious study, and
has suggested some changes in the accepted orthography, based on sound principles.[1] There is much
yet to learn in this important branch of investigation, and much useful work to be done. A really
critical text of *Ollantay* is a desideratum. There
are many ancient Quichua songs, possibly other
dramas, in private libraries. These should be diligently sought out, edited, and printed, with trans-
lations. A dictionary should be undertaken, with
references to all the words which occur in the
writings of ancient authors. There is a wide field
and a noble one, for young students in the land of
the Yncas, which is well deserving of careful, diligent,
and enthusiastic cultivation. Such discouraging
criticisms as that of General Mitré should have no

---

[1] I have received from Dr. Mujica a copy of a *Yarahui*, written
with the orthography he considers to be most accurate, and the
ordinarily accepted spelling, in parallel columns.

depressing effect. They should rather arouse the student to fresh efforts, both to secure the purity of his texts, and to illustrate their meaning by the acquisition of wider knowledge, and the cultivation of critical and accurate habits of thought.

Meanwhile, the conclusion that the drama of *Ollantay* is of Ynca origin, having withstood all the assaults of General Mitré's criticism, remains more firmly established, and on securer ground than before. The unsuccessful attack is an additional source of strength.

———————————

A PERUVIAN LOVE STORY.

THE assertion of General Mitré that conjugal devotion was not among the virtues of the ancient Peruvians, induces me to relate a story which is told by Miguel Cavello Balboa.[1] The events it records took place during the war between Huascar and Atahualpa. It, therefore, illustrates the closing chapters of the present volume.[2]

On the death of the great Ynca Huayna Ccapac in the province of Quito, he was succeeded by his legitimate son Huascar at Cuzco ; while the son who was with him, named Atahualpa, remained at the head of an army at Quito. But the body of the deceased sovereign was sent to Cuzco, accompanied by the widowed queen, Mama Rahua Ocllo, and her daughter the Princess Chuqui Uzpay, and by four venerable councillors who were executors of Huayna Ccapac. On approaching Cuzco these venerable men were arrested, ordered to explain why Atahualpa had remained behind, and, their defence not being satisfactory, they were put to death. The principal executor, who thus suffered, was named Auqui Tupac Yupanqui.

The Queen, Mama Rahua Ocllo, was much shocked at this cruelty on the part of her son Huascar. After

---

[1] He finished his book in 1586.   [2] Pages 224 to 235.

the funeral ceremonies, the new sovereign desired to marry his sister Chuqui Uzpay, and, after much hesitation, the Queen Mother reluctantly gave her consent.

Young Quilaco Yupanqui, a son of the murdered executor, Auqui Tupac Yupanqui, was sent by Atahualpa as an envoy to his brother Huascar. On reaching the valley of Xaquixaguana, Quilaco received a secret message from the Queen Mother, who loved him dearly, for he was a foster-brother of her child, the young queen Chuqui Uzpay. The Queen Mother ordered a procession of damsels to come out and meet the envoy ; among whom there was one more beautiful than all the rest, named Curi-coyllur.

At the coronation of Huascar, the chief of the valley of Yca arrived from the coast with a lovely daughter named Chumbillaya. She inspired the Ynca with a violent passion, and he gave her the name of Curi-coyllur, the "golden star." She bore him a daughter and died soon afterwards. His sister Corvaticlla, a beloved friend of Curi-coyllur, brought up the child with great care in a house near Cuzco, and her beauty was so marvellous that she inherited her mother's name of Curi-coyllur.

Curi-coyllur was fifteen when the girls assembled to meet the young envoy from Quito at Siquillabamba. Quilaco fell in love with her. He went on to Cuzco, and, finding that the Ynca Huascar had gone to Calca in the vale of Vilcamayu, he hurried thither, and laid the presents from the Ynca's brother Atahualpa at his feet. Huascar spurned both envoy and presents, and dismissed Quilaco with disdain. Quilaco returned to Cuzco, and told the queens what had befallen him at Calca. The guardian of Curi-coyllur, on hearing of his love, allowed him to visit the young girl. A few days afterwards Huascar sent him back with a message to Atahualpa, to the effect that he would be closely followed by an army to enforce obedience.

One day, at early dawn, Curi-coyllur was praying for the return of her lover. When a labourer appeared with his *taclla* (plough) on his shoulder, she mistook it for the *chuqui* (lance) of Quilaco. At last a troop of strangers appeared on the hill, taking the way to Xaquixaguana. She was shedding tears, when her lover came out of a field of maize close by, and threw himself at her feet. Quilaco told her and her aunt all that had happened at Cuzco, and asked Corvaticlla for the hand of her niece. It was promised when the times had become more quiet, and Quilaco continued his journey to Quito.

The great war then broke out between the two brothers, Huascar and Atahualpa. Quilaco had promised to return to Curi-coyllur in three years, and four had elapsed. Huascar was on the point of marrying her to one of his captains. She cut her hair, put on the dress of one of her servants, painted her face according to the usage of those who go to war, and mixed herself amongst the camp followers of the army of Huascar. The Ynca's general, named

Huanca Auqui, had retreated to the valley of Xauxa, where he met the reinforcements from Cuzco, and was superseded by Mayta Yupanqui. The army of Atahualpa, under the command of Quizquiz, advanced to Tarma, and the hostile forces met between Tarma and Xauxa. The battle lasted all day, but eventually the army of Huascar was defeated with great slaughter. Quilaco was wounded by an arrow, and fell on a heap of dead, while his men were too much occupied in chasing the fugitives to notice his fall.

Quilaco would have perished miserably from loss of blood; but he saw a lad searching among the bodies, and cried for help. The boy ran to him, drew out the arrow, and staunched the wound. He carried the wounded man to the banks of a stream, and washed the dirt off his face and body. Quilaco asked the motive of such kindness in a follower of Huascar.[1] "Brother," said the lad, "I am a native of this place; my name is Titu; I seek no advantage." He collected sticks, lighted a fire to warm the wounded chief; and so they passed the night. Next day the boy conveyed Quilaco to a neighbouring hut until he should be cured. A search was made for him by order of Quizquiz, and his disappearance caused profound sadness in the host of Atahualpa.

For many months Quilaco was unable to rise from his bed, and in the interval great events happened. Huascar was dethroned, his family was massacred

---

[1] Every *ayllu*, or lineage, was known by its head-dress.

at Cuzco, the usurper advanced to Caxamarca, Pizarro arrived on the coast with his Spaniards, and Atahualpa was made prisoner by them. Titu used to leave the hut, and collect news from passers-by on the great road. One day he told Quilaco that the power of Atahualpa and his generals had departed, and that strange men from the sea were now the rulers of the country. Titu spoke of the noble bearing and of the justice of the Viracochas, as he called the Spaniards, looking upon them as messengers from God. He entreated and at last persuaded the chief, who was now able to walk, to appear before the Spanish leader, who had arrived in the valley. It was the famous Hernando de Soto. They went together, and Titu, with the aid of an interpreter, related his history to the proud but noble-minded conqueror. Quilaco now for the first time discovered that Titu was his long-lost love, his Curi-coyllur, whom he had never hoped to see again.

They were baptized under the names of Hernando Yupanqui and Leonora Curi-coyllur, and married in conformity with the laws of the Church. But the young chief only survived for two years. The widow afterwards lived with Hernando de Soto, and bore him several children—Leonora de Soto, who married Fernando Carrillo, notary to his Majesty, and lived at Cuzco; Juana de Soto; Pedro de Soto; and others.

I know not whether the story of Quilaco and Curi-coyllur was ever dramatised like that of Ollantay. But we need not doubt that the " brilliant erudition"[1] of General Mitré would, if the play were brought to light, soon announce to us that it was a " *comedia de capa y espada*", with all the ideas and incidents borrowed from Homer, Herodotus, Tacitus, the Pentateuch, the Song of Solomon, Shakespeare, Lope de Vega, Mrs. Ratcliffe, and the Cid Campeador. Too much erudition is surely a dangerous thing.

The other story told by Balboa, of the love of Elfquen Pisan, Chief of Lambayeque, for the beautiful Chestan Xecfuin, is equally romantic, equally of native origin, and has as little to do with the old world classics as *Ollantay.* Among these people there was pride of caste, magnanimity towards the vanquished, a martial spirit, filial love, and conjugal devotion ; and these sentiments found natural expression in their literature. Cieza de Leon, in the following pages, bears ample testimony to Ynca civilisation.

[1] *Mercurio de Valparaiso*, 14th March 1853.

SECOND PART

OF THE

CHRONICLE OF PERU,

WHICH TREATS OF THE LORDSHIP OF THE INCAS YUPANQUIS, AND OF THEIR GREAT DEEDS AND GOVERNMENT.

WRITTEN BY

PEDRO DE CIEZA DE LEON.

SECOND PART

OF THE

CHRONICLE OF PERU.

CHAPTER III.

*　　　*　　　*　　　*　　　*
　*　　　*　　　*　　　*
*　　　*　　　*　　　*　　　*
　*　　　*　　　*　　　*

of them more than what I recount, go to a delightful place full of enjoyment and pleasure, where they all eat and drink and rejoice; and if, on the contrary, they have done evil, disobedient to parents, hostile to religion, they go to another place which is dark and dismal. In the first book I treated more fully of these things, so that I will now pass on, and relate in what manner the people of this kingdom lived before the Incas flourished and made themselves sovereign lords, in which time all affirm that they were in a state of anarchy, without any of the order, and reasonable government and justice which was afterwards established. I will also recount what there is to be said of Ticiviracocha, which is the name by which the Maker of all things was known.

CHAPTER IV.

Which treats of what the Indians of this kingdom say touching the state of things before the Yncas were known, and how they had fortresses in the hills, whence they came forth to make war one with another.

I OFTEN asked the inhabitants of these provinces what they knew of their condition before the Incas became the lords. On this subject they say that all men lived without order, and that many went naked like savages; that they had no houses, nor any habitations except the caves, many of which may be seen in the great cliffs and rocks, whence they came forth to eat what they could find in the fields. Others made fortresses in the mountains, called *pucara*, out of which they came forth, using strange languages, to fight, one with the other, over the cultivable lands, or for other reasons: and many were slain, the spoils and women of the vanquished being carried off. With all these things they went in triumph to the heights, where they had their castles, and there offered up sacrifices to their gods, shedding much blood of men and lambs before the stones and idols. All these people were in a state of anarchy, for they say for certain that they had no lords, but only captains to lead them in their wars. If some went about dressed, it was in slight clothing, and not such as they now use.

They say that the *llautu* or cords which they put on their heads that one tribe may be distinguished from another, were used then as they are now.

This people living in the condition that I have described, there rose up in the province of the Collao, a very brave lord named Zapana,[1] who so prevailed that he brought many people of that province under his rule. They relate another

[1] See Part I, p. 363.

thing; but whether it be true or not, the most High God who understands all things only knows. As for me, I have no other testimony or authority of books for what I relate than the statements of the Indians. What I want to relate is that they affirm of a certainty that, after that powerful captain arose in Hatuncollao,[1] there appeared in the province of the Canas,[2] which lies between the Canches[3] and Collao, near the village called Chugara, some women who were like valiant men. Taking up arms they subdued those who were in the district where they lived, and, almost like what is told of the Amazons, they made homes for themselves, without husbands. These people, after this had gone on for some years, and they had performed some famous deeds, came to fight with Zapana, he who had become Lord of Hatuncollao; and to defend themselves against his power, which was great, they made fortresses and walls, which still exist. But after they had done all to the utmost of their power, they were taken and killed, and their name disappeared.

There is a citizen in Cuzco named Tomás Vasquez,[4] who told me that he and Francisco de Villacastin,[5] being in the

---

[1] Hatun Colla (Great Colla), a village N.W. of Lake Titicaca.

[2] The Canas were a hardy mountain race on the water-parting between the Titicaca basin and the Vilcamayu. A proud, cautious, melancholy race of shepherds; constantly in revolt against the Yncas.

[3] The Canches inhabited the hills opposite the Canas, on the right bank of the Vilcamayu.

[4] Tomas Vasquez was one of the first conquerors, and had houses in Cuzco.—*G. de la Vega*, ii, p. 255.

[5] Francisco de Villacastin was also a householder in Cuzco. He married an Ynca princess, widow of Juan Balsa, who was killed at the battle of Chupas, fighting for young Almagro. Through her, Villacastin inherited Balsa's house at Cuzco. He died in prison at Cuzco, having taken the side of Gonzalo Pizarro. He owned the district of Ayaviri, and was one of the first conquerors, but a good man.—See *G. de la Vega*, ii, p. 524.

town of Ayavire,[1] seeing these enclosures, and asking the natives what they were, the above story was told them. They also relate what I have written in the first part, namely, that there were people with beards, in the Island of Titicaca, in past ages, white like ourselves; that, coming from the valley of Coquimbo, their captain, who was named Cari,[2] arrived at the place where Chucuito now stands, whence, after having founded some new settlements, he passed over with his people to the island. He made such war upon the inhabitants that he killed them all. Chirihuana, the governor of those settlements, which now belong to the Emperor,[3] told me what I have now written; and as this land was so extensive, and in parts so healthy and well suited for man's habitation, although they continued in the practice of petty warfare and indulgence of their passions, yet they established many settlements. Those captains who showed themselves to be valorous, continued as lords of several towns; and all, as is generally reported, had Indians of intelligence in their houses and fortresses, who spoke with the Devil. And the Devil, by permission of Almighty God, and for reasons known to Him, had very great power amongst these people

[1] A village on the ridge between the basin of Titicaca and the Vilcamayu. The Ayaviris bordered on the Canas.

[2] See Part I, p. 363.

[3] Chucuito was a fief of the crown.

CHAPTER V.

Touching what these natives say concerning Ticiviracocha, of the opinion held by some that an Apostle passed through this land, and of the temple there is in Cáchan, also what happened there.

BEFORE the Incas reigned in these kingdoms, or had ever been heard of, the Indians relate another thing much more notable than all things else that they say. For they declare that they were a long time without seeing the sun, and that, suffering much evil from its absence, great prayers and vows were offered up to their gods, imploring for the light they needed. Things being in this state, the sun, shining very brightly, came forth from the island of Titicaca, in the great lake of the Collao, at which every one rejoiced. Presently afterwards, they say, that there came from a southern direction a white man of great stature, who, by his aspect and presence, called forth great veneration and obedience. This man who thus appeared had great power, insomuch that he could change plains into mountains, and great hills into valleys, and make water flow out of stones. As soon as such power was beheld, the people called him the Maker of created things, the Prince of all things, Father of the Sun. For they say that he performed other wonders, giving life to men and animals, so that by his hand marvellous great benefits were conferred on the people. And such was the story that the Indians who told it to me say that they heard from their ancestors, who in like manner heard it in the old songs which they received from very ancient times. They say that this man went on towards the north, working these marvels along the way of the mountains; and that he never more returned so as to be seen. In many places he gave orders to men how they should live, and he spoke lovingly to them and with much gentleness, admonishing them that they should do good, and no evil or injury one to another, and that they should be loving and charitable to all. In most parts he is generally called *Ticiviracocha*,[1] but in the province of the Collao they call him *Tuapaca*, and in other places *Arnauan*. In many parts they built temples in which they put blocks of stone in likeness of him, and offered up sacrifices before them. It is held that the great blocks at Tiahuanacu were from that time. Although, from the fame of what formerly had passed, they relate the things I have stated touching Ticiviracocha, they know nothing more of him, nor whether he would ever return to any part of this kingdom.

Besides this, they say that, a long time having passed, they again saw another man resembling the first, whose name they do not mention; but they received it from their forefathers as very certain that wherever this personage came and there were sick, he healed them, and where there were blind he gave them sight by only uttering words. Through acts so good and useful he was much beloved by all. In this fashion, working great things by his words, he arrived at the province of the Canas, in which, near to a village which has the name of Cacha, and in which the Captain Bartolomé de Terrazas[2] holds an *encomienda*, the people rose against

[1] Garcilasso de la Vega says: "The Spaniards gave another name for God in their histories, which is *Ticiviracocha*, but neither I nor they know what it means." But he quotes Blas Valera in another place, who says that the god *Ticci Huira-ccoccha* was otherwise called *Pachacamac*. Montesinos suggests that *Tici* meant "bottom or foundation". I suspect it comes from *Atini*, "to conquer". *Atic*, "conquering". It may be from *Ticci*, "beginning".

[2] Terrazas was one of the first conquerors, and he accompanied Almagro in the expedition to Chile. Afterwards he became an active agriculturist. Garcilasso de la Vega says that he was very noble, liberal, magnificent, and possessed of all the knightly virtues. He planted vineyards, and in 1555 sent a large present of grapes to Garcilasso's father, when he was Corregidor of Cuzco, with a request that he

him, threatening to stone him. They saw him upon his knees, with his hands raised to heaven, as if invoking the divine favour to liberate him from the danger that threatened him. The Indians further state that presently there appeared a great fire in the heaven, which they thought to be surrounding them. Full of fear and trembling, they came to him whom they had wanted to kill, and with loud clamour besought him to be pleased to forgive them. For they knew that this punishment threatened them because of the sin they had committed in wishing to stone the stranger. Presently they saw that when he ordered the fire to cease, it was extinguished, so that they were themselves witnesses of what had come to pass ; and the stones were consumed and burnt up in such wise as that large blocks could be lifted in the hand, as if they were of cork. On this subject they go on to say that, leaving the place where these things happened, the man arrived on the sea coast, where, holding his mantle, he went in amongst the waves and was never more seen. And as he went, so they gave him the name of *Viracocha*, which means "the foam of the sea."

Soon afterwards they made a temple in this village of Cacha,[1] on the other side of a river which passes near, where they set up an idol of stone, very large, but in a somewhat narrow recess. This recess is not so large as those in Tiahuanaco, erected in memory of Ticiviracocha, nor does the figure appear to have the same kind of vestments. Some gold was found in holes near it.

When I passed through this province, I went to see the idol, for the Spaniards affirm that it may have been some apostle. I heard many declare that it had legends written

would send bunches to all the cavaliers in the town. These were the first grapes ever seen there. Terrazas was also the first to raise carrots in Peru.

[1] The best description of the very interesting temple of Cacha will be found in Mr. Squier's *Peru* (Macmillan, 1877), pp. 402 to 409.

on its hands. But this is nonsense, unless my eyes were blinded, for although I looked closely I could not see anything of the kind. The hands were placed over the haunches, the arms twisted, and on the girdle were indications that the vestments were fastened with buttons. Whether this or any other was intended for one of the glorious apostles who, in the days of his preaching, had passed this way, God Almighty knows. I know not, and can only believe that if he was an apostle, he would work with the power of God in his preaching to these people, who are simple and with little guile; and there would be some vestige of his visit. Yet what we see and understand is that the Devil had very great power over these people, God permitting it, and that in these places very heathenish and vain sacrifices were offered up. Hence I believe that, until our times, the word of the Holy Gospel was not heard. Now we see all the temples profaned, and the glorious Cross planted in all directions.

I asked the people of Cacha in remembrance of what god the temple had been built. The cacique, or lord, was an Indian of intelligence and good presence, named Don Juan, a Christian, who came with me himself to show me this piece of antiquity. He told me that it was built in honor of Ticiviracocha. Treating of this name Viracocha, I wish to disabuse the reader of the popular belief that the natives called the Spaniards by the name of Viracocha, which means foam of the sea. So far as the word is concerned it is true, for *vira* is the word for grease, and *cocha* is the sea. And seeing that the Spaniards came by sea, that name has been attributed to them. But this is a wrong interpretation, according to the explanation which I received at Cuzco, and which the Orejones give. They say that before Atahuallpa was taken prisoner by the Spaniards in the province of Caxamarca, there had been great wars between him and his brother Huascar Inca, the sole heir to the empire. At length, at the pass of Cotabamba over the river Apurimac, the king Huascar was taken prisoner, and cruelly treated by Chalicuchima.[1] Besides this, Quizquiz[2] did great mischief in Cuzco and, as is well known, killed thirty brothers of Huascar, committing other cruelties on those who were favourable to the legitimate heir and had not shown a desire to receive Atahuallpa. While these passions were at their height, Atahuallpa had been made prisoner and had agreed with Pizarro to give him a house of gold as his ransom. Martin Bueno, Zarate, and Moguer[3] went to Cuzco to receive it, the greater part being in the Sun temple called Curicancha. As these Christians arrived at Cuzco at the time when the party of Huascar was suffering under the above calamity, the oppressed Yncas rejoiced when they heard of the imprisonment of Atahuallpa, and with great supplications implored the aid of the Christians against their enemy, declaring that they must be sent by the intervention of their great God Ticiviracocha, and that they were his sons; and presently they called them so, giving them the name of Viracocha.

They ordered the High Priest and the other ministers of the temple to keep the sacred women there, and Quizquiz delivered all the gold and silver to the Spaniards. As these

[1] One of the generals of Atahualpa.

[2] Another of Atahualpa's generals.

[3] Zarate and Garcilasso de la Vega give the names of Hernando de Soto, and Pedro del Barco of Lobon, as those of the first Spaniards who were sent by Pizarro to Cuzco. Pedro Pizarro, who was at Caxamarca at the time, says that only two were sent, Martin Bueno and Pedro Martin de Moguer.

They left Caxamarca on February 15th, 1533, and remained one week at Cuzco. Xeres says that three men were sent. The truth seems to have been that three soldiers named Pedro Moguer, Francisco de Zarate, and Martin Bueno were first sent; but that they behaved with so much imprudence and insolence at Cuzco as to endanger their own lives and the success of their mission. Pizarro, therefore, ordered two officers of distinction, Hernando de Soto and Pedro del Barco, to follow the three soldiers to Cuzco.—See *G. de la Vega*, Part II, lib. i, cap. 31; *Herrera*, Dec. v. lib. i, cap. 1; *Zarate*, II, cap. vi; *Gomara*, cap. cxiv; *Xeres*, p. 72.

Spaniards were so free from all restraint, and held the honor
of the people so lightly, in return for the hospitality and
friendliness with which they were received, they corrupted
some of the virgins; which was the reason that the Indians,
who also saw how little reverence the Spaniards felt for the
Sun, and how shamelessly and without the fear of God they
violated the *mamaconas*,[1] which the Indians held to be a
great sacrilege, began to say that such people were not sons of
God, but that they were worse than *Supais*, which is their
name of Devil. Nevertheless, to comply with the order of the
Lord Atahuallpa, the captains of the city took leave of the
Spaniards without showing any anger whatever, soon afterwards sending the treasure. But the name of Viracocha continued from that day, and it was given, as I was informed, for
the reason I have already written down, and not owing to its
signification of foam of the sea.[2] And now I will relate what
I have been given to understand respecting the origin of the
Incas.

[1] Matrons in charge of virgins of the Sun. The word seems to be
used here, and elsewhere, for all females connected with the temples.

[2] *Uira* means "grease", and *Ccocha*, "a lake". The word for the
sea is *Mama-ccocha*. Montesinos says that *Uira*, in the word *Uiracocha*,
was a corruption of *Pirua*, meaning all things united together. *Pirua*
literally means a "granary". Garcilasso de la Vega pointed out that *Uira-
ccocha* would mean a "Sea of grease", not "Foam of the Sea": the
genitive always being placed first. *Ccochap-uira* would be "Foam of
the sea".

But the Ynca Garcilasso, though he points out the errors of other
writers, does not explain the meaning of the word himself. He simply
infers that it is a proper name, the original meaning of which is lost;
and adds that Blas Valera says that it signified "the will and power of
God", not because that is the etymology of the component words, but
because of the God-like qualities ascribed to Uira-ccocha.

CHAPTER VI.

*How certain men and women appeared in Pacaree-Tampu, and
what they relate touching their proceedings after they came
forth from there.*

I HAVE already stated more than once, how, as an exercise
and to escape from the vices caused by idleness, I took the
trouble to describe all that I obtained touching the Incas
and their system and good order of government. As I have
no other account nor writing beyond what they gave me, if
another should undertake to write more certainly than I have,
on this subject, he may well do so. At the same time, I have
not spared pains to make what I write clear; and to ensure
greater accuracy I went to Cuzco when the Captain Juan de
Saavedra was Corregidor.[1] Here he arranged that Cayu Tupac
should meet me, who is one of the surviving descendants of
Huaina Capac. For Sairi Tupac, son of Manco Inca, has
retired to Viticos, where his father took refuge after his great
war with the Spaniards at Cuzco. I also met others of the
Orejones, who are those that are held to be most noble
amongst themselves. With the best interpreters that could
be found, I asked these Lords Incas of what race they were,
and of what nation. It would seem that the former Incas,
to magnify their origin with great deeds, exaggerated the
story they had received, in their songs. It is this. When
all the races who lived in these regions were in a state of disorder, slaughtering each other and sunk in vice, there appeared three men and three women in a place not far from
the city of Cuzco, which is called Pacarec Tampu. And
according to the interpretation, Pacarec Tampu is as much as
to say the House of Production.

The men who came forth from there were, as they relate,

---

[1] In the beginning of 1550.

the one, Ayar Ucho, and the other, Ayar Cachi Asauca, and
the other, they say, was named Ayar Manco.   Of the women,
one had the name of Mama Huaco, the other Mama Cora, the
other Mama Rahua.[1]

Some Indians give these names after another fashion and

[1] Balboa says that four brothers and four sisters came out of Pacarec
Tampu or Tampu Toco, named Manco Capac, Ayar Cacha, Ayar Auca,
and Ayar Uchi; the women being Mama Guaca, Mama Cora, Mama
Ocllo, Mama Arahua.   Montesinos gives the names as—Ayar Manco
Tupac, Ayar Uchu Tupac, Aya Sauca Tupac, and Ayar Cachi Tupac,
and the women Mama Cora, Hipa Huacum, Mama Huacum, Pilco
Huacum.   Garcilasso de la Vega also says that there were four brothers
and four sisters, namely, Manco Capac, Ayar Cachi, Ayar Uchu, Ayar
Sauca, but he only gives the name of one of the women, Mama Ocllo,
wife of Manco Capac.   Juan de Betanzos gives the names in pairs, in
the order in which they came out of the mysterious cave, namely, Ayar-
cache and Mamaguaco, Ayaroche and Cora, Ayarauca and Raguaocllo,
Ayarmango and Mama Ocllo.

Fray Martin de Morua, in his *Historia del Origen y Genealogia de los
Incas*, a work written in 1590, but still inedited, gives the following
names of those who came out of Tambo Toco or Pacaric Tombo.   The
eldest, Guanacauri; the second, Cuzco Huanca; the third, Mango Capac;
and the fourth, Tupa Ayar Cache.   Of the women, the first was Tupa
Uaco; the second, Mama Coya : the third, Curi Ocllo; and the fourth,
Ipa Huaco.   Before reaching Cuzco they stopped at a place then called
Apitay, and now Guanacauri.   The third sister, Curi Ocllo, who was
considered most intelligent by the rest, was then sent forward to seek
for the best situation for a settlement.   Coming to the site of Cuzco, then
inhabited by Lares, Poques, and Huallas, a low and poor race, before
she arrived there she met one of the Poques.   She killed him with a
weapon called *raucana;* cut out his lungs; and, with them in her mouth,
all bloody, she entered the settlements.   The people were frightened at
the sight of her, thinking that she fed on men, and they left their houses
and fled.   Seeing that the place seemed good for a settlement, and that
the people were tame, she returned to her brothers and sisters, and
brought them all there except the eldest.   He preferred to stay at Apitay, where he died, and in memory of him they call that place and hill
Guanacauri.   The rest were received without opposition, and they
named the second brother to be the chief of the town, for which reason
the place was called Cuzco, for before its name was Acamama.   He died
in the Curicancha, and was succeeded by the third brother, named the
great Manco Capac.

in greater number, but I have put them down from the informations of the Orejones, who know better than any one else. They say that these people came forth, dressed in long mantles, and some vestments like a shirt without collar or sleeves, made of very fine wool, with patterns of different kinds, which they called *tacapu*, and in our language the meaning is "vestures of kings." And each of these lords held in the hand a sling of gold with a stone in it. The women came out dressed very richly like the men, and they had much gold. Going forward with this, they further say, that they obtained great store of gold, and that one of the brothers named Ayar Uchu spoke to his brethren that they should make a beginning of the great things that they had to do; for their presumption was such that they thought they were to make themselves sole lords of the land. They were determined to form in that place a new settlement, to which they gave the name of Pacarec Tampu; and this was soon done, for they had the help of the inhabitants of the surrounding country. As time went on, they put great quantities of pure gold and jewels, with other precious things, into that place, of which the fame goes that Hernando Pizarro and Don Diego de Almagro the lad, obtained a large share.

Returning to the history, they say that one of the three, named Ayar Cachi, was so valiant and had such great power, that, with stones hurled from his sling, he split the hills and threw them up to the clouds. When the other brothers saw this they were sorry, thinking that it was an affront to them who could not do such things, and they were enraged by reason of their envy. Then they asked him sweetly and with gentle words, though full of deceit, to return and enter the mouth of a cave where they had their treasure, to bring out a certain vase of gold that they had forgotten, and to pray to their father the Sun that he would prosper their efforts so that they might be lords of that land. Ayar Cachi, believing that there was no deceit in what his brother said, joyfully went to do what they required of him, but he had scarcely got into the cave when the other two so filled the mouth up with stones that it could not be seen. This done, they relate for a certainty that the earth trembled in such a manner that many hills fell into the valleys.

Thus far the Orejones relate the story of the origin of the Incas, because they wished it to be understood that as their deeds were so marvellous, they must have been children of the Sun. Afterwards, when the Indians exalted them with grand titles, they were called *Ancha hatun apu intipchuri!*[1] which means, "Oh very great lord, child of the sun." That which, for my part, I hold to be the truth in this matter is that as Zapana rose up in Hatuncollao, and other valiant captains did the same thing in other parts, these Incas must have been some three valiant and powerful brothers with grand thoughts who were natives of some place in those regions, or who had come from some other part of the mountains of the Andes ; and that they, finding the opportunity, conquered and acquired the lordship which they possessed. Even without this supposition it might be that what they tell of Ayar Cachi and the others was the work of magicians, who did what is told of them through the Devil. In fine, we cannot get from the story any other solution than this.

As soon as Ayar Cachi was secured in the cave, the other two brothers, with some people who had joined them, agreed to form another settlement, to which they gave the name of Tampu Quiru, which is as much as to say, "Teeth of a residence or of a palace", and it may be supposed that these settlements were not large nor more than sufficient for a small force. They remained at this place for some days, being now

---

[1] *Ancha*, the superlative ; *Hatun*, "great"; *Apu*, "a chief"; *Intip*, genitive of *Ynti*, "the sun"; *Churi*, "a son".

sorry at having so made away with their brother Ayar Cachi, who was also called Huanacaure.[1]

[1] Molina often mentions the worship of this hero, Huanacauri. Garcilasso de la Vega refers to Huanacauri four times (i, 65, 66 ; ii, 169, 230). He says that the first settlement made in the valley of Cuzco was on the hill called Huanacauri, and that a very sacred temple was built there. Molina refers to the sacrifices offered up there. The idol of Huanacauri was a great figure of a man, "their principal *huaca*, the brother of Manco Ccapac, whence they descend". The ceremonies of arming youths were a good deal connected with this Huanacauri idol.

CHAPTER VII.

*How the brothers, being in Tampu Quiru, beheld him whom
they had shut up in the cave by deceit, come forth with
wings; and how he told them that he went to found the
great city of Cuzco; and how they departed from Tampu
Quiru.*

PROCEEDING with the narrative that I took down in Cuzco,
the Orejones say that, after the two Incas had settled in
Tampu Quiru, careless now about seeing Ayar Cachi again,
they beheld him coming in the air with great wings of
coloured feathers, and they, by reason of the great fear that
this visit caused them, wanted to flee away; but he quickly
removed their terror by saying to them, "Do not fear,
neither be afflicted; for I only come that the empire of the
Incas may begin to be known. Wherefore leave this settlement that you have made, and advance further down until
you see a valley, and there found the Cuzco, which will be of
great note. For here are only hamlets, and of little importance; but that will be a great city, where the sumptuous
temple must be built that will be so honoured and frequented, and where the sun will be so worshipped. I shall
always have to pray to God for you, and to intercede that
you may soon become great lords. I shall remain in the
form and fashion that you will see on a hill not distant from
here; and will be for you and your descendants a place of
sanctity and worship, and its name shall be Guanacaure.
And in return for the good things that you will have received from me, I pray that you will always adore me as
God, and set up altars in that place, at which to offer sacrifices. If you do this, you shall receive help from me in war;
and as a sign that from henceforward you are to be esteemed,
honoured, and feared, your ears shall be bored in the manner

that you now behold in mine." And when he had so spoken they say that he appeared with ear ornaments of gold set round as with a gem.

The brothers, astonished at what they saw, were as men struck dumb and without speech. When their perturbation had ceased, they replied that they were content to do as he commanded, and presently they went in haste to the hill called the Hill of Guanacaure, which, from that time forward, was accounted sacred. In the highest part of it, they again saw Ayar Cachi, who, without doubt, must have been some devil, if there is any truth in what they relate; and, God permitting, he made them understand his desire that they should worship and sacrifice to him under these false appearances. They say that he again spoke to them, telling them to assume the fringe or crown of empire, such of them as were to be sovereign lords, and how they should order the arming of youths to make them knights and nobles. The brothers answered that they would comply with all his commands, as they had already promised, and in sign of obedience, with hands joined and heads bowed down, they made the *mocha*[1] or reverence, that he might the better understand them. The Orejones further say that the practice of assuming the fringe and of arming the knights began here, so I put it in this place, that there may be no necessity for repeating it further on.

This may be received as pleasant and very certain history, for Manco Inca assumed the fringe or sovereign crown in Cuzco, and many Spaniards are still living who were present at the ceremony, and I have heard it from them. It is true that the Indians say that the ceremony was more solemn and magnificent in former times, and was performed with such sumptuous riches as could not be enumerated.

It would seem that these lords arranged the ceremony for assuming the fringe or crown, and they say that Ayar Cachi

---

[1] *Mucha*, "adoration", from *Muchani*, "I worship".

dressed in the same manner, on this same hill of Guanacaure. He who was to become Inca was dressed, on one day, in a black shirt painted with red patterns and no collar, and on his head a fawn-coloured plait twisted round. And he wore a long grey mantle, in which dress he came forth from his lodging and went into the fields to gather a wisp of straw, and he had to stay out all day doing this, without eating or drinking, for it was his duty to fast. And the mother and sisters of the former Inca had to remain spinning with such diligence that, during that one day, they had to spin and weave four dresses, fasting all the time. One of these dresses consisted of a grey shirt and white mantle, and another had to be all white, and the other had to be blue, with cords and trimmings. He who was to become Inca had to wear these dresses, and to fast for the appointed time, which is one month, and they call this fast *zaziy*.[1] It is kept in a lodging of the royal palace, without seeing light or having connection with a woman. During this time of fasting the ladies of his lineage have to work very hard to make a great quantity of *chicha* with their own hands, making it from maize, and they must be richly dressed. After the time of fasting is passed, he who was to be lord came forth, carrying a halberd of gold and silver in his hands, and he proceeded to the house of some venerable relative, where his hair had to be shorn. Then, clothed in one of these dresses, he left Cuzco, where this festival was held, and went to the hill of Guanacaure, and performed certain ceremonies and sacrifices. He then proceeded to where the wine was kept, and drank. The Inca then went to a hill called Anaquar, and from the foot of it he ran, that the people might see whether he was agile, and would be valiant in war. Presently he came down, carrying a little wool on the halberd, in token that when he fought with his enemies, he would bring away their hair and the heads with

---

[1] *Sasi*, "a fast". See *G. de la Vega*, Part I, lib. vii, cap. 6.

it. This done, the Inca returned to the hill of Guanacaure. Here he and his courtiers gathered straw, and he who was to be Inca had a very large bundle of it, made of very fine gold of equal lengths. With this he went to another hill called Yahuira, and there he put on another of the dresses, and on his head a plait or *llautu* called *pillaca*,[1] which is like a crown, underneath which were ear-ornaments of gold, and on the top a tuft of feathers sewn like a diadem, which they call *puruchuco*.[2] On the halberd they fastened a girdle of gold which reached to the ground, and on his breast was placed a moon of gold. In this dress, and before all who were present, he killed a sheep, the body and blood being divided among all the principal people, to be eaten raw. The signification of the ceremony was that if they were not valiant their enemies would eat them, as they were eating the sheep that had been killed.

At this place they took a solemn vow, according to their usage, in the name of the Sun, that they would maintain the order of knighthood, and would die in defence of Cuzco, if it should be necessary. Next their ears were opened, and the apertures were so large that they could hold a geme each one in circumference. This done, they put on the heads of fierce lions, and returned to the square of Cuzco with great noise. In the square there was a great chain of gold going all round, and supported on prongs of gold and silver. Here they danced, and there were marvellous great festivities, according to their fashion. Those who had been made knights had on the heads of lions, as a sign that they would be valiant and fierce. At the end of the dancing the knights remained armed, and were called Orejones. They had privileges and enjoyed great dignities, and are worthy, if selected, to assume the crown, which is the fringe.

---

[1] This word, in Quichua, is used also for a kind of cloak.

[2] *Puhura* is "a feather", and *chuccu*, "a cap". The distinctive head-dress of each tribe was called *chuccu* or *umachuccu*.

When this was given to the lord who was to be sovereign, greater festivities were held, a vast concourse of people assembled, and he who is about to be Emperor must first take his own sister for his wife, that no base lineage may succeed. He also performed the great *zaziy*, which is the fast. And during the intervals that these ceremonies occupied, the lord being engaged in the business of sacrifices and fasting, he could not attend to private or public concerns. It was, therefore, a law among the Incas that, when the sovereign died, or handed over the crown or fringe to another, one of the principal nobles was selected, who, with mature counsel and great authority, might govern the whole empire of the Incas, as if he were the lord himself, during these days, and he was allowed to have a guard and to be addressed with reverence.

These ceremonies being completed, and the blessings having been given in the temple of Curicancha, the Inca received the fringe, which was large and descended from the *llautu* that he had on his head, so as to fall over his eyes, and he was then held and reverenced as the sovereign.

At the festivals were present the principal lords for more than five leagues round, and there appeared in Cuzco very great store of gold and silver and precious stones, and rich plumes, all round the long chain of gold, and the marvellous figure of the Sun. This chain was of such size that it weighed, according to what the Indians assert for a certainty, more than four thousand hundred weights of gold. If the Sovereign did not receive the fringe in Cuzco, they looked upon it as an absurdity that he should be called Inca, for his possession was not assured. Thus Atahuallpa is not counted among the kings, although, owing to his great valour and to his having killed so many people, he was obeyed by many nations from fear.

Returning to those who were on the hill of Guanacaure, after Ayar Cacha had spoken of the order that was to be taken for the arming of knights, the Indians relate that turning to his brother Ayar Manco, he told him to go on with the two women to the valley he had pointed out, and to found there the Cuzco, without forgetting to come and perform sacrifices in that place, as he had commanded. And as soon as he had done speaking, both he and the other brother were turned into two figures of stone in the shape of men. This was seen by Ayar Manco, who, taking the women with him, went to the place where Cuzco now stands and founded a city, naming himself from that time forward Manco Capac,[1] which means the rich King and Lord.

---

[1] The word *Manco* has no meaning in Quichua. *Ccapac* means "rich", and, as applied to the sovereign, it is explained as signifying rich in power and in virtues.

CHAPTER VIII.

*How Manco Capac, when he saw that his brothers had been
turned into stones, went to a valley where he met some
people, and how he founded and built the ancient and very
rich city of Cuzco, which was the capital of the whole
empire of the Incas.*

WHEN Manco Capac had seen what had happened to his
brothers, and had come to the valley where now is the city
of Cuzco, the Orejones say that he raised his eyes to heaven
and, with great humility, besought the Sun that he would
favour and aid him in forming the new settlement. Then
turning his eyes towards the hill of Guanacaure he addressed
the same petition to his brother, whom he now held and reverenced as a god. Next he watched the flight of birds, the
signs in the stars, and other omens, which filled him with confidence, so that he felt certain that the new settlement would
flourish, and that he would be its founder and the father of all
the Incas who would reign there.

In the name of Ticiviracocha, and of the Sun, and of the
other Gods, he laid the foundation of the new city. The
original and beginning of it was a small stone house with a
roof of straw that Manco Capac and his women built, to
which they gave the name of Curicancha,[1] meaning the place
of gold. This is the place where afterwards stood that celebrated and most rich temple of the Sun, and now a monastery
of monks of the order of St. Domingo. It is held for certain
that, at the time when Manco Inca Capac built this house,
there were Indians in large numbers in the district; but as he
did them no harm and did not in any wise molest them, they
did not object to his remaining in their land, but rather
rejoiced at his coming. So Manca Capac built the said house,

---

[1] *Ccuri*, " gold"; "*cancha*", "a place".

and it was devoted to the worship of his Gods, and he became
a great man and one who represented high authority.

One of his wives was barren and never had children. By
the other he had three sons and one daughter. The eldest
was named Inca[1] Roca Inca and the daughter Ocllo. The
names of the others are not recorded, nor is more said than
that the eldest was married to his sister, and that he taught
them how to make themselves beloved by the people and not
hated, with other important matters. In those days the descendants of Zapana had made themselves powerful in Hatuncollao, and sought to occupy all that region by tyranny. But
Manco Capac, as the founder of Cuzco, had married his sons,
and brought into his service, by love and good words, some
people who enlarged the house of Curicancha. After he had
lived for many years, he died at a great age, and his obsequies,
were sumptuously performed. Besides that, a figure of him
was made, to be reverenced as a child of the Sun.

[1] Sinchi.

CHAPTER IX.

In which notice is given to the reader of the reason that the Author, leaving the account of the succession of the kings, prefers to explain the government of the people, their laws, and customs.

ALTHOUGH I might write the events of the reign of Sinchi Roca Inca, son of Manco Capac the founder of Cuzco, in this place, it has seemed to me that there will be confusion further on if the system of the government of these lords is not explained as one whole. For one ordered one set of laws, and others others. For example, one introduced the system of *mitimae*,[1] others the plan of having garrisons of soldiers in fixed positions for the defence of the kingdom. All these regulations are important and worthy to be remembered, that the learned statesmen who regulate the affairs of civilized governments may be informed of them, and may feel astonished at the knowledge that a barbarous people without letters should have been found to have had institutions such as we know that they possessed, both with reference to internal polity and to their plans of extending their dominion over other nations. Under a monarchy they obeyed one Lord, who alone was deemed worthy to reign in an empire which the Incas possessed, extending over more than one thousand two hundred leagues of coast. In order to avoid the necessity for saying that some assert that particular institutions were introduced by one lord, and others by another, on which points many of the native accounts differ, I will relate, in this place, what I understand and hold for certain, in conformity with the statements that I took down from their mouths in the city of Cuzco, which are corroborated by the

---

[1] Colonists.

remains that they have left, and which are visible to those who have travelled through Peru.

It should not appear to learned persons that, in adopting this course, I deviate from the plan of my work; for my aim is to make the matter more clear and intelligible, as I have declared. I propose to write with brevity, and not to dwell on minute details, and in the same way I shall afterwards proceed to narrate the events of the reigns of the Incas, and their succession, down to the death of Huascar, and the entry of the Spaniards which brought them to an end. I desire that those who may read my work, should understand that among all the Incas, the number of which was eleven, three were most capable of governing their lordships, insomuch that the Orejones who relate their history do not cease to praise them. These were Huayna Capac, Tupac Inca Yupanqui his father, and Inca Yupanqui, father of one and grandfather of the other. It may also be assumed that, as these monarchs flourished in recent times, the kingdom must still be full of people who knew Tupac Inca Yupanqui, and accompanied him in his wars, and that they heard from their fathers what Inca Yupanqui did during his reign; so that it may be said that the events took place almost before their eyes. They, therefore, have more light to throw upon this period, and are well able to relate the events; although much has been forgotten touching the history of the earlier reigns. Yet it is certain that they do not lose the memory of events for many years, although they know not the use of letters, as I have already observed in the first part of this Chronicle.[1] The use of letters has not been found either in any part of this kingdom or throughout the whole of the Indies. With these remarks we will now proceed with the narrative.

[1] Cap. xxxviii, in which he refers his reader to this second part. He observes that the Yncas were very intelligent and learned, without having letters, which had not been invented in the Indies.—See p. 136 of my Translation.

CHAPTER X.

*How the lord, after he had assumed the fringe of sovereignty,
was married to his sister the Coya, which is the name of
the queen, and how it was permitted that he should have
many women, although among them all the Coya alone
was the legitimate and principal wife.*

IN former chapters I have briefly explained how those who
were to become nobles were armed as knights, as well as the
nature of the ceremonies that took place when the Incas
were crowned as kings, by taking the crown, which is the
fringe falling as far down as their eyes. And it was ordained by them that he who became king should take
his sister, being the legitimate daughter of his father and
mother, as his wife; in order that the succession of the
kingdom might by that means be confirmed in the royal
house. It appeared to them that by this means, even if such
a woman, being sister of the king, should not be chaste, and
should have intercourse with another man, the son thus born
would still be hers, and not the son of a strange woman.
They also considered that if the Inca married a strange
woman, she might do the same and conceive in adultery, in
such a way that, it not being known, the child would be received as a natural born son of the lord. For these reasons,
and because it seemed desirable to those who ordained the
laws, it was a rule among the Incas that he amongst them all
who became emperor should take his sister to wife. She had
the name of *Coya*, which means the Queen, as when the
King of Spain marries any princess, who before had her own
name, she is called Queen so soon as she enters the kingdom,
so they called those of Cuzco *Coya*. If by chance he who
became lord had no sister, it was permitted that he should
marry the most illustrious lady there was, and she was held

to be the principal among all his women. For none of these lords had less than 700 women for the service of their house and for their pleasure. So that they all had many children by these women, who were well treated, and respected by the people. When the king was lodging in his palace or wherever he might be, the women were watched and guarded by porters and *camayos*,[1] which is the name of the guards. If any had intercourse with a man she was punished with death, and the man suffered the same penalty.

The sons whom the lords had by these women, as soon as they were grown up, received lands and fields, which they call *chácaras*,[2] and they were given clothes and other necessaries from the government stores for their use. But it was not thought fit that they should have lordships, because, in the event of any troubles in the kingdom, it was not desired that they should be in a position to be looked upon as legitimate sons of the king. Thus none of them was entrusted with the rule over a province, although in time of war many were captains and were preferred to those who were of purer lineage. The legitimate lord who inherited the kingdom favoured them; but if they joined in any revolt they were cruelly punished. None of them was allowed to speak to the king, even if he was a brother, without first putting a light burden on his shoulders and taking off his shoes, as was the custom with all other subjects.

---

[1] *Caman* is a particle which, when added to a noun, denotes a task or occupation. *Nocap-camay* means "my task"; *Campa-camayqui*, "your task". It also means fitness, as *Apupac-caman*, "fit to be a chief". *Camayoc* is a word attached to offices and occupations. *Siray-camayoc*, "a tailor"; *Llacta-camayoc*, "a village officer". *Pucara-camayoc*, "a castellan".   [2] A farm.

CHAPTER XI.

*How it was the custom among the Incas that they celebrated
in their songs, and by making statues of those who were
valorous and extended the bounds of the empire, and performed any other deed worthy of memory; while those who
were negligent or cowardly received little notice.*

I UNDERSTOOD, when I was in Cuzco,[1] that it was the custom
among the kings Incas, that the king, as soon as he died
should be mourned for with much lamentation, and that
great sacrifices should be offered up in accordance with their
religion. When these ceremonies were over, the oldest
people of the country discussed the life and acts of the
recently deceased king, considering whether he had done
good to the country, and what battles he had gained over the
country's enemies. Having settled these questions, and
others which we do not entirely understand, they decided
whether the deceased king had been so fortunate as to merit
praise and fame, and to deserve that his memory should for
ever be preserved. They then called for the great *quipos-
camayos*[2] who preserve the records, and understand how to
give an account of the events that occur in the kingdom.
Next they communicated with those who were most expert,
and who were selected for their skill in rhetoric and the use
of words. These knew how to narrate the events in regular
order, like ballad singers and romance writers. These compose the songs, so that they shall be heard by all at marriage
ceremonies and other festivities. Thus they were instructed
what to say concerning the deceased lord, and, if they
treated of wars, they sang, in proper order, of the many
battles he had fought in different parts of the empire. And

---

[1] In August 1550.

[2] *Quipu-camayoc*, the officer in charge of the records.

for other events, there were songs and romances to celebrate them on suitable occasions, so that the people might be animated by the recital of what had passed in other times.

Those Indians who, by order of the kings, had learnt the romances, were honoured and favoured, and great care was taken to teach their sons and other men in their provinces who were most able and intelligent. By this plan, from the mouths of one generation the succeeding one was taught, and they can relate what took place 500 years ago, as if only ten years had passed.

This was the order that was taken to prevent the great events of the empire from passing into oblivion. When a king died, if he had been valiant and a good ruler, without having lost any province inherited from his father, nor been guilty of mean or paltry actions, it was permitted and ordained that songs in his honour should be composed, in which he should be praised in such wise as that all the people should be astonished to hear of deeds so mighty. These songs were not to be recited always and in all places; but only on occasions when there was a great and solemn assembly of people from all parts of the empire, or when the principal lords met together before the king on special occasions, or when they held their *taquis*,[1] or drinking bouts. Then, those who knew the romances, standing before the Inca, sang, with loud voices, of the mighty deeds of his ancestors. If any of his predecessors had been negligent, cowardly, or vicious, or preferred pleasure to the labour of extending the bounds of the empire, it was ordered that such a king should receive little or no mention. If the name was preserved, it was merely to complete the line of succession. On other points there was silence concerning him, and the good and valiant alone were kept in memory.

---

[1] *Taqui* is "music"; *Taquiz*, "a song". The *taquis* was an assembly to hear the legendary songs.

The memory of those who were great and good was so venerated that the successor of such an one sought no inheritance from him, but he succeeded to the empire alone. It was the law that the riches and the royal insignia of one who had been King of Cuzco should never pass to another, and should never be forgotten. With this end, a figure was made in the resemblance of the deceased king, which was called by his name.[1] These figures used to be placed in the square of Cuzco on festivals, and round each figure stood the women and servants of the dead king, with his food and drink. For the Devil was accustomed to speak out of these figures. And each figure had its orators, who pleased the multitude with pleasant speeches. All the treasure which the deceased lord possessed was left in the care of his servants and confidential attendants, who brought it out at the festivals, with great ceremony. Besides this, the servants and attendants had their *chacaras*, which is their name for fields where they cultivate maize and other crops, and with these the women and family of the deceased lord were maintained, although he was dead and gone. No doubt this custom explains the fact that, in this empire, there was such vast treasure as we here beheld with our eyes. The Spanish conquerors heard that when, in discovering the provinces of the kingdom, they entered Cuzco, the figures of the deceased kings were there. This appears to have been true, for when Manco Inca Yupanqui, son of Huayna Capac, desired to assume the fringe, these figures were publicly brought out into the square of Cuzco, in the sight of all the Spaniards and Indians who were present on that occasion.

It is true that the Spaniards got possession of a great part of the treasure ; but the remainder is concealed in such wise as that few or perhaps none know where it is. Of the figures

---

[1] It was the mummified body, as will be seen presently.

and of their other wonderful things, there is now no memory except what is preserved in their songs.[1]

[1] Twenty years after this was written, the Licentiate Polo de Ondegardo discovered where five of these figures were concealed, which proved to be the actual mummies of the Yncas and their wives, dressed in their clothes. Ondegardo, who was corregidor of Cuzco, showed them to Garcilasso de la Vega in 1570. One mummy was that of the Ynca Uira-ccocha; the second of Tupac Ynca Yupanqui; the third of Huayna Ccapac; the fourth of Mama Runtu, queen of Uira-ccocha; the fifth of Ccoya Mama Ocllo, mother of Huayna Ccapac. They were perfect, wanting neither hair, nor eye-lashes, and were dressed in the clothes they wore when alive, with the *llautu* or fringe. They were seated with the arms crossed on the breast, and eyes cast down.

Acosta, who also saw them, says that the eyes were made of small pellets of gold, "so well imitated that no one would have missed the real ones". The mummies were taken to Lima by order of the Viceroy Marquis of Cañete, and eventually interred there, at the hospital of San Andres.

CHAPTER XII.

How they had chroniclers to record their deeds, and of the
QUIPOS, *what they were, and what we see of them.*

WHAT I have written respecting the placing of the images in
the square was done by order of the Incas, and some of the
most learned of the people were chosen to make known the
lives of those lords in songs, and the events of their reigns,
with the object I have already described. And it is also to be
noted that besides this, it was the custom among them, and a
law much kept and observed, for each king, during his reign
to select three or four old men, known for their intelligence
and ability, who were instructed to retain in their memory
all the events that happened in the provinces, whether they
were prosperous, or whether they were the reverse, and to
compose songs to be handed down, so that the history of the
reign might be had in remembrance in after times. But these
songs could not be recited or made public, except in the
presence of the lord, and those who were charged with this
duty, during the reign of the king, were not allowed to say
anything which referred to him. But after his death they
spoke to his successor in the empire, almost in these very
words: "Oh! great and powerful Inca, the Sun, the Moon, the
earth, the hills and the trees, the stones, and thine ancestors,
may they all preserve thee from misfortune and make thee
prosperous, happy, and successful over all that are born!
Know that the events which occurred in the days of thy
fathers are these." Then, in the narration, they stood in
great humility, with eyes cast on the ground and hands
lowered. They could well do this, for there were among
them some men with very good memories, sound judgments,
and subtle genius, and full of reasoning power, as we can bear
witness, who have heard them even in these our days.

As soon as the king understood what was related to him,

he caused other aged men to be called, and charged them with the duty of learning the songs which were handed down from memory, and to prepare others touching the events which might occur in his own reign. The expenditure and the account of contributions from the provinces were recorded in the *quipus*, that it might be known how much was paid in the former reign, and also during that of the new lord. No one was allowed to treat of historical events, except only on days of great rejoicing, or on days of mourning and sadness for the death of some brother or child of the king. If the histories were recited on other occasions, those who did so were severely punished.

They had another method of knowing and understanding what had been received from the contributions in the provinces, what provisions were stored on the routes that the king would take with his army or when he was visiting the provinces, how much was in each place of deposit, how much was delivered out. And this method exceeded in artifice the *carastes* used by the Mexicans for their calculations.[1] The system of the Peruvians was by *quipus*. These were long ropes made of knotted cords, and those who were accountants and understood the arrangement of these knots, could, by their means, give an account of the expenditure, and of other things during a long course of years. On these knots they counted from one to ten, and from ten to a hundred, and from a hundred to a thousand. On one of the ropes are the units, on another the tens, and so on. Each ruler of a province was provided with accountants who were called *quipucamayos*, and by these knots they kept account of what tribute was to be paid in the district, with respect to silver, gold, cloth, flocks, down to fire-wood and other minute details. By the same *quipus* they could report to those who were commissioned to take the account at the end of a year, or of ten or

---

[1] See Prescott's *Conquest of Mexico* (i, p. 83), where the Aztec system of notation and arithmetic is explained.

twenty years, with such accuracy that so much as a pair of *alpargatas*[1] would not be missing.

I was incredulous respecting this system of counting, and although I heard it described, I held the greater part of the story to be fabulous. But when I was at Marcavillca, in the province of Xauxa, I asked the lord Guacarapora to explain it in such a way as that my mind might be satisfied, and that I might be assured that it was true and accurate. He ordered his servants to bring the *quipus*, and as this lord was a native, and a man of good understanding, he proceeded to make the thing clear to me. He told me to observe that all that he, for his part, had delivered to the Spaniards from the time that the Governor Don Francisco Pizarro arrived in the valley, was duly noted down without any fault or omission. Thus I saw the accounts for the gold, the silver, the clothes, the corn, sheep, and other things ; so that in truth I was quite astonished.

There is another thing that should be known, for I take it to be very certain. The long wars, cruelties, robberies, and tyrannical treatment which these people have suffered from the Spaniards would have led to their complete destruction, if it had not been for the excellent order and concert of their regulations. But they, having been trained in the intelligent system of accounts which was established by their wise princes, made an agreement among themselves that if an army of Spaniards passed through any of the provinces, and did such damage as would be caused by the destruction of growing crops, sacking of houses, and other mischief of still worse kinds, all the accountants should make the best provision possible in the districts through which our people passed, in order that all might not be devastated. So it was arranged, and as soon as the Spaniards were gone, the chiefs assembled, the *quipus* were examined and checked, and if one province had lost more than another, that which had suffered less

---

[1] The canvas shoes with rope soles, used in the Basque Provinces.

made up the difference : so that the burden was shared equally by all.

To this day these accounts are kept in each valley, and there are always as many accountants as there are lords, and every four months the accounts are made up and balanced. Through their former orderly government they have been able to endure such great oppression, and if God should be served by all ending with the good treatment that the people now receive, and with the decent order and justice that has been introduced, this kingdom might again be, to some extent, what it once was. But I believe that such a result will come tardily or never.

It is true that I have seen towns, and towns of considerable size, and after Christian Spaniards have passed through but one single time, they are left in such a state as to appear as if a fire had consumed them. And where the people were not so well trained, they did not help each other, and afterwards perished from pestilence and famine. For among some of them there is little charity, and each one is lord of his house and does not wish to take account of others. But this systematic order in Peru was due to the lords who commanded, and knew how to arrange all things as we see in those matters which have been described. And with this I will pass onwards.

CHAPTER XIII.

How the Lords of Peru were beloved on the one hand, and feared on the other, by all their subjects; and how no one, even a great lord of very ancient lineage, could come into the presence, except with a burden, in token of great obedience.

IT should be well understood that great prudence was needed to enable these kings to govern such large provinces, extending over so vast a region, parts of it rugged and covered with forests, parts mountainous, with snowy peaks and ridges, parts consisting of deserts of sand, dry and without trees or water. These regions were inhabited by many different nations, with varying languages, laws, and religions, and the kings had to maintain tranquillity and to rule so that all should live in peace and in friendship towards their lord. Although the city of Cuzco was the head of the empire, as we have remarked in many places, yet at certain points, as we shall also explain, the king stationed his delegates and governors, who were the most learned, the ablest, and the bravest men that could be found, and none was so youthful that he was not already in the last third part of his age. As they were faithful and none betrayed their trusts, and as they had the *mitimaes*[1] on their side, none of the natives, though they might be more powerful, attempted to rise in rebellion; or if such a thing ever did take place, the town where the revolt broke out was punished, and the ringleaders were sent prisoners to Cuzco.

Thus the kings were so feared that, when they travelled over the provinces, and permitted a piece of the cloth to be raised which hung round their litter, so as to allow their vassals to behold them, there was such an outcry that the

---

[1] Colonists. See chapter xxii.

birds fell from the upper air where they were flying, inso-much that they could be caught in men's hands. All men so feared the king, that they did not dare to speak evil even of his shadow. And this was not all. If any of the king's captains or servants went forth to visit a distant part of the empire on some business, the people came out on the road with presents to receive them, not daring, even if one came alone, to omit to comply with all his commands.

So great was the veneration that the people felt for their princes, throughout this vast region, that every district was as well regulated and governed as if the lord was actually present to chastise those who acted contrary to his rules. This fear arose from the known valour of the lords and their strict justice. It was felt to be certain that those who did evil would receive punishment without fail, and that neither prayers nor bribes would avert it. At the same time, the Incas always did good to those who were under their sway, and would not allow them to be ill-treated, nor that too much tribute should be exacted from them. Many who dwelt in a sterile country where they and their ancestors had lived with difficulty, found that through the orders of the Ynca their lands were made fertile and abundant, the things being supplied which before were wanting. In other districts, where there was scarcity of clothing, owing to the people having no flocks, orders were given that cloth should be abundantly provided. In short, it will be understood that as these lords knew how to enforce service and the payment of tribute, so they provided for the maintenance of the people, and took care that they should want for nothing. Through these good works, and because the lord always gave women and rich gifts to his principal vassals, he gained so much on their affections that he was most fondly loved. I remember having seen old Indians with my own eyes, when I was in sight of Cuzco, who gazed at the city and raised a great shout, followed by tears of sorrow at the contemplation of

the present state of things, and the thought of what was
passed, when for so many years they had lords in that city, of
their own people, who knew how to receive their service and
friendship after another fashion than that of the Spaniards.

It was a custom and inviolable law among these lords of
Cuzco, for their grandeur and in recognition of the royal
dignity, that when the king was in his palace, or travelling,
either with his army or without it, no one, even if he should
be the greatest and most powerful among the lords of the
empire, could speak to him or enter into his presence without first removing his shoes, which they call *oxotas*,[1] and
placing on his shoulders a burden, with which to appear
in the presence of the lord. In the presence, no account was
taken whether a man was great or humble ; but only that he
should understand the recognition he was bound to show to
his lord. Having entered, he turned his back in the presence
of the lord, having first made the reverence, which they call
mocha ;[2] and then he said what he had to say, or heard the
command he was to receive. This done, if he remained some
days at court, or was a person of importance, he did not
again enter the presence with a load. For it was always
those who arrived first from the provinces, by invitation or
on other duty, who performed this ceremony on entering the
presence of the lord.

[1] *Usutas.*

[2] *Muchani* means " I kiss ", " adore ", " worship ". Hence *Mucha*, the
act of adoration or worship.

CHAPTER XIV.

How the riches possessed by the Kings were very great, and how the sons of the lord were ordered always to be in attendance at court.

THE great wealth that we have seen in these parts enables us to believe what is said of the riches possessed by the Incas. For I believe what I have already affirmed several times, that there is no other country in the world so rich in metals. Every day they are discovering great veins both of gold and silver. They also collected gold in the rivers in many parts of the provinces, and obtained silver from the mountains, and all was for one king. So that he must have possessed very great riches. I am not, therefore, astonished at these things, nor even if the whole city of Cuzco and its temples had been built of pure gold. That which brings necessity upon princes, and prevents them from accumulating riches, is war. We have a clear example of this in the expenditure of the Emperor from the year in which he was crowned to the present time. For, having received more silver and gold than the Kings of Spain ever had, from the king Don Rodrigo to himself, none of them were in such necessity as His Majesty. Yet if he had no wars, and his residence was in Spain, in truth, what with his dues and with the treasure from the Indies, all Spain would be as full of riches as Peru was in the time of its kings.

I make the comparison because all the treasure of the Incas was expended in no other thing than in personal array and ornaments for the temples, and for the service of the houses and lodgings. In war time the provinces supplied all the men, arms, and provisions that were necessary; and if they gave some payment of gold to some one of the *mitimaes* during war, it was little more than had been extracted from the mines in one day. As the gold and silver was highly valued and much esteemed by them, they ordered it to be procured in great quantity, from many parts of the empire, in the manner and with the order that I will explain presently.

Such vast sums were collected because the son was obliged to leave all the wealth of the father with his image as a memorial, which had been amassed during many years. For all the service of the king's house, including the vases for his use and the kitchen utensils, were of gold and silver. These treasures were not collected in one place, but were scattered, especially at the chief places in the provinces, where there were many workers in silver who made these things for the king's service. In the palaces and royal lodgings there were plates and sheets of these metals, and the royal clothes were enriched with silver work, torquoises, emeralds, and other stones of great value. For the women they had still greater riches to ornament their persons and for their service; and their litters were encrusted with gold and silver. Besides this, there were vast quantities of gold in ingots, and of silver; besides many *taquiras*,[1] or beads, some very small, and other ornaments for their *taquis*[2] and drinking-bouts. For their sacrifices they also had great store of treasure. As they also had the foolish practice of burying treasure with the dead, it is incredible the quantity that was interred at the obsequies of a great king. In short, the drums and musical instruments and arms for royal use were of the precious metals. Moreover, to add to the grandeur of their capital, a law was made that neither gold nor silver that once entered Cuzco should ever leave it again, on pain of death to be inflicted on the transgressor. Owing to this law, the quantity that entered being great, while none went out, there was such store that if when the Spaniards entered they had not committed other tricks,

---

[1] Small beads. It should be *chaquira*. The word occurs several times in the First Part.　　　　[2] Recital of songs.

and had not so soon executed their cruelty in putting Atahu-allpa to death, I know not how many great ships would have been required to bring such treasure to Spain as is now lost in the bowels of the earth, and will remain so, because those who buried it are now dead.

As these Incas required so much, they ordered further that some sons of the lords of the provinces throughout the empire should reside at court all the year round, that they might understand the ceremonials and behold the great majesty of the sovereign, and they were assured that, as they obeyed and served, so they would inherit their lordships and *curaca*-ships ;[1] and when those of one province departed, those of another arrived. Thus the court was always well attended, for besides these, it was never without many knights of the *Orejones* and aged councillors, with whom to consult touching what had to be provided and ordained.

[1] *Curaca*, a great lord.

CHAPTER XV.

*How they built the edifices for the Lords, and the royal road
along which to travel over the kingdom.*

ONE of the things which I admired most, in contemplating
and noting down the affairs of this kingdom, was to think how
and in what manner they can have made such grand and admirable roads as we now see, and what a number of men
would suffice for their construction, and with what tools and
instruments they can have levelled the mountains and broken
through the rocks to make them so broad and good as they
are. For it seems to me that if the Emperor should desire to
give orders for another royal road to be made, like that which
goes from Quito to Cuzco, or the other from Cuzco to go to
Chile, with all his power I believe that he could not get it
done; nor could any force of men achieve such results unless
there was also the perfect order by means of which the
commands of the Incas were carried into execution. For if
the road to be made was fifty leagues long, or one hundred
or two hundred, and though the ground was of the most
rugged character, it would be done with diligent care. But
their roads were much longer, some of them extending for
over one thousand one hundred leagues along such dizzy and
frightful abysses that, looking down, the sight failed one. In
some places, to secure the regular width, it was necessary to
hew a path out of the living rock; all which was done with fire
and their picks. In other places the ascents were so steep and
high that steps had to be cut from below to enable the ascent
to be made, with wider spaces at intervals for resting-places.
In other parts there were great heaps of snow, which were
more to be feared, and not at one spot only, but often recur-
ring. Where these snows obstructed the way, and where
there were forests of trees and loose clods of earth, the road
was levelled and paved with stones when necessary.

Those who read this book, and have been in Peru, will remember the road which goes from Lima to Xauxa by the rugged mountains of Huarochiri and the snowy heights of Pariacaca, and will understand if they have heard or seen more than I write. Besides this, they will remember the path which descends to the river Apurimac, and how the road passes along the mountains of Paltas, Caxas, and Ayancas, and other parts of this kingdom where it is fifteen feet wide, a little more or less; and in time of the kings it was kept clean, so that there was neither a loose stone nor a growing weed on it, for it was always kept in good order. In the inhabited parts, near the towns, there were great palaces and lodgings for the soldiers. In the snowy wildernesses and plains, shelter-houses were built, where travellers could take refuge from the cold and rain. In many places, as in the Collao and other parts, there were distance-marks like the heaps in Europe which indicate boundaries, except that those in Peru are larger and better made. They called them *topos*,[1] and the distance between them is a Castillian league and a half.

The manner of making these roads and their grandeur being understood, I will explain the ease with which they were constructed by the natives, without increasing the death-rate, or causing excessive labour. When any king determined to have any of these famous roads made, much preparation was not necessary, but it was merely needful that the king should give the order. For then the overseers went over the ground to make a trace, and the Indians received instructions to construct the road from among the inhabitants who were on either side. One province completed the section within its

---

[1] *Tupu* is the general name for a measure. The measure of land which the Ynca apportioned to each vassal, sixty paces long by fifty wide, was called *tupu* or *topu*. See also the First Part, p. 146 of my Translation, and of *G. de la Vega*, I, v, cap. 3. A large pin for securing a mantle is also called *topu*.

limits, and when it reached the boundary it was presently taken up by the next: and if it was urgent, they all worked at one time. When they reached the uninhabited parts, the Indians of the nearest inhabited districts brought provisions and tools, in such wise that, with much rejoicing and little fatigue, it was finished. For there was no apprehension, and the Yncas or their servants interfered in nothing.

They also made great paved causeways of excellent construction, such as that which passes by the valley of Xaquixaguana, leading from the city of Cuzco to Muhina. There were many of these royal roads, both in the mountains and along the coast. Among them all there are four which are considered most important. They are those starting from the central square of the city of Cuzco, as from a cross-road, to the provinces of the kingdom, as I have mentioned in the First Part of this Chronicle, where I treat of the founding of Cuzco.[1] The lords were so respected, that when they travelled on these roads, the attendant guards went by one, and rest of the retinue by another. Their grandeur was so considered that, one being dead, the son, on occasion of a long journey, caused a road to be made for himself, larger and wider than that of his predecessor. This was when such a king set out on some conquest, or to achieve something worthy of memory, that it might be said that the road prepared for him was larger than any made before. This is clearly the case, for I have seen three or four roads near Vilcas, and I even lost my way on one, believing that I was on the one which is now in use. These roads are called, one the road of the Ynca Yupanqui, another that of Tupac Ynca; and that which is now used, and always will be hereafter, is that of Huayna Ccapac, reaching to the river Ancasmayu in the north, and to the south far beyond what we now call Chile; so long, indeed, that from one end to the other the distance is over one thousand two hundred leagues.

<hr>

[1] Chapter xcii.

CHAPTER XVI.

*How and in what manner they made the royal hunts for the
Lords of Peru.*

IN the First Part[1] I related how, in this kingdom of Peru.
there was a very great quantity of flocks, both wild and tame,
of *urcos*[2] sheep, *pacos*, *vicuñas*, and *llamas*, and excellent
pastures in all parts, so that they could be well maintained.
Although they were so numerous, it was forbidden by the
kings, on pain of severe punishment, to kill females, and if
the rule was broken, punishment followed, so that they were
never eaten. They multiplied so that the number when the
Spaniards arrived in the country is incredible. The principal
reason for this order was to ensure the growth of sufficient
wool to make clothing; for in many parts, if the flocks were
wanting, I certainly do not know how the people could
preserve themselves against the cold, if they had not any wool
wherewith to make clothes. But by this arrangement there
were many store-houses in all parts, where they kept the
clothing, as well for the soldiers as for the rest of the people,
and most of this cloth was made of the wool of guanacos
and vicuñas.

When the lord desired to enjoy a royal hunt, it is noteworthy how many animals were taken and killed; as many
as thirty thousand head. Tents were pitched in a position
selected by the lord, on such occasions as he was pleased to
amuse himself with the chase. For, on the high parts of the
mountains, in whatever place was chosen. there were sure to
be flocks in such quantities as we have stated. Having
assembled fifty thousand or sixty thousand people. they surrounded the plains and broken ground in such sort that they
gradually approached each other, at the same time descending

---

[1] Chapter cxi.
[2] Male.

from the steeper heights to the more level plains, and making the country resound with the noise of their voices. Gradually they approached each other, until they formed a ring with hands joined, and in the enclosed space bounded by their bodies the flocks were detained and secured. The lord was so placed as to witness the slaughter. Then certain Indians entered the enclosure armed with *ayllos*,[1] which are used to secure the legs, and others with sticks and clubs, and began to seize and kill. Among the great quantity of captured animals there were many guanacos, which are rather larger than small donkeys, with long necks like camels. They tried to escape by spitting into the faces of the men and rushing about with great leaps. They say that it was a marvellous thing to hear the noise made by the Indians in catching them, and to see the efforts made by the animals to escape in all directions. If the king wished to kill any of the chase without entering into the tumult, it was arranged in any way he pleased.

Many days were passed in these hunts, and a multitude of animals was killed. Then the overseers ordered the wool to be taken to the store-houses, and to the temples of the Sun, where the *mamaconas* were expert in making very fine cloth for the lords, the fineness being such that it appeared to be of silk, and of various colors. The flesh of the slaughtered animals was eaten by those who were present with the king, and some of it was dried in the sun,[2] to be kept in the store-houses, as provisions for soldiers on the march. All these animals, it must be understood, were in wild flocks and not domesticated. They also took many deer and *biscachas*,[3] as well as foxes, and some bears and small lions.

[1] *Ayllu* means the "*bolas*", or stones sewn round with leather and attached to lines, which were thrown to bring down animals, by twining round their hind legs. See the *Life of Don Alonzo de Guzman*, p. 101. Also *Balboa* and *G. de la Vega*. The word *Ayllu* also means "lineage", or "family".   [2] Called *charqui*, whence " jerked" beef.

[3] A large rodent, in the loftier parts of the Andes. *Lagidium Peru-rianum.*

CHAPTER XVII.

Which treats of the order maintained by the Incas, and how in many places they made the waste places fertile, by the arrangements they made for that purpose.

ONE of the things for which one feels envious of these lords is their knowledge of the way to conquer the wild lands and to bring them, by good management, into the condition in which they were found by the Spaniards when they discovered this new kingdom. I often remember, when in some wild and barren province outside these kingdoms, hearing the Spaniards themselves say, "I am certain that if the Incas had been here the state of things would be different." So that the advantage they were to us was well known. For under their rule the people lived and multiplied, and barren lands were made fertile and abundant, in such manner and by such admirable means as I will describe.

They always arranged matters, in the commencement of their negotiations, so that things should be pleasantly and not harshly ordered. Afterwards, some Incas inflicted severe punishments in many parts; but formerly, it is asserted on all sides, that they induced people to submit by great bene-volence and friendliness. They marched from Cuzco with their army and warlike materials, until they were near the region they intended to conquer. Then they collected very complete information touching the power of the enemy, and whence help was likely to reach them, and by what road. This being known, the most effective steps were taken to prevent the succour from arriving, either by large bribes given to the allies, or by forcible resistance. At the same time forts were ordered to be constructed on heights or ridges, consisting of circles with high walls, one inside the other and each with a door. Thus if the outer one was lost, the defenders could retire into the next, and the next, until refuge was taken in the highest. They sent chosen men to examine the land, to see the roads, and learn by what means they were defended, as well as the places whence the enemy received supplies. When the road that should be taken and the necessary measures were decided upon, the Inca sent special messengers to the enemy to say that he desired to have them as allies and relations, so that, with joyful hearts and willing minds they ought to come forth to receive him in their province, and give him obedience as in the other provinces; and that they might do this of their own accord he sent presents to the native chiefs.

By this wise policy he entered into the possession of many lands without war. In that case, he gave orders to his soldiers that they should do no harm or injury, nor commit any robbery or act of violence; and if there were not sufficient provisions in the province, he ordered that it should be sent from other parts. For he desired that his sway should not appear heavy to those who had newly come under it, so as to know and hate him at the same time. If any newly conquered province had no flocks, he ordered that so many thousand heads should be sent there, to be well looked after, so as to multiply and supply wool to clothe the people; and none were to be killed for eating until the lapse of a certain number of years. If, on the other hand, they had flocks, but needed some other thing, a similar course was pursued to supply the want. If the people lived in caves or thickets, they were led, by kind words, to build houses and towns on the more level parts of the mountains; and when they were ignorant as regards the tilling of their land, they were instructed, and the method of making channels to irrigate their fields was taught to them.

In all things the system was so well regulated that when one of the Incas entered into a new province by friendly agreement, in a very short time it looked like another place, the natives yielding obedience and consenting that the royal governors and *mitimaes*[1] should remain with them. In many others, which were conquered by force of arms, the order was that little harm should be done to the property and houses of the vanquished ; for the lord said, "These will soon be our people, as much as the others." For this reason the war was made with as little injury as possible, although great battles were often fought, where the inhabitants desired to retain their ancient liberty and their religion and customs, and not to adopt new ways. But during such wars the Incas always had the mastery, and when the enemies were vanquished, they were not destroyed; on the contrary, orders were given to release the captives and restore the spoils, and allow them to retain their estates. For the Inca desired to show them that they should not be so mad as to revolt against his royal person and reject his friendship ; rather they should wish to be his friends, as were those in the other provinces. In saying this to them, he gave them beautiful women, pieces of rich cloth, and some gold.

With these gifts and kind words, he secured the good-will of all, in such sort that those who had fled into the wildernesses returned, without fear, to their houses, and all cast aside their weapons ; while those who saw the Inca most frequently, looked upon themselves as most fortunate.

All were ordered to worship the Sun as their god. Their own customs and religious usages were not prohibited, but they were enjoined to conform to the laws and customs that were in force at Cuzco, and all were required to use the general language of the empire.

Having established a governor, with garrisons of soldiers, the army then advanced, and if the new provinces were large, it was presently ordered that a temple of the Sun should be built, and women collected for its service, and that a palace should be erected for the lord. Tribute was collected, care

---

[1] Colonists.

being taken that too much was not exacted, and that no injustice was done in anything ; but that the new subjects were made acquainted with the imperial policy, with the art of building, of clothing themselves, and of living together in towns. And if they needed anything, care was taken to supply it, and to teach them how to sow and to cultivate their lands. So thoroughly was this policy carried into effect, that we know of many places where there were no flocks originally, but where there has been abundance since they were subjugated by the Incas ; and others where formerly there was no maize, but where now they have large crops. In many provinces they went about like savages, badly clothed, and barefooted, until they came under the sway of the Incas ; and from that time they have worn shirts and mantles, both men and women, so that they always hold the change in their memories. In the Collao, and in other parts, the lord gave orders that *miti-maes* should go to the mountains of the Andes[1] to sow maize and coca, fruits and edible roots, for each town the quantity that was required. These colonists, with their wives, always lived in the places where the crops were sown and harvested, and the produce was brought from those parts, so that the want of it was never felt. And no town, however small, was without these *mitimaes* in the valleys. Further on we shall treat of the lot of these *mitimaes*, and what they did, as well as how they fared.

[1] That is to say, that colonists were sent from the cold and lofty plateau of the Collao to the warm and deep valleys of the Andes, where maize and coca can be cultivated. There was thus an exchange of products between the cold and the more genial regions. For another account of the *mitimaes* or colonists, see *G. de la Vega*, part I, lib. iii, cap. 19.

The people of the Collao were also sent to settle in the coast valleys, and thus Arequipa, Tacna, and Moquegua were colonised. To this day, it is remembered in the villages of the coast from what particular districts in the Collao their ancestors came as *mitimaes*. Those who colonised Arequipa came from Cavanilla near Lake Titicaca ; the colonists of Moquegua were from Acora and Ilave, villages on the lake ; of Tacna, from Juli and Pisacoma.

CHAPTER XVIII.

*Which treats of the order they adopted in the payments of tri-
bute by the provinces to the Kings, and of the system by which
the tribute was regulated.*

As in the last chapter I wrote of the method adopted by the
Incas in their conquests, it will be well in this one to relate
how they levied tribute from so many nations. It is a thing
very well understood that there was no village, either in the
mountains or in the valleys of the coast, which did not pay
such tribute as was imposed by those who were in charge.
It is said that when, in one province, the people represented that
they had nothing wherewith to pay the tribute, the king ordered
that each inhabitant should be obliged, every four months, to
give a rather large cane full of live lice, which was a sign of
the care taken by the Inca to make every subject contribute
something. Thus we know that they paid their tribute of
lice until such time as, having been supplied with flocks, they
had been industrious enough to multiply them, and to make
cloth wherewith to pay more suitable tribute in the time to
come.

The system which the Orejones of Cuzco and the other
native lords of the land say that the Incas adopted in imposing tribute was as follows : He who reigned in Cuzco, sent
some of his principal officers to visit the empire, one by each
of the four royal roads of which I have already written.[1] One
was called Chincha Suyo, which included all the provinces as
far as Quito, with all the valleys of Chincha towards the
north. The second was Conde Suyo, which includes the provinces on the sea coast, and many in the mountains. The
third was called Colla Suyo, including all the provinces to the
south as far as Chile. The last road led to Ande Suyo,

---

[1] In chapter xcii of the First Part.

which included the lands covered with forests at the foot of
mountains of the Andes.[1]

So it was that when the lord desired to know what tribute
would be due from all the provinces between Cuzco and
Chile, along a road of such great length, as I have often explained, he ordered faithful persons whom he could trust, to
go from village to village, examining the condition of the
people and their capacity for payment. They also took note
of the productiveness of the land, the quantity of flocks, the
yield of metals, and of other things which they required and
valued. Having performed this service with great diligence
they returned to the lord to submit their reports. He then
ordered a general assembly of the principal persons of the
kingdom to meet. The lords of the provinces which had to pay
the tribute being present, he addressed them lovingly, saying
that as they received him as their sole lord and monarch of
so many and such vast districts, they should take it in good
part, without feeling it burdensome, to give the tribute that
was due to the royal person, who would take care that it was
moderate, and so light that they could easily pay it. Having
been answered in conformity with his wishes, the lords of
provinces returned to their homes, accompanied by certain
Orejones who fixed the tribute. In some parts it was higher
than is paid to the Spaniards at present. But, seeing that the
system of the Incas was so perfect, the people did not feel the
burden, rather increasing and multiplying in numbers and
well being. On the other hand, the disorder introduced by
the Spaniards, and their extreme covetousness, have caused the
prosperity of the country to decrease in such sort that a great
part of the population has disappeared. Their greed and
avarice will destroy the remainder, unless the mercy of God
should grant a remedy by causing the wars to cease. Those
wars have certainly been permitted as a just scourge. The

[1] The four great divisions comprised in *Ttahuantin Suyu* (the four
provinces) were *Chincha Suyu*, *Cunti Suyu*, *Colla Suyu*. *Anti Suyu*.

country can only be saved by the taxation being fixed by moderate rules, so that the Indians may enjoy liberty and be masters of their own persons and estates, without other duty than the payment by each village of what has been fixed by rule. I shall treat of this subject a little more fully further on.

When the officers sent by the Incas made their inspection, they entered a province and ascertained, by means of the *quipus*, the number of men and women, of old and young. Then they took account of the mines of gold and silver, and, with so many thousand Indians at work, the quantity that should be extracted was fixed. An order was given that such quantity should be delivered to the overseers. As those who were employed to work at the extraction of silver could not attend to the cultivation of their fields, the Inca imposed the duty upon the neighbouring province to find labour for the sowing and reaping of the crops of the miners. If the mining province was large, its own inhabitants were able both to carry on the mining works and to cultivate the ground. In case one of the miners fell ill, it was arranged that he should return to his home, and that another should take his place. No one was employed in the mines who was not married, because the wives had to supply their food and liquor; besides which, arrangements were made to send sufficient provisions to the mines. In this manner, although men might be at the mines all their lives, they were not overworked. Besides, there was provision to rest for certain days in each month, for their festivals and for pleasure. But in fact the same Indians did not always remain at the mines; for there were periodical reliefs.

The Incas so arranged the mining industry, that they extracted great abundance of gold and silver throughout the empire, and there must have been years when more than fifty thousand *arrobas* of silver and fifteen thousand of gold were produced. It was always used for the royal service. The metal was brought to the principal place of the province, and in the manner that the mines were worked in one district in the same way were they ordered in all the others throughout the empire. If there were provinces where no metal could be extracted as a tribute, the people paid taxes in smaller things, and in women and boys, who were taken from the villages without causing any discontent. For if a man had an only child it was not taken, but if he had three or four children, one was required in payment of his dues.

Other provinces made their contributions in the form of so many thousand loads of maize, at each harvest. Others provided, on the same scale, a certain number. of loads of dried *chuñus*,[1] in the same way as the maize, and others again paid in *quinua*,[2] or other products. In other provinces the tribute consisted of so many cloth mantles, and in others of shirts, according to the number of inhabitants. Another form of tribute was the supply of so many thousand loads of lances, another of slings and *ayllos*, and all other kinds of weapons that they used. Other provinces were required to send so many thousand labourers to Cuzco, to be employed on the public edifices of the city and of the kings, with supplies of their needful provisions. Other provinces contributed cables to move the great stones, while others paid tribute in coca. The system was so arranged that all the provinces of Peru paid something to the Incas in tribute, from the smallest to the most important. Such perfect regularity was maintained that while the people did not fail to provide what was required, those who made the collections never took even a grain of maize too much. All the provision and warlike stores that were contributed, were served out to the soldiers, or supplied to the garrisons which were formed in different parts, for the defence of the empire.

When there was no war, a large proportion was eaten and used by the poor; for when the kings were at Cuzco they

---

[1] Potatoes frozen and dried in the sun.—See *G. de la Vega*, i, lib. v, cap. 5.　　　　　[2] *Chenopodium Quinoa.*

were served by the *anaconas*,[1] which is the name for perpetual servants who sufficed to till the royal fields, and do service in the palaces. Besides which, there was always brought for the royal table, from the provinces, many lambs and birds, fish, maize, coca, edible roots, and all kinds of fruits.

Such order was maintained in the tribute paid by the Indians that the Incas became very powerful, and never entered upon any war which did not extend their dominions.

To understand how, and in what manner, the tributes were paid, and the other taxes were collected, it must be known that in each *huata*,[2] which is the name for a year, certain Orejones were sent as judges, but only with powers to inspect the provinces, and give notice to the inhabitants that if any felt aggrieved he was to state his complaints, in order that the officer who had done him the injury might be punished. Having received the complaints, and also ascertained whether any tribute had not been paid, the judges returned to Cuzco ;

---

[1] *Yanacuna.* *Yana* means "a servant". Also "black". Literally, *Yanacuna* seems to be merely the plural form of *Yana.* But the word was applied to Indians bound to service. Balboa says that six thousand Indians, accused of rebellion against Tupac Ynca Ynpanqui, were assembled in the village of Yanayacu. They were pardoned, but they and their descendants were ordered henceforth to be employed solely in the service of the Yncas and of the temples. They were called *Yanayacu-cuna*, or men of Yanayacu, corrupted to *Yanaconas.* Hence, domestic servants were called *Yanaconas* by the Spanish settlers.—*Balboa*, p. 120.

In the time of the Viceroy Toledo (1570), the *Yanaconas* numbered about forty-six thousand souls. The Viceroy Marquis of Montes Claros, in 1601, described them as Indians domiciled in the houses or on the estates of Spaniards, like servants. Their masters found them in food and clothes, and gave them a patch of land, also paying their tribute for them. Lest the system should degenerate into slavery, the King of Spain declared that the *Yanaconas* were free, and desired that this should be made known to them.—*Memorias de los Vireyes*, i, p. 27.

[2] *Huata*, "a year". A sun circle for astronomical observations was called *Ynti-huatana.* *Huatana* means "a halter", from *huatani*, "I seize". "The place where the sun is tied up or encircled." Hence, *huata* means "a year".

whence others set out with power to inflict punishment on those who were in fault. Besides this, it was the rule that, from time to time, the principal men of the provinces should be permitted to appear before the lord, and report upon the condition of the provinces, on their needs, and on the incidence of taxation. Their representations then received attention, the Lords Incas being certain that they did not lie, but spoke the truth; for any deceit was severely punished, and in that case the tribute was increased. The women contributed by the provinces were divided between the service of the kings, and that of the temples of the Sun.

CHAPTER XIX.

How the Kings of Cuzco ordered that every year an account should be taken of all persons who died and were born throughout their dominions, also how all men worked, and how none could be poor by reason of the storehouses.

THE Orejones who gave me information at Cuzco concurred in saying that formerly, in the time of the Kings Incas, orders were given throughout all the towns and provinces of Peru, that the principal lords and their lieutenants should take note, each year, of the men and women who had died, and also of the births. For as well for the assessment of tribute, as for calculating the number of men that could be called upon to serve as soldiers, and for the defence of the villages, such information was needed. This was easily done, because each province, at the end of the year, was ordered to set down in the *quipus*, by means of the knots, all the men who had died in it during the year, as well as all who were born. In the beginning of the following year, the *quipus* were taken to Cuzco, where an account was made of the births and deaths throughout the empire. These returns were prepared with great care and accuracy, and without any fraud or deceit. When the returns had been made up, the lord and his officers knew what people were poor, the number of widows, whether they were able to pay tribute, how many men could be taken for soldiers, and many other facts which were considered, among these people, to be of great importance.

As this empire was of such vast extent, a fact which I have frequently pointed out in many parts of this work, and as in each province there were a great number of storehouses for provisions and other necessaries for a campaign, and for the equipment of soldiers, if there was a war these great resources were used where the camps were formed, without touching the supplies of allies, or drawing upon the stores of different villages. If there was no war, all the great store of provisions was divided amongst the poor and the widows. The poor consisted of those who were too old to work, or who were maimed, lame, or infirm; but those who were well and able to work received nothing. Then the storehouses were again filled from the obligatory tributes; and if, by chance, there came a year of great sterility, the storehouses were, in like manner, ordered to be opened, and the necessary provisions were given out to the suffering provinces. But as soon as a year of plenty came, the deficiencies so caused were made up. Although the tributes given to the Incas did not serve for other purposes than the above, yet they were well expended, and the kingdom was well supplied and cared for.

It was not permitted that any should be idle, or should profit by the labour of others, all being commanded to work. Each lord, on certain days, went to his farm, took the plough in his hand and made a furrow, besides working at other things. Even the Incas themselves did so, to give a good example to others; for they intended it to be understood that there must not be any one so rich that, on account of his riches, he could affront the poor: and by this system, there was no one in the whole land, being in good health, who did not work. The infirm were fed and clothed from the storehouses. No rich man was allowed to wear more ornaments than the poor, nor to make any difference in his dress, except the lords and the *Curacas*. These, as well as the Orejones, to maintain their dignity, could use great freedom in this respect, and they were made much of, among all the nations.

CHAPTER XX.

How Governors were appointed to the provinces, and of the manner in which the Kings visited their dominions, and how they bore, for their arms, certain waving serpents with sticks.

IT is well known that the lords of this kingdom had their lieutenants or representatives in the principal places, in the time of their sovereign power; such as Vilcas,[1] Xauxa,[2] Bombon,[3] Caxamalca,[4] Guancabamba,[5] Tomebamba,[6] Latacunga,[7] Quito, Coranqui,[8] and on the other side of Cuzco towards the south, in Hatuncana, Hatuncolla,[9] Ayavire,[10] Chuquiabo,[11] Chucuito,[12] Paria,[13] and others as far as Chile.

In these places there were larger houses and more resources than in many of the other towns of this great empire, so that they were the central positions or capitals of the provinces; for the tribute was brought into these centres from certain distant places at so many leagues distance to one, and at

[1] Vilcas is between Cuzco and Ayacucho, on the left of the road, and near the left bank of the river Pampas. The buildings of the Yncas are described by our author in his First Part (chap. lxxxix, p. 312 of my Translation). The only modern traveller who has visited and described the ruins is M. Wiener. They are called Vilcas Huaman.—See *Pérou et Bolivie, Récit. de Voyage par Charles Wiener*, Paris, 1880, pp. 264-271.

[2] The principal place in the valley of the same name, in the *sierra* east of Lima. The valley of Xauxa was inhabited by the tribe of Huancas.

[3] On the heights above the river Pampas, on the road from Ayacucho to Cuzco.

[4] The city in the north of Peru, where Atahualpa was seized and put to death by Pizarro.　　[5] North of Caxamarca.

[6] In the kingdom of Quito.　　[7] In Quito.

[8] In the northern part of Quito.　　[9] See p. 3.

[10] See p. 4.

[11] On the site of the modern city of La Paz, in Bolivia.

[12] On the western shore of lake Titicaca.

[13] In the province of Charcas.

so many to another. The rules were so clear that every village knew to which centre it had to send its tribute. In all these capitals the kings had temples of the Sun, and houses with great store of plate, with people whose only duty it was to work at making rich pieces of gold and great vases of silver. There were also many soldiers as a garrison, and also a principal agent or lieutenant who was over all, and to whom an account had to be rendered of all that came in, while he was expected to keep the account of all expenditure. These governors were not allowed to interfere in the administration of any neighbouring province; but within his own jurisdiction, if there was any disturbance or uproar, he had the power of inflicting punishment, much more if there was any treasonable movement or rebellion of one denying allegiance to the king. For it is certain that full powers were entrusted to these governors.[1]

If the Incas did not make these appointments and establish colonists, the natives would often rise and assume the royal power for one of themselves. But with so many soldiers, and such resources, it was not easy to set any treason or insurrection on foot. For the governors had the full confidence of their sovereign and all were Orejones, generally with *chacaras* or estates in the Cuzco district, with their houses and families. If one proved to be incompetent as a ruler with an important charge, another was presently appointed in his place.

If the governors, at certain times, came to Cuzco on private business or to consult with the king, they left lieutenants in their place, not men selected by favour, but those who knew their duties and would perform them with greatest fidelity, and with most care for the service of the Incas. If one of the

---

[1] The governors or viceroys were called *Tucuyricoc.*—See *Balboa*, p. 115; *Montesinos*, p. 55; *G. de la Vega*, Part I, lib. II, cap. 14, says that the *Tucuyricoc* was a commissioner who secretly visited the provinces and reported the shortcomings of officials.

governors or lieutenants died at his post, the natives quickly sent a report of the cause of the death, with proofs, to the lord ; and even the bodies of the dead were sent by the post road when it was considered desirable.

The tribute which was paid to the central station by the natives, as well gold and silver as weapons, clothes and all other things, was delivered to the *camayos* who had charge of the *quipos*, that an account might be taken. These officers kept the records with reference to the issue of stores to the armies, or to others, respecting whom they might receive orders, or to be sent to Cuzco. When overseers came from the city of Cuzco to examine the accounts, or the officers went there to submit their *quipus* for inspection, it was necessary that there should be no mistake, but that the accounts should be balanced. And few years were allowed to pass without these examinations of the accounts being made.

These governors had full authority to assemble soldiers and organize an army if any disturbance or rising should make it necessary to meet a sudden emergency, either to put down an insurrection or to oppose an invasion. The governors were honoured and favored by the lords, and many of them continued in perpetual command in the provinces when the Spaniards came. I know some of them who are now in office, and the sons of others who have inherited their posts.

When the Incas visited the provinces of their empire in time of peace, they travelled in great majesty, seated in rich litters fitted with loose poles of excellent wood, long and enriched with gold and silver work. Over the litter there were two high arches of gold set with precious stones, and long mantles fell round all sides of the litter so as to cover it completely. If the inmate did not wish to be seen, the mantles remained down, but they were raised when he got in or came out. In order that he might see the road, and have fresh air, holes were made in the curtains. Over all parts of these mantles or curtains there was rich ornamentation. On some were embroidered the sun and the moon, on others great curving serpents, and what appeared to be sticks passing across them. These were borne as insignia or arms. The litters were raised on the shoulders of the greatest and most important lords of the kingdom, and he who was employed most frequently on this duty, was held to be most honoured and in highest favour.

Round the litter marched the king's guard with the archers and halberdiers, and in front went five thousand slingers, while in rear there were lancers with their captains. On the flanks of the road, and on the road itself, there were faithful runners who kept a lookout and announced the approach of the lord. So many people came out to see him pass, that the hill sides were covered, and they all blessed their sovereign, raising a great cry and shouting their accustomed saying, which was:—"*Ancha hatun apu intip churi, canqui zapalla apu tucuy pacha ccampa uyay sullull.*"[1]   This means, "Very great and powerful lord, son of the Sun, thou only art lord, all the world hears thee in truth."   Besides this they said other things in a loud voice, insomuch that they went little short of worshipping their king as a god.

Along the whole road Indians went in front, cleaning it in such a way that neither weed nor loose stone could be seen, but all was made smooth and clean.   The Inca travelled as far as he chose each day, but generally about four leagues. He stopped at certain places where he could examine into the state of the country ; hearing cheerfully those who came with complaints, punishing those who had been unjust, and doing

---

[1] *Ancha* is a superlative form. *Hatun*, "great". *Apu*, "chief" or "lord". *Yntip* is the genitive of *Ynti*, "the sun". *Churi*, "a son". *Canqui*, second person singular, present indicative of *Cani*, "I am". *Sapa*, "only"; *lla*, a particle expressive of love. *Apu*, "lord". *Tucuy*, "entire". *Pacha*, "the earth". *Ccampa*, genitive of *Cam*, "thou". *Uyay*, from *Uyani*, "I obey". *Sullull*, "truth". "*Most high Lord, Child of the Sun Thou art the sole and beloved lord. The whole earth truly obeys thee.*"

justice to those who had suffered. Those who came with him, did not demand anything, neither did they go a single pace off the road. The natives supplied what was necessary, besides which there was more than enough of all provisions in the storehouses, so that nothing was wanting. By the way, many men and women and lads came to do personal service if it was needed. The lords were thus carried from one village to another, where they were taken up by those of the next village, and as it was only one day, or at most two, they did not feel this service to be any hardship. Travelling in this way, the lord went over his dominions for as long a time as pleased him, seeing what was going on with his own eyes, and giving necessary instructions on great and important matters. He then returned to Cuzco, the principal city of the whole empire.

CHAPTER XXI.

How the Posts of the Kingdom were arranged.

THE empire of Peru is so vast, that the Incas ordered a road to be made, as I have already stated on many occasions, from Chile to Cuzco, and even from the river of Maule[1] as far as the river Angasmayu.[2] If the king was at one of these extreme points, he could be informed of what had taken place at the other; but for one man to make such a journey, even by very long marches, it would take a considerable time. At the end of a journey, of a 1,000 leagues, there might be no time left to take the needful measures, and to remedy any wrong step that had been made. The Incas therefore, with a view to the efficient government of the empire, invented a system of posts, which was the best that could be thought of or imagined. The system is entirely due to the Inca Yupanqui, who was son of Viracocha Inca, and father of Tupac Ynca, according to the accounts given in the songs of the people, and in the statements of the Orejones. The Inca Yupanqui not only invented the system of the posts, but he did other great things, as I shall presently relate.

From the time of his reign, throughout all the royal roads, there were built, from half-league to half-league, a little more or less, small houses well roofed with wood and straw; and among the mountains they were constructed against the rocks. Thus the roads were lined with these small houses at regular intervals. The order was that in each house there should be two Indians with provisions, stationed there by the neighbouring villages.[3] They were not permanently left there, but were relieved by others from time to time; and

---

[1] The extreme southern limit of the empire, in Chile.

[2] The northern limit of the empire, to the north of Quito.

[3] These post-runners were called *Chasqui*.

the system of government was so efficient that it was only necessary to give the order, to ensure that these men should always be at their stations so long as the Incas reigned.

Each province took charge of the posts within its boundaries, including those which were on the coast deserts or in the region of snowy heights. When it was necessary to give notice to the kings in Cuzco, or in any other part, of any event that had taken place, or which was connected with their service, the men at the posts set out from Quito or Tomebamba, or from Chile or Caranqui, or from whatever other part of the empire, whether along the coast or in the mountains, and they ran with great speed, without stopping, each one over his half league. For the Indians who were stationed at the post houses, were chosen from among the most active and swiftest of all their countrymen. When one approached the next post house, he began to call out to the men who were in it, and to say :—"Start at once, and go to the next post with news that so and so has happened, which such a Governor wishes to announce to the Inca." When the other runner heard what was shouted to him, he started with the utmost speed, while the runner who arrived went into the house to rest, and to eat and drink of what was always kept in store there ; while the other did, in like manner, at the next post house.

So well was this running performed, that in a short time they knew, at a distance of 300 leagues, 500, and even 800, what had passed, or what was needed or required. With such secrecy did the runners keep the messages that were entrusted to them, that neither entreaty nor menace could ever extort a relation of what they had thus heard, although the news had already passed onwards. The roads pass over rugged mountains, over snow covered ridges, over stony wildernesses, and forests full of thorny thickets, in such sort that it may be taken as quite certain that the news could not have been conveyed with greater speed on swift horses or on mules, than by these foot posts. For the men on foot have no impediments, and one of them can do more in a day than a mounted messenger could do in three. I do not mean one single Indian, but one running for one half league, and another for the next, according to the established order. And it must be understood that neither storms nor anything else prevent the due service of the posts in the wildest parts, and as soon as one started another arrived to wait in his place.

In this way the lords were kept informed of all that happened in every part of the empire, and they arranged all that was needful for the ordering of the government, in the same way. In no other part of the world do we read of any such invention ; although I am aware that when Xerxes the Great was defeated, the news was conveyed by men on foot, in a short time. Certainly this system of posts was very important in Peru, and by it we may well see how good was the government of these lords. At the present day some of these post-houses may be seen near the royal roads, in many parts of the mountains, and they bear testimony to the truth of what has been said. I have also seen some of the *topos*, which as I have already explained, are like heaps for landmarks, except that these are larger and better made, and were used for counting the distance, each interval between them being one and a half leagues of Castille.

CHAPTER XXII.

How the Mitimaes were established, and of the different kinds of them, and how they were highly esteemed by the Incas.

In this chapter I wish to describe that which appertains to those Indians called *mitimaes*, for many things are related concerning them in Peru, and they were honoured and privileged by the Incas, being next in rank to the Orejones, while in the History which they entitle *Of the Indies*, it is written by the author,[1] that they were slaves of Huayna Capac. Into this error all those writers fall who depend upon the relations of others, without having such knowledge of the land concerning which they write, as to be able to affirm the truth.

In most, if not in all parts of the provinces of Peru there were and still are these *mitimaes*, and we understand that there were three classes of them. The system conduced greatly to the maintenance, welfare, and peopling of the empire. In considering how and in what manner these *mitimaes* were stationed, and the nature of their services, my readers will appreciate the way in which the Incas under-

---

[1] Francisco Lopez de Gomara was the author in question. In the chapter referred to, entitled "The Rule made by Gasca respecting the Tribute", he confuses the *mitimaes* with the *yanaconas*. The latter were not exactly slaves, but hereditary domestic servants. The words of Gomara are—"Also he left many whom they call *mitimaes*, and who are in the position of slaves in the manner they were held to service by Guainacapa, and he ordered the others to return to their homes. But many of them wished for nothing but to remain with their masters, saying that they were well with them, and could learn Christianity by hearing mass and sermons, and could earn money by selling, buying, and by service." Clearly he is referring to the *yanaconas*, not to the *mitimaes*.

This criticism of our author proves that this Second Part was written after 1552, in which year the first edition of the work of Gomara was published.

stood how best to order and regulate the government of so many regions and provinces.

Mitimacs is the name of those who are transported from one land to another. The first kind of *mitimaes*, as instituted by the Incas, were those who were moved to other countries, after a new province had been conquered. A certain number of the conquered people were ordered to people another land of the same climate and conditions as their original country. If it was cold, they were sent to a cold region, if warm, to a warm one, where they were given lands and houses such as those they had left. This was done that order might be secured, and that the natives might quickly understand how they must serve and behave themselves, and learn all that the older vassals understood concerning their duties, to be peaceful and quiet, not hasty to take up arms. At the same time, an equal number of settlers was taken from a part which had been peaceful and civilized for a long time, and sent into the newly conquered province, and among the recently subjugated people. There they were expected to instruct their neighbours in the ways of peace and civilization; and in this way, both by the emigration of some and the arrival of others, all was made secure under the royal governors and lieutenants.

The Incas knew how much all people feel the removal from their country and their home associations, and in order that they might take such banishment with good will, they did honour to those who were selected as emigrants, gave bracelets of gold and silver to many of them, and clothes of cloth and feathers to the women. They were also privileged in many other ways. Among the colonists there were spies, who took note of the conversations and schemes of the natives, and supplied the information to the governors, who sent it to Cuzco without delay, to be submitted to the Inca. In this way all was made secure, for the natives feared the *mitimaes*, while the *mitimaes* suspected the natives, and all learnt to

serve and to obey quietly. If there were turmoils or disturbances they were severely punished. Among the Incas there
were some who were revengeful, and who punished without
moderation and with great cruelty.

The *mitimacs* were employed to take charge of the flocks
of the Inca and of the Sun, others to make cloth, others as
workers in silver, and others as quarrymen and labourers.
Some also were sculptors and gravers of images; in short,
they were required to do such service as was most useful, and
in the performance of which they were most skilful. Orders
were also given that *mitimacs* should go into the forests of
the Andes to sow maize and to cultivate coca and fruit-trees.
In this way the people of the regions where it was too cold
to grow these things were supplied with them.

The second class of *mitimacs* were those who formed garrisons under captains, some of whom were *Orejones*, on the
frontiers, in forests east of the Andes. For the Indians, such
as the Chunchos, Moxos, Chiriguanas, and others whose
lands are on the slopes eastward of the Andes, are wild and
very warlike. Many of them eat human flesh; and they
certainly came forth to make war and destroy the villages
and fields of their neighbours, carrying off those they could
capture as prisoners. To guard against this evil, there were
garrisons in many parts, in which there were some *Orejones*.
In order that the burden of war might not fall upon one
tribe, and that they might not be able quickly to concert a
rising or rebellion, it was arranged that the *mitimacs* should
be taken from provinces that were conveniently situated, to
serve as soldiers in these garrisons; whose duty it was to hold
and defend the forts, called *pucaras*, if it should be necessary.
Provisions were supplied to the soldiers of the maize and
other food which the neighbouring districts paid as tribute.
The recompense for their service consisted in orders that
were given, on certain occasions, to bestow upon them
woollen clothing, feathers, or bracelets of gold and silver,

after they had shewn themselves to be valiant. They were also presented with women from among the great number that were kept, in each province, for the service of the Ynca, and as most of these were beautiful they were highly valued. Besides this, the soldiers were given other things of little value, which the governors of provinces were required to provide, for they had authority over the captains whom these *mitimacs* were obliged to obey.

Besides the frontiers already mentioned, they maintained these garrisons in the borders of Chachapoyas and Bracamoros, and in Quito, and Caranque, which is beyond Quito to the northward, next to the province called Popayan, and in other parts where it was necessary, as well in Chili, as in the coast valleys and the mountains.

The other manner of stationing *mitimacs* was more strange. The system of planting captains and garrisons on the frontiers, although done on a large scale, is no new thing, for there are not wanting other governments who have adopted a similar policy. But the other manner of colonising was different. In the course of the conquests made by the Yncas, either in the mountains, or plains, or valleys, where a district appeared to be suitable for cultivation, with a good climate and fertile soil, which was still desert and uninhabited, orders were at once given that as many colonists as would be sufficient to people it should be brought from a neighbouring province with a similar climate. The land was then divided amongst them, and they were provided with flocks and all the provisions they needed, until they had time to reap their own harvests. These colonists worked so well, and the king required their labours to be proceeded with so diligently, that in a short time the new district was peopled and cultivated, insomuch that it caused great content to behold it. In this way many valleys on the coast and ravines on the mountains were peopled, both such as had been personally examined by the Yncas, and such as they knew of from report. No tribute was required from the new settlers for some years; and they were provided with women, provisions, and *coca*, that they might, with more goodwill, be induced to establish themselves in their new homes.

In this way there were very few cultivable lands that remained desert in the time of the Incas, but all were peopled, as is well known to the first Christians who entered the country. Assuredly, it causes no small grief to reflect that these Incas, being gentiles and idolaters, should have established such good order in the government and maintenance of such vast provinces, while we, being Christians, have destroyed so many kingdoms. For wherever the Christians have passed, discovering and conquering, nothing appears but destruction.

It must be understood that the city of Cuzco was also full of strangers, all occupied in some industry. As there were many different tribes and lineages of men, it was necessary to guard against risings or other troubles which would be contrary to the wishes of the king. To this day there are in Cuzco men of Chachapoyas and Cañaris, and people from other parts, descended from the settlers who had been placed there.

It is held as certain, that these systems of colonisation have been in use since the days of Inca Yupanqui, the same who established the posts, and the first who planned the enrichment of the temple of Curicancha, as will be recounted in its place. Although some Indians say that the *mitimaes* were planted from the time of Viracocha Inca, the father of Inca Yupanqui, those may believe it who please to do so. For my part, I took such pains to ascertain the facts, that I do not hesitate to affirm the colonising system to have been instituted by Inca Yupanqui. Such is my belief; and this being the case we will now pass on to another part of the subject.

CHAPTER XXIII.

Of the great preparations that were made when the Lords set out from Cuzco on warlike expeditions; and how robbers were punished.

IN former chapters I related the manner in which the lords travelled, when they went to examine the condition of the provinces; and now I wish to explain to the reader the way in which the same lords set forth on their warlike expeditions. As these Indians are all brown and noisy,[1] and are so like each other, as we, who have dealings with them, can see at the present day; in order that they might be intelligible to each other, it was ordered that they should all speak the language of Cuzco. If this rule was not made, each man would talk in his native tongue when the *Orejones* visited the provinces. The same rules applied to the camps. It is clear that when the Emperor assembles a camp in Italy, and the army consists of Spaniards, Germans, Burgundians, Flemings, and Italians, each would speak in his own language. Here this confusion was avoided. Each tribe was also distinguished by differences in the head-dress. If they were Yuncas of the coast, they went muffled like gipsies. The Collas wore caps in the shape of a pump box made of wool. The Canas wore another kind of cap, larger, and of greater width. The Cañaris had crowns of thin lathes, like those used for a sieve. The Huancas had short ropes, which hung down as low as the chin, with the hair plaited. The Canchis had wide fillets, red or black, passing over the forehead. These and all other tribes were known, one from the other, by their head-dresses, and these were so clear and distinct that, when fifteen thousand men assembled, one tribe could easily be distinguished from another. To this day, when we see an assemblage of people,

---

[1] *Alharaquientos;* those who make a great noise, from *alharaca,* confused noise.

we presently say that these come from such a part and those from such another part; for in this way, as I have explained, they were known one from another.

The kings established the following order in their wars, that the great concourse of people might not cause confusion. In the great square of Cuzco was the stone of war, in the shape of a sugar loaf, well enclosed, and full of gold. The king came forth, with his councillors and favourites, to a place where the chiefs of provinces were assembled, to learn from them who were most valiant among their people, and best fitted to be leaders and captains. One Indian had charge of ten men, another received authority over fifty, another over a hundred, another over five hundred, another over a thousand, another over five thousand, and another over ten thousand. All these had authority over men of their own tribe, and all obeyed the captain-general of the king. Thus, if it was intended to send ten thousand men to any battle or campaign, it was only necessary to open the mouth and give the order; and the same with five thousand or any other number; and in the same way with smaller parties for exploring the ground or going the rounds, when fewer men were required. Each captain carried his banner, and some led men armed with slings, others with lances, darts, *ayllos* or slings, and some with heavily knobbed sticks.

When the Lord of Cuzco set out, the greatest order was preserved, even when there were three hundred thousand men in his army. The march was regulated each day, from *tambo* to *tambo*, where sufficient food was found for all, so that none were forgotten, besides arms, sandals, tents for the soldiers, and porters and women to carry the loads from *tambo* to *tambo*. The lord lodged in a house provided at each stage, with the guard near him, and the rest of the soldiers all round; and there were always dances and drinking bouts, the soldiers rejoicing among themselves.

The natives of the districts through which the army passed

were not allowed to be absent, or to fail in supplying all that was wanted, on pain of severe punishment. But neither soldiers nor captains, nor even the sons of the Incas, were allowed to ill-use or oppress the people, or to take from them so much as a grain of maize; and if this command was infringed, the punishment was death. Robbery was punished by whipping with greater severity than in Spain, and frequently the punishment of death was inflicted. All things were ordered and regulated on an established system. The natives did not fail to supply the soldiers sufficiently, while the soldiers had no desire to do evil or to rob, fearing the punishment. If there were any outbreaks of rebellion or mutiny, the principal ringleaders were brought to Cuzco, well guarded, where they were cast into a prison full of wild animals, such as serpents, vipers, tigers, bears, and other evil creatures. If any one denied the accusation, it was said that those serpents would do him no harm, but that if he lied they would kill him; and this they held and kept for certain. In this dreadful prison they always kept many people for crimes they had committed, whom they looked at from time to time. If their fate had been that they had not been bitten by any of the wild creatures, they were taken out, great sorrow was shown at their evil case, and they were allowed to return to their homes. In these prisons there were keepers sufficient to guard the captives, and to give food as well to them as to the evil lizards. Certainly, I laughed heartily when I heard that they used to have this prison in Cuzco; but although they told me the name, I do not remember it, and for that reason I have not put it down.[1]

---

[1] It was called *Samca-huasi*, or *samca-cancha*.

CHAPTER XXIV.

How the Incas ordered the people to form settled towns, dividing the lands concerning which there was any dispute, and how it was ordered that all should speak the language of Cuzco.

In former times, before the Incas reigned, it is well understood that the natives of these provinces had no towns as is now the case, but only strong places with forts, which they call *pucaras*, whence they came forth to make war one with another; and so they always passed their time, living in great trouble and unrest. The Incas, reigning over them, considered their manner of living to be evil, and induced them, partly by menaces and partly by favours, to see the wisdom of ceasing to live like savages, but rather as reasonable beings, establishing themselves in towns, both on the plains of the coast and in the mountains, and settling on the land according to the regulations that were made. In this way the Indians abandoned the *pucaras* in which they originally dwelt, and formed themselves into communities in towns, as well in the valleys of the coast as in the mountains, and on the plain of the Collao. The Incas caused the boundaries of fields to be set up, in order to prevent quarrels, settling the land which each man was to occupy, for their knowledge and for that of those who might be born after them. The Indians at the present day clearly state that this division was made. They told me at Xauxa that one of the Incas divided the plains and valleys amongst them which they now hold, and that this arrangement was then in force, and would continue. In many places in the mountains there are irrigating channels taken from the rivers with great skill and ingenuity, while all the towns were full of lodgings and store-houses of the kings, as I have already stated in many places.

It was understood by them that it would be very troublesome to travel for great distances over the land, and at each league to have a new language; while it would be very difficult to find interpreters for all of them. Selecting the best language, the Incas ordered, on pain of serious punishment, that all the natives of the empire should understand the tongue that was spoken at Cuzco, as well the men as the women. Even a child had scarcely left the breast of its mother before they began to teach it the language which it was bound to know. Although this rule was difficult to enforce at first, and many only wished to talk in their own native tongue, yet the power of the kings was such that they succeeded in enforcing their intention, and the people found it to be best to comply with their order. So completely was this policy enforced, that in a few years the language was understood and used over an extent of more than twelve hundred leagues. Yet although this language was used, all the tribes also spoke their own, which were so numerous that if they should be written down it would not be believed.

When a captain of Cuzco, or some one of the Orejones, set out to take an account of the revenues, or to act as judge on commission among the provinces, or on any other duty, he did not speak any other language than that of Cuzco to the people, nor they to him. This language is very good, concise, and comprehensive, and composed of many words. It is so clear, that in the few days that I studied it, I knew sufficient to ask for many things in the part where I wished to travel. They call

A man -	- *Runa.*	Night - - - *Tuta.*
A woman -	- *Huarmi.*	Head - - - *Uma.*
A father -	- *Yaya.*	Ear - - - *Rincri.*
A brother -	- *Huauque.*	Eye - - - *Ñaui.*
A sister -	- *Ñaña.*	Nose - - - *Senca.*
The moon (month) -	*Quilla.*	Teeth - - - *Quiru.*
The year -	- *Huata.*	Arm - - - *Maqui.*
Day - -	- *Punchau.*	Leg - - - *Chaqui.*

I only insert these words in my chronicle because I now see, that even as regards the language that was formerly used in Spain, they are varying and altering it bit by bit; and as regards the days that are to come, it is only God that knows what will happen in them. If the time should come when a language which was used by so many people shall be forgotten, it should at least be known which words belonged to the first and general language, and whence they came. Further, I declare that it was a great advantage to the Spaniards to have found this language, for with it they could travel in all directions; but now in some places it is beginning to be lost.

CHAPTER XXV.

How the Incas were free from the abominable sin, and from other evil customs which have been seen to prevail in the world, among other princes.

IN this kingdom of Peru, the public fame among all the natives is that the abominable sin was practised in some of the villages of the district of Pueblo Viejo, as well as in other lands where there were evil people, as in the rest of the world. I shall record a great virtue in these Incas; for, being lords with such freedom, and with no one to whom to give an account, besides being able to take their pleasure with women, night and day, and enjoy themselves as their fancies dictated, it has never been alleged, or even hinted, that any of them committed the above crime. On the contrary, they abhorred those who were guilty of it, looking upon them as vile wretches for glorying in such filthy conduct. Not only were they free from such vices in their own persons, but they would not permit any one who was guilty of such practices to remain in the royal houses or palaces. I believe, also, and I have heard it related that, even if it came to their knowledge that any one had committed an offence of that kind, they punished it with such severity that it was known to all.

It therefore should not be doubted, but rather believed implicitly, that this vice was unknown among the Orejones and many other nations. Those who have written generally of the Indians, condemning them for being guilty of this sin, should retract what they have said as regards many nations who are innocent. With the exception of Puerto Viejo, sinners of this class were unknown throughout Peru, except that, as is the case in all countries, there may be eight or ten here and there who do evil secretly. Those who were kept as priests in the temples, with whom it was rumoured that the lords joined in company on days of festivity, did not meditate the committing of such sin, but only the offering of sacrifice to the demon. If the Incas, by chance, had some knowledge of such proceedings in the temple, they may have ignored them, thinking that it was enough if they ordered that the Sun and their other gods should be worshipped in all parts, without considering it necessary to prohibit other ancient customs and religions, to abandon which would have been as bad as death itself, to those who were born in their practice.

We understand that in ancient times, before the Yncas reigned, the inhabitants of many provinces went about like savages; coming forth to make war upon each other, and eating their prisoners, as is now the case in the province of Arma[1] and others in that neighbourhood. But as soon as the Incas began to reign, being a reasonable people, with good and holy customs and laws, they not only did not themselves eat such food, but they exerted their power to put a stop to it among all the people with whom they came in contact, with many of whom it was much esteemed. Such was their energy, that in a short time the practice was forgotten throughout their vast empire, where no such food had been eaten for many years before the Spaniards came. Those who have now succeeded the Incas give evidence that they conferred a great benefit by not imitating their ancestors in eating such food, in the sacrifices of men and children.

Some have published—among those who hastily write down what they hear—that the Incas, on their days of festival, killed a thousand or two thousand children, and a greater number of Indians. This and other things are proofs that we Spaniards falsely impute crimes to the Indians, using the stories they recount to us to justify our ill-treatment of them and the bad usage they have suffered at our hands. I do not say that they did not sacrifice, and that they did not kill men and

---

[1] See chapter xix of my translation of the First Book, p. 71.

children in such sacrifices; but it was not in the way that
has been asserted, nor were the victims so numerous. They
sacrificed animals from their flocks, but fewer human beings
than I thought, as I shall explain in its place.

I know, from the statements of the aged Orejones, that
these Incas were innocent of any abominable sin, that they
did not practise the evil custom of eating human flesh, nor
were they guilty of public vices and irregularities. On the
contrary, they punished such crimes in others. If God had
permitted that one influenced by Christian zeal, and not by
avarice, should have given them complete knowledge of our
sacred religion, they were a people who would have been im-
pressed by it, as we now see in the good order in which con-
version works. But we must leave what has been done to
the judgment of God, who knows all; and in what may be
done hereafter we must beseech Him to give us grace to
enable us in some measure to repay those people to whom we
owe so much, and who had given such slight offence to justify
the injury we have done them, Peru and the rest of the Indies
being so many leagues from Spain, and separated by so vast
an ocean.

CHAPTER XXVI.

How the Incas employed councillors and executors of justice; and of their method of reckoning time.

As Cuzco was the principal city in all Peru, where the kings resided during the greater part of their time, many of the chief people of the empire lived there also, whose knowledge and ability fitted them for royal councillors. All affirm that, before any measure of importance was decided upon, these councillors were consulted. The most trustworthy travelled much, in all parts, inspecting the roads, superintending the government of the city, seeing that no offences were overlooked, and that culprits were punished. The Incas understood so well the administration of justice that no one ventured to commit an offence. This is to be understood with regard to such crimes as robbery, rape, or conspiracy. But many provinces carried on wars, the one with the other, and the Incas were not always able to prevent them.

Justice was executed at the river which flows near Cuzco, on those who were taken there, or who were brought as prisoners from other parts. Here their heads were cut off, or death was inflicted in other ways. Mutinies and conspiracies were punished more severely than other crimes. Thieves, and those who were convicted as such, were also severely punished, and their women and children were looked upon as degraded.

In observing natural things these Indians were much advanced, as well the movements of the sun as of the moon. Some of them said that there were four great heavens, and all affirm that the seat and residence of the great God, the Creator of the world, is in the heaven. I often asked them if they understood that the world would some day come to an end, but at this they laughed. For they understand little on this subject; and if they know anything, it is what God permits the devil to tell them. They call the whole world *pacha*, understanding the movements of the sun, and the increasing and waning of the moon. They count the year by the moon, and call it *huata*, consisting of twelve moons. They had small towers, many of them near Cuzco, but now in a ruined state, and by the shadow which the sun threw from them they calculated the time of sowing and other matters.[1] These Indians watched the heavens and the signs very constantly, which made them such great soothsayers. When the stars fall, great is the cry that they make, and the murmurings between one and another.

[1] Garcilasso de la Vega (i, p. 177) gives a fuller account of these solstitial towers; and Cieza de Leon himself refers to them in his first part (chap. xcii, p. 225). Acosta also describes them (ii, p. 395).

CHAPTER XXVII.

*Which treats of the riches of the temple of Curicancha, and of
the veneration in which the Incas held it.*

HAVING completed an account of some things that it is necessary for my purpose that I should describe, we will then
return to the succession of the kings that ruled down to
Huascar, recounting the events of each reign with great
brevity. But now I will speak of the great, most wealthy,
and most renowned temple of Curicancha, which was the
principal one in all these kingdoms.

It is a received fact among the Indians that this temple is
as ancient as the city of Cuzco itself. But the Inca Yupanqui,
son of Viracocha Inca, increased its riches to the extent in
which it was found when the Christians arrived in Peru.
Most of the treasure was brought to Caxamarca for the
ransom of Atahualpa, as we shall relate in its place. The
Orejones say that after the doubtful war between the inhabitants of Cuzco and the Chancas, who are now chiefs of the
province of Andahuaylas, the Inca Yupanqui found himself very rich and powerful, and people came to serve him
from all parts, bringing presents; and the provinces contributed great service in gold and silver. For in those
days there were very rich mines and veins of the precious
metals. Finding himself so rich and powerful, the Inca resolved to ennoble the house of the Sun, which in their language is called *Inti-huasi*, and also *Curi-cancha*, meaning "the
place of gold", and to increase its wealth. That all those who
may see and read this may understand how rich the temple
at Cuzco was, and the merit of those who built and completed
such great things, I here will preserve the memory of it. I
will relate what I saw, and what I heard from many of the

first Christians, who received the account from the three men[1]
that first came from Caxamarca, and who saw everything.
But the Indians themselves tell us so much, and are so truth-
ful, that other evidence is unnecessary.

This temple was more than four hundred paces in circuit,
entirely surrounded by a strong wall. The whole edifice was
of excellent masonry, the stones very well placed and fixed.
Some of the stones were very large. There was no mortar,
either of earth or lime, but a sort of bitumen with which
they used to fix their stones. The stones themselves are so
well worked that no joining or cement can be seen. In all
Spain I have not seen anything that could be compared with
the masonry of these walls, except the tower which they call
Calahorra, near the bridge of Cordova, and a work which I
saw at Toledo, when I came there to present the First Part of
my Chronicle to the Prince Don Felipe.[2] I allude to the
hospital which the Archbishop of Toledo, Tavera, ordered to
be built.[3] Although these edifices have some resemblance to
those I have mentioned, yet they are the best as regards the
masonry of the walls, the stones being so admirably worked,
and placed with such great ingenuity. The encircling wall
was straight, and very well traced out.

The stone appeared to me to be of a dusky or black colour,
and most excellent for building purposes. The wall had
many openings, and the doorways were very well carved.
Round the wall, half way up, there was a band of gold, two
palmos wide and four *dedos* in thickness. The doorways and
doors were covered with plates of the same metal. Within

---

[1] According to Cieza de Leon, these three men were Martin Bueno,
Zarate, and Pedro de Moguer. Pedro Pizarro, an eye-witness, says
there were only two, Martin Bueno and Pedro de Moguer. But see the
note at page 9.   [2] In 1552.

[3] The Hospital of San Juan Bautista. It was commenced on Decem-
ber 9th, 1541, and up to 1624 the first Mass had not yet been said in
its chapel The activity in forwarding the work ceased on the death of
the founder, Archbishop Tavara, in 1545.

there were four houses, not very large, but with walls of the same kind, and covered with plates of gold within and without, as well as the woodwork. The covering was of straw, which served as a roof. Against the wall there were two benches, from which the Sun could be seen when it rose. The stone in front was subtly bored, and the holes were adorned with emeralds and other precious stones. These benches were for the kings, and no one else was allowed to use them on pain of death.

At the doors of these houses porters were stationed to keep guard over the virgins, many of whom were daughters of great lords, the most beautiful and charming that could be found. They remained in the temple until they became old. If one of them had knowledge of a man, they killed her by burying her alive; and the same penalty was suffered by the man. These women were called *mama-cunas*. Their only occupations were to weave and dye woollen cloth for the service of the temple, and to make *chicha*, which is the wine they make, of which they always kept large full jars.

In one of these houses, which was the richest, there was the figure of the sun, very large and made of gold, very ingeniously worked, and enriched with many precious stones. This temple also contained some of the figures of the former Incas who had reigned in Cuzco, and also a vast quantity of treasure.

Round the temple there were numerous small dwellings of Indians who were employed in its service; and there was an enclosure where they kept the white lambs, children, and men for sacrifice. They had also a garden, the clods of which were made of pieces of fine gold; and it was artificially sown with golden maize, the stalks, as well as the leaves and cobs, being of that metal. They were so well planted, that even when there was a high wind they were not torn up. Besides all this, they had more than twenty golden sheep with their lambs, and the shepherds with their slings and crooks to watch

them, all made of the same metal. There was a great quantity
of jars of gold and silver, set with emeralds; vases, pots, and
all sorts of utensils, all of fine gold. On other walls were
sculptured and painted various notable things; and, in fine, it
was one of the richest temples in the world.

The High Priest, called Villac Umu, resided in the temple,
and offered up the ordinary sacrifices, accompanied by super-
stitious rites, with the help of the other priests, according to
their custom. At the important festivals the Inca was present at the sacrifices, and there were great rejoicings. Within
the enclosure of the temple there were more than thirty
granaries of silver in which the maize was stored; and many
provinces sent their tribute for the service of the temple. On
certain days the devil was seen by the priests, who gave them
deceptive answers, in conformity with what might be expected from him.

Many other things might be said of this temple, which I
omit because it seems to me that I have said enough to shew
what a grand place it was; so I shall not treat further of the
silver work, of the *choquira*, of the plumes of gold and other
things, which, if I wrote down, I should not be believed. That
which I have described has been seen, or the greater part, by
Christians who are still alive, when it was brought to Caxamarca as a ransom for Atahualpa. But a great deal was
hidden by the Indians, and is now buried and lost. Although
all the Incas added to the adornment of the temple, in the
time of the Inca Yupanqui its riches were increased to such
an extent that when he died, and his son Tupac Inca succeeded,
it remained in its complete state.

CHAPTER XXVIII.

Which treats of the other principal temples, and of their names.

MANY were the temples in this land of Peru, and some were looked upon as very ancient because they were founded before the time of the Incas, as well in the high mountains as in the valleys of the coast. During the reigns of the Incas many other new temples were built, where sacrifices and festivals were celebrated. It would take very long to enumerate each temple in the different provinces, so I have determined only to allude, in this place, to those which were held in most esteem.

Next after the temple of Curicancha, the second *huaca* of the Incas was the hill of Guanacauri, which is within sight of the city, and was much honoured and frequented. For some say that the brother of the first Inca was turned into stone in that place, at the time when they set out from Pacari Tambo, as was explained at the beginning of this work. In ancient times there was an oracle in this place from which the accursed devil spoke. A great amount of treasure was buried around it; and on certain days they sacrificed men and women, to whom, before they were put to death, the priest addressed a discourse, explaining to them that they were going to serve that god who was being worshipped, there in the glorious place that they, in their ignorance, believed that he inhabited. Those who were to be sacrificed also believed it for certain, and dressed themselves in clothes of fine cloth, with fringes of gold, and bracelets, and with gold lace in their sandals. After they had heard the discourse which those liars of priests addressed to them, they were given much *chicha* to drink, out of great vases of gold. The sacrifice was celebrated with songs, declaring that such lives were offered up to serve the gods, the victims holding themselves fortunate to receive death in such a place. Having thus celebrated the rites, the victims were strangled by the ministers. A *cccpi*[1] of gold and a small jar of gold were placed in the hands of each body, and they were buried in tombs around the oracle. These victims were looked upon as canonized saints, for the people believed that, without any doubt, they were in heaven serving their Guanacauri. The women who were sacrificed also came richly dressed in fine cloths and plumes of feathers, with their *topus* of gold, like spoons, and small breastplates all of gold. And they also, after they had drunk deeply, were strangled and interred, both they and those who killed them believing that they went to serve their demon or Guanacaure. They celebrated these and similar sacrifices with much dancing and singing. This idol was kept where they heard the oracle, with its farms, *yanaconas* or servants, flocks, virgins, and priests who profited by all the rest.

The third oracle or *huaca* of the Incas was the temple of Vilcañota, renowned throughout these kingdoms. Here the devil, our Lord God permitting it, had great power, and spoke by the mouths of the false priests who were there to serve the idol. This temple of Vilcañota was a little more than twenty leagues from Cuzco, near the village of Chungara. It was very much esteemed and venerated, and many offerings and gifts were presented to it, as well by the Inca and lord, as by the rich men of the districts whence people came to sacrifice. The temple had its priests, virgins, and cultivated lands, and almost every year the offering of *capacocha* was made, which is what I will now explain. They gave great credit to what the devil said in his replies, and on certain occasions they offered up sacrifices of birds, sheep, and other animals.

The fourth temple that was venerated and frequented by the Incas and the natives of the provinces was the *huaca* of Ancocagua, where there was also a very ancient oracle which was famous. It was in the province of Hatun Cana, and on

---

[1] Burden or load.

certain occasions people came from many parts, with great veneration, to hear the vain replies of the demon. Here there was great store of treasure offered up by the Incas and other worshippers. They say also that, besides the numerous animals sacrificed to this demon, whom the people believed to be God, they also sacrificed some men and women, in the same way as I have described in recounting the offerings made on the hill of Guanacauri.

That the treasure alleged to have been in this temple was really there, seems clear from the following circumstance. After the Spaniards had occupied Cuzco for more than three years, and the priests and chief lords had produced the great treasures which all these temples contained, I heard that a Spaniard named Diego Rodriguez Elemosin took from this *huaca* more than 30,000 *pesos* of gold. Besides this, still more has been found; and there is a rumour that an immense quantity of gold and silver is in places which no one but God knows, and they will never be discovered, except by accident or good luck.

Besides these temples, there was another which was as much venerated and frequented by them, named Coropuna, in the province of Condesuyo. It is on a very lofty mountain which is covered with snow both in summer and winter. The kings of Peru, with the principal lords, visited this temple, making presents and offerings as at the others. It is. held for very certain that among the gifts and *capacocha* offered to this temple, there were many loads of gold, silver, and precious stones buried in places which are now unknown. The Indians concealed another great sum which was for the service of the idol, and of the priests and virgins who attended upon it. But as there are great masses of snow, people do not ascend to the summit, nor is it known where these great riches are hidden. This temple possessed many flocks, farms, and service of Indians and *yanaconas*. There was always a large concourse of people in it, from many parts, and the devil talked here more freely than in the other oracles, for he constantly gave numerous replies, and not occasionally, as in the other temples. Even now, at the present time, for some secret reason known to God, it is said that devils visibly walk about in that place, and that the Indians see them and are much terrified. I have also heard that these devils have appeared to Christians in the form of Indians, appearing and disappearing in a very short space of time. Occasionally they offered great services to this oracle, killing many sheep and birds, and some men and women.

Besides these oracles there was that of Aperahua, where the oracle answered out of the trunk of a tree, and near it a large quantity of gold was found. Also that of Pachacamac, which is in the country of the Yuncas, and many others, as well in the provinces of Anti-suyu, as in Chincha-suyu, Omasayu, and other parts of this empire, of which I might say somewhat more. As in the first part of my work I treat of the founding of temples, I shall now only dwell upon the oracles. To those which the Incas and other nations held in most veneration, they sacrificed some men and women, with many sheep. But before those which were not so much respected, they did not shed human blood nor kill men, only offering up gold and silver. The *huacas* of little account, like our chapels, were worshipped by offering *chaquira*, plumes, and other small things of slight value. I say this owing to the opinion held by us Spaniards, that they sacrificed human beings in all the temples, which is false. What I have stated is the truth, so far as I have been able to obtain it, without deducting or putting down more than I myself understand and hold to be certainly true.

CHAPTER XXIX.

*How the Capacocha was made, and to what extent it was prac-
tised by the Incas; by which is to be understood the gifts
and offerings that were made to idols.*

IN this place it will be well that I should explain what was
understood by the *Capacocha*, as all that has just gone before
related to the service of the temples. I speak on the authority
of old Indians who are still living, and who saw what passed
concerning this matter, and I shall write what I gather from
them to be the truth.

It was the custom in Cuzco for the kings to cause all the
statues and figures of idols in the *huacas* or temples where
they were worshipped, to be brought to the city once a year.
They were conveyed with much veneration by the priests
and *camayocs* or guardians, and when they entered Cuzco
they were received with great feasting and processions, being
deposited in the places that were set apart for that purpose.
A great number of people having come from the neighbourhood of the city, and indeed from all parts of the empire, as
well men as women, the reigning sovereign, accompanied by
all the Incas and Orejones, courtiers, and principal men of
the city, inaugurated a succession of great festivals, drinking
bouts, and *taquis*.

The great chain of gold which encircled all was brought out
into the square of Cuzco, and such riches and precious stones
as he is able to imagine who has read what has been written
touching the treasures possessed by these kings. The business of this annual ceremony was to receive a forecast of
the events of the year to come, from the statues and figures
and their priests; whether it would be fertile or sterile;
whether the Inca would have a long life or would die; whether
enemies would come from any direction; and, in conclusion,

other enquiries, of more or less import, were made, such as whether there would be any pestilence, or murrain in the flocks, and whether the flocks would be largely multiplied. These enquiries were not made of all the oracles together, but of each one by itself. If the Incas did not do this every year, they felt discontent and fear, and did not consider their lives to be safe.

First, the people made merry, with their solemn drinking bouts, banquets, great *taquis* or musical entertainments, and other festivities, which are entirely different from ours. Then the Inca invited those around him, with great triumph; and at this feast there were great jars of gold and silver; for all the service of his kitchen, down to the pots and pans, was of that metal. The High Priest was also present at the festival with the same pomp and magnificence as the king, accompanied by the *mama conas* and priests who had come together for the occasion. Those who were appointed for the purpose were commanded to put the questions concerning future events to each of the idols; and the idols replied by the mouths of the priests who had charge of their images. These, having drunk deeply, answered in the way which seemed to be most to the taste of those who made the enquiries, finding out what to say from the devils who were in the statues. The enquiry being made of each idol, the priests, being so cunning in their wicked art, asked for some time to answer, that their nonsense might be listened to with more credit and respect. They said that they must offer up sacrifices that, their great gods being pleased, it might please them to answer as to what would happen. So many animals, such as sheep and lambs, *cuis*[1], and birds, exceeding the number of 2,000 sheep and lambs, were beheaded. Meanwhile the prests made their diabolical exorcisms and vain sacrifices, according to their custom. Presently they announced what they had dreamt or imagined, or perhaps what the devil had told them. Great

---

[1] Guinea pigs.

attention was paid to what they said, and to the number which concurred in foretelling good or evil. The same thing was gone through with regard to the other replies, and care was taken to note who spoke truly, and ascertained what was about to come to pass in the coming year.

This being done, the almoners of the king came forth with the offerings which they call *capacocha*, and the general almsgiving having been gone through, the idols were taken back to their temples. If, before the year had passed, the saying of any one of those dreamers happened to come true, the Inca joyfully sent for him, to be one of his household.

The *capacocha*, as I have said, was an offering paid instead of a tithe to the temples. It consisted of many vases of gold and silver and precious stones, loads of rich mantles, and large flocks. In the following years no gifts were bestowed on those whose sayings proved to be false or uncertain, and they forfeited their reputations. At these ceremonies great things were done at Cuzco, much more than I have written. In these days, after the Royal Audience had been established, and Gasca had returned to Spain,[1] mention was made of this *capacocha* in certain lawsuits, and it is certain that the custom prevailed, as well as all else that we have written. We will now describe the great festival of *Hatun Raymi*.

[1] In January 1550.

CHAPTER XXX.

*How they made great festivities and sacrifices at the grand and
solemn feast called Hatun Raymi.*

THE Incas held many festivals during the year, at which they
offered great sacrifices according to their custom; but to
notice them all would require a separate volume. It is also
well not to dwell long on the sorceries and follies that were
practised on these occasions; but only to describe the feast
of Hatun Raymi, which is very famous. It was kept in
many provinces, and was the principal ceremony of the
whole year, and the occasion on which the greatest number of
sacrifices was offered up.

This festival was celebrated in the end of August, when
the maize harvest had been got in, as well as the potatoes,
quinuas,[1] *oeas,*[2] and the other seeds that they sow. They call
this feast Hatun Raymi, which in our language means "a very
solemn festival"; and in it they had to offer up thanks and
praise to God, the Creator of Heaven and Earth, whom they
called, as has often been mentioned before, Ticiviracocha, as
well as to the Sun, to the Moon, and to their other gods, for
having granted them a good harvest of food for their support.
In order to celebrate this festival with greater devotion and
solemnity, it is said that they fasted for ten or twelve days,
abstaining from too much food, and from intercourse with
women; drinking *chicha* only in the morning, which is the
time when they eat, and at other times only water; abstaining
from the use of *aji* and from carrying anything in the mouth,
and practising other usages such as were observed on these
occasions of fasting. This time of fasting being over, the
people brought to Cuzco a great number of lambs, of sheep,

---

[1] *Chenopodium Quinua.*   [2] *Oxalis tuberosa.*

of doves and *cuys*, and of other birds and beasts which were killed for the sacrifices. Having killed a vast number, they anointed the statues and figures of their gods, or rather devils, with the blood, as well as the doors of the temples and oracles. After an interval, the soothsayers and diviners looked for omens in the entrails, announcing what they prognosticated, to which the people gave great credit.

When the sacrifice was finished, the High Priest, with the other priests, went to the temple of the Sun; and, after reciting their accursed psalms, they ordered the *mama conas*, or virgins, to come forth richly dressed, with the great store of *chicha* they had prepared; and all those who were in the great city of Cuzco ate of the sheep and birds which had been killed for the vain sacrifices, and drank of that *chicha* which was held to be sacred. It was contained in jars of silver, out of the great numbers there were in the temple; and they drank it out of cups of gold.

Having eaten and drunk many times, and the Inca, High Priest, and all the rest being merry in consequence, it was still only a little after noon. They then formed in procession, and the men began to sing, with loud voices, the romances and chaunts which had been prepared for use at this festival by their ancestors. The purport of them all was to give thanks to the gods, promising to do them services for the blessings received. To accompany the songs they had many drums of gold, some of them encrusted with precious stones, which their women played upon, who, together with the sacred *mama conas*, joined in the songs.

In the centre of the plaza it is said that a great theatre was placed, with steps, adorned with cloths and plumes richly embroidered with golden beads, very large mantles of their exceedingly fine cloth, also garnished with silver and gold work, and precious stones. On the summit of this throne was placed the figure of Ticiviracocha, large and richly adorned. As they held it to be the sovereign God, maker of

all created things, they gave it the highest place ; and all
the priests were near it.   The Inca and all the principal men
and the people came to worship it, taking off their sandals
with much humility, bending their shoulders, filling out their
cheeks, and sighing towards it, thus performing *mucha*, which
is their word for worship.

Below this throne was placed the figure of the Sun, but
they do not state of what it was made, and also that of the
Moon, and other figures of idols sculptured in wood and
stone.   We hold it to be very certain that neither in Jeru-
salem, nor in Rome, nor in Persia, nor in any other part of
the world, by any state or king of this earth, was such wealth
of gold and silver and precious stones collected together, as
in this square of Cuzco when this festival and others like it
were celebrated.   For the images of the Incas, their deceased
kings were brought out, each one with its service of gold and
silver.   That is to say, such of them as had been good and
brave fathers of their people, generous in granting favours,
pardoners of injuries.   These were canonized as saints, in
their blindness, and their bones were honoured by those who
did not comprehend that their souls were burning in hell,
thinking that they were in heaven.

It was the same with some other Orejones, or chiefs of
another nation, whom, for some cause or other, they, in their
heathen minds, looked upon as saints.   They call those who
were canonized in this way *Ylla*, which signifies the body of
him who did good in his lifetime.   Another meaning of *Yllapa*
is thunder and lightning.   Hence the Indians call discharges
of artillery *Yllapa*, from the loud report.

The Inca and High Priest, with all the courtiers, and the
great concourse of people that came from the neighbourhood,
did *mucha* (which means reverence and worship), to the gods
arranged round the square.   They also made many offerings,
such as small golden figures of idols, sheep, women, and many
other trinkets.   This festival of Hatun Raymi continued for

fifteen or twenty days, during which there was much singing and dancing, drinking bouts, and other feasting, according to their custom. At the end of the time they finished with the sacrifices, and put back the images of the idols into the temples, and those of the deceased Incas into their houses.

The High Priest enjoyed that dignity during his life. He was married, and was so respected that he vied in dignity with the Inca, and had jurisdiction over all the oracles and temples, appointing and removing priests. The Inca and the High Priest often played together at their games, and these functionaries were of high lineage and had powerful relations. The dignity was not conferred upon obscure persons, even if they should possess great merit. All those who lived in the parts of Cuzco which they called Hurin-Cuzco and Hanan-Cuzco, and their descendants, were considered to be noble, although they should reside in other parts. I remember when I was in Cuzco in the year 1550, during the month of August, after the harvests had been got in, that a great crowd of Indians entered the city with their wives, making much noise. They carried their ploughs in their hands, and some stalks of maize, to make a festival by merely singing and reciting as had been their custom at harvest time. The *Apus* and Priests do not consent that these heathen festivals shall be performed in public as in former times, nor in secret if they can prevent it. But as there are so many thousands of Indians who have not become Christians, it is probable that these rites are still performed in secret.

The figure of Ticiviracocha, and those of the Sun and Moon, and the great chain of gold, besides other recorded pieces of great value, have not been found. There is neither Indian nor Christian who knows where they are. But although their value is great,[1] it is small when compared with all that has been buried in Cuzco, in the places of the oracles, and in other parts of this great empire.

[1] The statue of the Sun was found by the Spaniards in 1572, in possession of Tupac Amaru, at the time when this Ynca and his camp were captured by the expedition under the command of Garcia de Loyola.

CHAPTER XXXI.

*Of the second king or Inca who reigned in Cuzco, named
Sinchi Roca.*

WITH as much conciseness as I am able to use, I have written
what I learnt touching the government and customs of the
Incas; and I now propose to return to my narrative of what
happened from the time of Manco Capac to that of Huascar,
as I have already promised. Touching the first Inca, and
those who followed him, the Orejones do not give many particulars, because, in truth, they did not perform many great
deeds. For the most valorous of all were the Inca Yupanqui,
and Tupac Inca his son, and Huayna Capac his grandson.
But the reason may be that which I have already written,
namely, that these kings were the most modern.

As soon, then, as Manco Capac was dead, and the general
mourning and obsequies had been performed for him, Sinchi
Roca[1] assumed the fringe or crown, with the accustomed
ceremonies. He contrived to enlarge the house of the Sun,
and induced as many people as possible to flock to the new
settlement, by gifts and large offers. The place was then, as
it is now, called Cuzco. Some of the natives of it affirm that,
in the place where was the great square, being the same then
as now, there was a small lake and slough of water, so that it
was difficult to raise the great edifices which they had begun
to build. As soon as this was known to the king, Sinchi
Roca, he contrived, with the aid of his allies and neighbours,
to get rid of this swamp, covering it with great slabs and
huge beams, and levelling the ground on the top, where the
water used to be, in such sort that it remained as we now see

---

[1] *Sinchi* means strong, valiant. *Rocca* has no meaning in the Quichua
language.

it. They further state that the whole valley of Cuzco was barren, and that the land never yielded good fruit from the seed which they sowed. So they brought many thousands of loads of earth from the great forests of the Andes, and spread it all over the land ; by which means, if the tale be true, the valley became very fertile, as we now see it.

This Inca had, by his sister and wife, many children : and they named the eldest Lloque Yupanqui. The people round Cuzco beheld the good order in which the settlers lived, and how they brought people under their friendly influence more through love and benevolence than by recourse to severity and force. Some of the captains and principal men came to hold discourse with those of the city, and rejoiced to see the temple of Curi-cancha, and the good order that reigned around it. By this means treaties of friendship were made in many directions. They relate that, among those chiefs that I have mentioned, there came to Cuzco a captain of the town called Zañu, which is not very distant. He asked Sinchi Roca, with great vehemence, that he would see fit to take his very fair and beautiful daughter as a wife for his son. When the Inca understood the request he was very sorry, for what the chief asked was contrary to the rule established and ordained by his father. Yet, if he did not grant the request of this captain, he and others would hold the Incas to be in-human men, declaring that they only thought of themselves. Having taken counsel with the Orejones and principal men of the city, it appeared to all that the maiden ought to be received for marriage with the Inca's son. It was thought that, until they became more powerful, it would not be prudent to follow the mandate of the Inca's father in this matter. Thus it was that the answer to the father of the proposed bride was that she should be brought, and the marriage was solemnised according to their method and custom, and she was called *Coya* in Cuzco.[1] The king's daughter, who

[1] Garcilasso de la Vega says that the legitimate wife of Lloque Yupanqui was named Mama Cava.

was to have been the wife of her brother, was immured in the temple of Curi-cancha, where priests were appointed to offer up sacrifices before the statue of the Sun, and where there were men to guard the sacred women in the manner already described.

By reason of this marriage, the Indians relate that the bride's people united with the citizens of Cuzco, making great rejoicing, thus confirming their union of brotherhood and friendship. On account of this, great sacrifices were offered up on the hill of Guanacauri[1] and at Tampu-quiru,[2] as well as in the temple of Curi-cancha. This being done, there was an assembly of more than 4,000 youths, and the ceremonies were performed which had been ordained for them. They were armed as knights, and continued to be looked upon as nobles. Their ears were bored, and the round pieces were put in them, in accordance with custom.

When these things had taken place, and others of which we have no record, in the time of the king Sinchi Rocca, he became old, and was surrounded by many sons and daughters. So he died, and was mourned for, and his obsequies were celebrated in a very sumptuous fashion. His image was preserved as a memorial that he had been a good ruler, and that his soul rested in heaven.[3]

---

[1] See p. 17. [2] See p. 14.

[3] Garcilasso de la Vega also says that Sinchi Rocca waged no wars ; but that the Canches submitted to him, and that by peaceful means he extended his dominions as far as Chuncara, about twenty leagues beyond his father's frontier.

CHAPTER XXXII.

Of the third king that reigned in Cuzco, named Lloque Yupanqui.

THE Inca Sinchi Rocca being dead in the manner that has been described, his son, Lloque Yupanqui,[1] was received as lord, having first performed a fast during the days appointed. As, in his divinations and omens, he found great reason to hope that the city of Cuzco would flourish in the future, the new king began to ennoble it with new edifices. He asked his father-in-law, with all his allies and confederates, to come and live in the city, where their honour would be respected and they would receive such a share of the land as they needed.

The lord or captain of Zañu consented, and the more western part of the city was assigned to him, which, being on hills and slopes, was named Anan-Cuzco. The lower part remained for the king, with his house and retinue. As all were now Orejones, which is as much as to say nobles, and nearly all had been concerned in the foundation of the new city, the people who lived in the two parts of the city, called Hanan-Cuzco, and Hurin-Cuzco, were always held to be illustrious. Some Indians even wished to have it understood that one Inca had to be of one of these lineages, and the next of the other. But I do not hold this to be certain, nor is it what the Orejones relate, and that is what is here written down. In most parts of the city there were large wards on the hill-slopes, because the ground was broken up into ravines and hills, as I explained in the first part of this chronicle.[2]

---

[1] *Lloque* means left-handed, and *Yupanqui* is the second person singular of the indicative future of a verb meaning "to count". "*You will count*", and it is understood that he will count as great, virtuous, and excellent.   [2] Chapter xcii.

They do not give any account of notable wars in those times. On the contrary, they affirm that those of Cuzco, little by little, through the good policy they employed, succeeded in making friends with many neighbouring people, and in enlarging the temple of Curi-cancha, both as regards edifices and riches. For now they sought for gold and silver, of which much came to the market held in the city; and they shut up women in the temple, who were not allowed to come forth, as has been explained in other places.

Reigning in this manner in Cuzco, and passing most of his time there, Lloque Yupanqui became very old, without having any children by his wife. The people of the city showed much grief at this, making many sacrifices and offering up prayers as well in the Curi-cancha, as at Guanacauri and Tampu-quiru. They say that, through one of those oracles whence issued vain replies, they heard that the Inca would beget a son who would succeed in the kingdom. At this they were well satisfied, and, rejoicing with the hope, they put the old king on his wife the Coya, so that at the end of some days it was known that she had conceived, and in due time she gave birth to a son.

Lloque Yupanqui died,[1] leaving orders that the fringe or crown of the empire should be deposited in the temple of Curi-cancha until his son was of an age to reign. The name given to the son was Mayta Capac, and, as governors, they say that the old Inca nominated two of his brothers, whose names I did not hear.

The Ynca Lloque Yupanqui was mourned for by all the servants of his household, and in many parts of the city, and, in conformity with their heathen blindness, they killed many women and boys, in the belief that they would go to serve the dead lord in heaven, where they held it to be certain that

---

[1] According to Garcilasso de la Vega, this Ynca Lloque Yupanqui not only conquered the Canas and Ayaviri, but the whole Collao submitted to him, as far as Hatun-colla and Chucuito.

his soul rested. Considering him to be a saint, the chief
people of the city ordered that his image should be made, to
be brought out at their festivals.   Assuredly the preparations
they make for the obsequies of one of these kings are very
great. Generally they mourned in all the provinces, and in
many of them the women were shorn, and their heads bound
with cords of reed.   At the end of a year they make greater
lamentations and heathen sacrifices than can be imagined. As
regards this, those who were at Cuzco in the year 1550, beheld
what took place in honour of Paullu,[1] when they celebrated
the end of his mourning year.   It was such that most of the
ladies of the city went to his house to see the ceremony, and
I was myself present.   Certainly it was calculated to excite
admiration, and we were given to understand that it was
nothing compared to what used to take place in former days.
Now I will speak of Mayta Capac.

[1] Paullu Tupac Yupanqui was a son of the Ynca Huayna Ccapac. He
lived at Cuzco, in the house which belonged to his brother Huascar;
much beloved and respected both by Spaniards and Indians. The
Governor Vaca de Castro induced him to be baptised with the name of
Christóbal. He died in May 1549.

CHAPTER XXXIII.

Of the fourth Inca who reigned at Cuzco, named Mayta Capac,
and of what happened during his reign.

WHAT has been described having taken place, Mayta Capac[1]
began to increase in stature. So, after the usual ceremonies,
his ears were bored. Then, when he was still nearer to man's
estate, he received the crown or fringe of empire in presence
of a great multitude, as well natives as strangers, who assembled for the purpose. As he had no sister with whom to
marry, he took for his wife the daughter of a lord or captain
of a place called Oma, which is at a distance of two leagues
from Cuzco. Her name was Mama Cahua Pata.[2]

After the marriage, there was a district near the city where
dwelt a tribe called Alcaviquiza,[3] who had shown no desire to
form a friendship with those of Cuzco. They were full of sus-
picion, the one of the other. It is related that, when a
woman went to certain springs to draw water, a boy came
forth from the other district, and broke her pitcher, making
use of I know not what words. She went back to Cuzco
shrieking; and presently the two parties came forth with
their arms, which they had taken up on hearing the noise.
The Inca, with his followers, arrived, and they put themselves in array to fight, having taken as the pretext so slight
a cause as this quarrel between the woman and the boy.
This was the motive for subjugating that tribe, and for making
all memory of it to disappear.

---

[1] *Mayta* has no special meaning in Cuzco. *Ccapac* means rich, not
in gold, but in the qualities of mind.

[2] According to Garcilasso de la Vega, the Ynca Mayta Ccapac married
his sister Mama Cuca.

[3] *Allcay-villcas*, as written by Balboa; and *Alcaviya*, according to
Betanzos. In the report on the first Lords of Cuzco by the Viceroy
Don Francisco de Toledo, written in 1572, it is *Alca-uizas*.

The object was well understood by those of Alcaviquiza, and, as valiant men, they resolutely came forth to the battle, which was the first that took place in those days. They fought together for a long time, and, as the affair had arisen so suddenly, those of Alcaviquiza had not been able to seek for help. Though they fought well, they were defeated in such sort that nearly all were killed, scarcely fifty of them escaping with life. Then the king Mayta Capac took possession of the fields and inheritances of the dead as conqueror, and divided them among the people of Cuzco. There was great rejoicing for the victory, and sacrifices were offered up to the oracles, which they held to be sacred.

Of this Inca the Orejones do not relate more than that Mayta Capac reigned in Cuzco several years; and, when people were arriving to set out for the province called Condesuyo, he became so ill that he died,[1] leaving, as his heir, his eldest son, named Capac Yupanqui.

---

[1] Garcilasso de la Vega gives a very different account of the reign of Mayta Ccapac, whom he makes out to have been a great conqueror. He says that Mayta Ccapac marched to the river Desaguadero, crossed it, and conquered the great province called Hatun-pacasa, on the other side. His captains crossed the Cordilleras to Moquegua, where the Ynca established a colony. Mayta Ccapac then conquered the provinces on the eastern side of lake Titicaca, including Caravaya, and eventually overran the whole of Charcas as far south as the lake of Paria. Not satisfied with this great acquisition to the south, Garcilasso also attributes to this Ynca the annexation of the provinces of Chumpivilicas, Parinacochas, and Pumatampu to the west of Cuzco; and the colonisation of Arequipa. —See my Translation, i, pp. 210-234.

CHAPTER XXXIV.

Of the fifth king who reigned at Cuzco, named Capac Yupanqui.

IT seems to me that the Indians related few things of those Incas who reigned in Cuzco soon after the foundation of that city. Certainly it must be as they say that three or four of the Incas were those who ordained and performed all that has already been written.

Mayta Capac being dead, his obsequies were performed in the usual way, and, his image having been placed in the temple, he was canonized as a saint in conformity with their blindness. Capac Yupanqui then assumed the fringe. This was done with great feasting, and people came from all parts to attend the solemnity of the coronation. These rejoicings having been completed, drinking and singing being the chief part of them, the Inca determined to go and make sacrifice on the hill of Guanacauri, accompanied by the High Priest, the ministers of the temple, and many Orejones and inhabitants of the city.

In the province of Condesuyo it was known that at the time when the late Inca died he had intended to make war, and the people were prepared, that they might not be taken unawares. After a few days they received news of his death, and of the intended visit of Capac Yupanqui to Guanacauri. So they determined to make war upon him, and to secure spoils if they obtained the victory. Setting out from a town in that district called Marca, they came to the place where the Inca then was. He had been warned of what was going on, and was ready for their coming. Many days did not pass before they joined battle one with the other, the struggle continuing for a long time, as both sides fought with spirit. In the end, those of Condesuyos were defeated with much slaughter. The sacrifice was then performed with great rejoicing, some men and women being offered up in accordance with their blindness, and many flocks of sheep and lambs, in the entrails of which they prognosticated their extravagancies and follies. When these sacrifices were finished, the Inca returned to Cuzco, where there was great feasting and rejoicing for the victory.

Those of the enemy who escaped, returned to their homes as best they could, where they again began to assemble troops, declaring that they would either die or destroy the city of Cuzco, and kill all the strangers who were in it. Inflamed with pride and anger, they hurried their preparation, and before they had seen the temple of Curi-cancha, they divided the ladies who were in it among themselves. Having assembled together, they marched towards the hill of Guanacauri, whence they intended to enter Cuzco. Capac Yupanqui had been informed of their movements, and had called together all the people of Cuzco and the confederates. With the Orejones, he then waited until he knew the enemy were near Cuzco. He then went forth to meet them, and there was a battle, in which each captain animated his troops. Although those of Condesuyo fought obstinately, they were defeated a second time, with a loss of more than 6,000 men, and those who escaped, turned and fled to their own land.

Capac Yupanqui followed the fugitives to their homes, where he waged war upon them in such wise that they came to sue for peace, offering to recognise the Lord of Cuzco, as the other tribes had done which were in friendship with him. Capac Yupanqui pardoned them, and showed himself very friendly to them all, ordering his people not to do any harm to those whom he now considered as friends. Some beautiful maidens were then looked for in that land, to be conveyed to the temple at Cuzco. Capac Yupanqui travelled for some days in the conquered region, requiring the people to live in an orderly way, and not to build their towns in the heights or on the snow-covered rocks. All was done as he ordered, and he returned to Cuzco.

He continued to enrich the city and the temple more and more; and he ordered a house to be built for his residence, which was the best that up to that time had been erected in Cuzco. They relate that he had legitimate sons to succeed him by the Coya, that the fame of his state and of the temple he had founded spread abroad among all the neighbouring provinces, and that all the people were astonished at the good order and reason that reigned in Cuzco, and at the inhabitants being well dressed, in-so-much that these things were noised abroad in all directions.

In those days, the people who occupied the region to the west of Cuzco as far as Andahuaylas, having heard the tidings, sent ambassadors to Capac Yupanqui with gifts and offerings, and the request that he would receive them as friends and confederates. The Inca gave a very favourable answer, giving them rich pieces of gold and silver to deliver to those who sent them. These messengers were several days in the city, receiving kind treatment and hospitality, judging more by what they saw than by what they had heard; and thus they recounted all things on their return. Some of the Orejones of Cuzco affirm that the general language used in all the provinces was that which was spoken by these Quichuas,[1] who were held by their neighbours to be very valiant until the Chancas destroyed them.[2] After the Inca

---

[1] The language was first called *Quichua* by Friar Domingo de Santo Tomas, in his grammar printed at Valladolid in 1560. *Quehani* is " I twist", and the participle *quehuasca* means twisted. *Ychu* is "straw"— together, *Quehuasca-ychu*, " twisted straw", corrupted and abbreviated into *Quichua*. A Quichua is properly au Indian who inhabits the temperate slopes, so called from the abundance of straw in that region. According to Garcilasso de la Vega the name of Quechua was applied to the basin of the river Abaucay (i, p. 243).

[2] Garcilasso refers to the enmity between the Quichuas and Chancas (i, p. 345).

Capac Yupanqui had lived many years, he died at a great age.[1] When the days of mourning were passed, his son was received without any opposition as King of Cuzco, as his father had been. The new king's name was Inca Rocca.

[1] Garcilasso attributes the conquest of the provinces of Cotabambas and Aymaraes to Ccapac Yupanqui; as well as the sea-coast from Acari to Quilca. He also attributes the settlement of the feud between Cari and Sapana, two great chiefs of the Collao, to Ccapac Yupanqui. It will be seen further on that Cieza de Leon places that event in the reign of the Ynca Huira-ccocha. Ccapac Yupanqui is also made, by Garcilasso, to extend his conquests to Cochabamba, Chayanta. and the extreme south of Charcas; while his son Rocca, during his life-time, overran Lucanas and advanced the limits of the empire to the valley of Nasca on the coast.

CHAPTER XXXV.

*Of the sixth king who reigned in Cuzco and of what hap-
pened in his time; and of the fable or history they relate
touching the river that passes through the midst of the city
of Cuzco.*

CAPAC YUPANQUI being dead in the way that has been related, he was succeeded in the lordship by Inca Rocca his son;
and a vast concourse of people came from all directions to be
present at the ceremony of his taking the fringe. Great
sacrifices were offered up at the oracles and temples in
accordance with their blindness. These Indians relate that
when the ears of this Inca were bored, to place in them those
round plates which are worn by the Orejones to this day, one
of them hurt him very much. The pain was such that he
went forth from the city to a very high hill which they call
Chaca, where he summoned his women and the Coya his
sister, named Macay Cuca, whom he had received as his wife
in his father's time. They further relate that, at the time,
there happened a mysterious event, which was this. Previously, neither stream nor river flowed by the city, and this
was felt to be no small want and inconvenience. For, when
it was warm, the inhabitants went to bathe in the rivers that
flowed in the neighbourhood of the city, and they even
bathed when it was not warm; and there were small foun-
tains for the use of the people, as there are at the present
day.

The Inca being on this hill, somewhat apart from his
people, he began to offer up a prayer to the great Ticiviracocha and to Guanacauri, and to the Sun, and to the Incas
his ancestors, that they would be pleased to declare how and
from what direction, a river could be brought by human

labour to the city. While he was praying he heard a great peal of thunder, insomuch that all present were terrified. The Inca himself, owing to the fright he received, bowed his head until the left ear touched the ground, from which flowed much blood. Suddenly he heard a great noise of running water underneath that place. So, with great joy, he ordered many Indians of the city to come, who quickly dug down until they reached the water which had opened for itself a way in the bowels of the earth, and had hitherto flowed without being of any use.

Continuing this narrative, they say further that, after they had dug much and seen the source of the water, solemn sacrifices were offered to the gods, for they believed that this benefit had come to them through divine interposition. With great rejoicing they contrived so skilfully that they led the water through the centre of the city, having first paved the ground with large flags, and raised walls with strong foundations on either side of the watercourse, placing some bridges of stone across, to pass from one side to the other.

I have seen this river, and it is true that it flows in the way they describe, coming from its source in the direction of that hill. But, as for the rest, I know not the truth, and merely write down what they assert. Yet a stream might well flow under the ground without being either seen or heard; for, in many parts of this great kingdom, both large and small rivers flow under the ground, as those report who have travelled over the plains and mountains. In these days there are large sewers on the banks of this river, full of filth and refuse. But, in the time of the Incas, it was kept very clean, the water flowing over the large flags, and occasionally the Inca and his women went to bathe there. At divers times some Spaniards have found a quantity of gold, not crude, but worked into small ornaments and *topus*, which had been left or had fallen when the Incas and their retinue bathed in the river.[1]

After this event, the Inca Rocca came forth from Cuzco to make sacrifices, contriving by great subtilty and kind words to bring as many people as he could into friendship with him. He advanced towards the region called Condesuyo, where, in a place called Pomatambo,[2] he fought a battle with the natives of that district, and remained conqueror and lord of them all. He pardoned them, conferred many benefits on them, instructed them in his rules and order of government, and they offered to become his subjects and to pay tribute. After having been for some days in Condesuyo, and having visited the oracles and temples in that region, the Inca returned in triumph to Cuzco, the principal chiefs marching before him to guard his person, with axes and halberds of gold.

[1] There are two rivulets which flow through Cuzco, the Huatanay and Tulumayu or Rodadero, coming from either side of the Sacsahuaman hill on which the Ynca fortress was built. The two streams unite beyond the convent of San Domingo, at *Pumap-chupan* or the "lion's tail". Both these streams are confined by walls of cut stone, with stairways descending to the water, and stone bridges, consisting of long slabs at frequent intervals. The houses on the western side of the great square are built over the Huatanay river; but these are modern, and did not exist in the time of the Yncas. Garcilasso de la Vega says that the Huatanay was lined and paved with masonry, the floor being of large flags, and that this masonry work extended for a quarter of a league beyond the city. Although there is very little water in ordinary times, the stream is subject to violent freshes, when the rush of water sometimes injures the masonry. The name is composed of two words, *Huata* (a year), and *Ananay* an ejaculation of weariness, indicating the fatigue caused by the yearly necessity for renewing the river banks.

Garcilasso de la Vega mentions other springs which conveyed water to the temple and gardens of the sun, under the Huatanay. He says that, in 1558, a flood tore up the flag-stones in the bed of the river, just over the place where the pipe leading water to the temple was laid down, and broke the pipe itself. The silt then covered the place, concealing the position of the pipe, so that no sign was left of it (i, p. 281).

[2] According to Garcilasso it was Mayta Ccapac who conquered the province of Puma-tampu (corruptly Pomatambo).

This Inca had many sons and not a single daughter. After having ordained some important matters relating to the government, he died, having first married his eldest son, named Inca Yupanqui, to a lady who was a native of Ayamarca, named Mama Chiquia.[1]

[1] Garcilasso says that Inca Rocca made the bridge over the Apurimac, and conquered Curampa, and the tribe of Chancas in Andahuaylas. He is also said to have annexed Vilca, and two provinces called Sullu and Utunsullu, while his son subdued Paucartambo and part of the forest region to the eastward. Inca Rocca is also said, by Garcilasso, to have founded schools at Cuzco, and to have built his own palace near them. He left a son, named Yahuar-huaccac, by his legitimate wife Mama Micay.

Blas Valera relates that Inca Rocca reigned for more than fifty years; and this writer preserved some of his laws, regulations for his schools, and wise sayings, which are given in *Garcilasso* (i, p. 336).

CHAPTER XXXVI.

*Of the seventh King or Inca who reigned in Cuzco, named Inca
Yupanqui.*

WHEN Inca Rocca died, many people, both men and women
came from Condesuyo, Vicos, and Ayamarca, and there was
great mourning for the deceased king. Many women, from
among those who in life had loved and served him, in accordance with the general blindness of those Indians, hung themselves by their own hair, and others were killed in divers
ways; that their souls might go quickly to serve their lord.
In the sepulchre, which was sumptuous and magnificent, they
put great treasures, and a still greater number of women and
servants, with provisions and fine clothing.

No sepulchre of these kings has been found, but to form a
judgment as to whether they were rich or not, it is not necessary to seek further proof than the fact that in ordinary burying places 60,000 *pesos* of gold, more or less, have been found.
What then must have been the quantity deposited in a royal
tomb, when they possessed so much of the precious metals,
and held it to be most important to leave this life well provided with riches?

They also made an image of Inca Rocca, accounting him as
one of their gods, and believing that he took his rest in
heaven.

As soon as the mourning was over, and the obsequies were
completed, the new Inca retired to perform his fast; and lest
any sedition or disturbance should be caused by his absence,
he ordered that one of the principal nobles of his lineage
should represent his person in public; to whom he gave
authority to punish offences, and to maintain the city in
peace and rest, until the Inca should come forth with the

royal insignia of the fringe. They say that they have the tradition that this Inca was of gentle presence, grave, and of imposing mien. He retired into the most secret part of his palace, where he remained to perform his fast on maize. At the end of the fast he came forth, the people showing great joy on beholding him. They made feasts and great sacrifices, and afterwards the Inca ordered that quantities of gold and silver should be brought from all parts for the temple. And in Cuzco they made the stone which they called "of the war" It was large, and was enriched with gold and stones.[1]

[1] " Y se hizo en el Cuzco la piedra que llaman de la guerra, grande, y las engastonadas en oro y piedras." So in the Escurial copy, but the meaning is not clear.

CHAPTER XXXVII.

*How when this Ynca wanted to make war in the province of
Collao, a certain disturbance arose in Cuzco; and how the
Chancas conquered the Quichuas, and got possession of their
dominions.*

INCA YUPANQUI being in Cuzco with the desire of ennobling
it, he determined to go to Colla-suyu, which includes the provinces to the southward of the city, because he had received
intelligence that the descendants of Zapana, who reigned in
Hatun-colla, were very proud and powerful, and that they
had assembled forces to march upon Cuzco. So he ordered
his people to prepare. The Indians relate that many men had
arrived for the campaign which Inca Yupanqui wanted to
undertake, and, being on the point of setting out, some captains of Condesuyo, with their warriors, plotted amongst
themselves to kill the Inca. For they said that if he returned
victorious, he would be in such high estimation that he would
desire to bring all men under vassalage and servitude. At
the time when the Inca was engaged in his festivities, and
somewhat joyous from the quantity of wine he had drunk,
one of the conspirators approached and delivered a blow with
a stick on the royal head. The Inca, disturbed and excited,
rose up saying, "What do you do, traitor?" By this time, the
men of Condesuyos had killed many persons, and the Inca
himself thought of seeking safety in the temple. But it was
of no avail to think, for he was overtaken by his enemies and
killed, with many of his women.[1]

[1] This Ynca Yupanqui of Cieza de Leon, son of Ynca Rocca, is the
Yahuar-huaccac of Garcilasso and other writers. When he was a child
he is said to have wept blood, and hence the name. *Yahuar* (blood), and
Huaccac (weeping). Others declared that he was born weeping blood.
During his reign, according to the account of Garcilasso, all the coast

There was great confusion in the city, insomuch that one man could not understand another. The priests had retired to the temple, and the women tore their hair, horrified at the death of the Inca by bloodshed, as if he had been some vile person. Many of the inhabitants were preparing to abandon the city, and the murderers wanted to plunder. They relate that at this juncture there was a great noise of thunder with lightning, and there fell so much water from heaven that those of Condesuyo were afraid. Without following up their success, they retired, contenting themselves with the mischief they had done.

They further state that, at that time, the Quichuas were lords of the province called Andahuaylas, and that from the neighbourhood of a lake called Choclococha there came a great multitude of people under two captains named Huaraca and Uasco; who went forward, conquering as they advanced, until they came to that province. When the inhabitants knew

region from Arequipa to the desert of Atacama was annexed to the empire by the Ynca's general and brother named Apu Mayta. The Ynca was much troubled by the headstrong disposition of his son, whom he banished to a lofty plateau called Chita, to the eastward of Cuzco, to live with shepherds who tended the flocks of the Sun. Three years afterwards, the son returned to Cuzco and told the Ynca his father that an apparition, calling itself Uira-ccocha Ynca, had appeared to him while he slept under a rock. It ordered him to repair to Cuzco and report that there was a great rebellion in the western province, threatening the existence of the empire. Yahuar-huaccac did not believe the story, and ordered his son to return to his banishment in the pastures of Chita. But soon the news came of the great rebellion of the Chancas, Yahuar-huaccac fled to Muyna, five leagues south of Cuzco, while his son put himself at the head of the army, and defeated the rebels. He took the name of the apparition, calling himself Ynca Uira-ccocha, and dethroned his father.

There is little resemblance between the stories told by Cieza de Leon of Ynca Yupanqui, and by Garcilasso of Yahuar-huaccac, except that they were both unfortunate. It will be seen further on that Cieza de Leon places the great rebellion of the Chancas after the reign of Uira-ccocha, and tells quite a different story about it.

of their approach, they prepared for war, encouraging each other, and saying, that it would be right to kill those who had come to attack them. Coming forth by a pass which leads towards the Aymaraes, these Chancas with their captains approached their opponents, until they were close together, when some speeches were made between them. Then they joined battle. According to the tradition, the fighting was desperate, and the result long doubtful. Finally, the Quichuas were defeated and cruelly treated, for all who fell into the hands of the enemy were killed, without sparing tender youth or helpless old age, and carrying off the women. Having done other evil things, they made themselves lords of that province, and possessed it as their descendants do to this day. And I have related this event because hereafter there will be frequent mention of these Chancas.

Returning to the previous subject of the retreat of the Condesuyos from Cuzco, the city was cleared of the dead, and great sacrifices were offered up. Moreover, it is said to be certain that, in the interment of Inca Yupanqui, the same honors as were done to his ancestors were not accorded to him, nor was his image set up, and he left no son.

CHAPTER XXXVIII.

*How the Orejones considered who should be Inca, and what
passed until Viracocha Inca assumed the fringe, who was
the eight Inca that reigned.*

WHEN what has been related, in accordance with the account
given by the Orejones of Cuzco of these things, had taken
place, there was great lamentation for the death of the Inca.
Then the principal people of the city considered who should
be chosen for king, and who was worthy to be raised to such
a post of dignity. There were several opinions, some proposing that there should be no king, but that the city should
be governed by those who might be elected ; while others
maintained that all would be lost if there was no head.

Over this question there was a great dispute, and while it
was at its height, they say that a woman came forth, in front
of the Anan-Cuzcos and said, "What are you about? Why do
you not take Viracocha Inca, seeing that he is so worthy?"
On hearing these words, the people left their cups of wine,
and went hastily for Viracocha Inca, son of Inca Yupanqui,[1]
saying, as soon as they saw him, that he should perform the
accustomed fast, and then receive the fringe, which they
desired to confer upon him. Viracocha agreeing, he commenced the fast, and committed the charge of the city to his
relation Rocca Inca. In due time he came forth with the
crown, and they celebrated solemn festivals in Cuzco, which
lasted for many days, all showing great satisfaction at the
election of the new Inca.

Some have pretended that this Inca was called Viracocha because he came from other parts and brought with him a different

---

[1] He contradicts himself, for, at the end of the last chapter, he said
that Ynca Yupanqui had no son.

dress, and that in his features and aspect he appeared like a Spaniard, because he had a beard.[1] They relate other things which would be tedious if they were written down. I inquired touching this matter, of Cayu Tupac Yupanqui, and the other principal people in Cuzco, who gave me the account of the Incas which I am now writing, and they replied that it was nonsense, without any foundation. For Viracocha was born and brought up in Cuzco like his parents and grandparents, and the name of Viracocha was given him as a special name, such as each one receives.

As soon as he received the crown, he married with one of the principal ladies named Runtu Coya,[2] who was very beautiful. When the festivities were concluded he resolved to set out for the conquest of some people near Cuzco, who had not consented to come into friendly relations with former Incas, confiding in the strength of their *pucaras*. With the force that he saw fit to assemble, he set out from Cuzco in a rich litter guarded by the principal people, and directed his march to a place called Calca,[3] where his messenger had been received with much insolence. When those of Calca knew that the army of Cuzco was approaching, they assembled in arms and posted themselves in the heights, whence they hurled great stones on the troops of the Inca, that they might kill those who were struck. The Incas climbed up the hills, and, in spite of opposition, succeeded in occupying one of the forts or strongholds. When those of Calca saw the Cuzco soldiers in their fastnesses, they came forth in a body, and fought resolutely. The battle continued from morning until noon, and many were killed on both sides, still more being made prisoners. The victory remained with those of Cuzco.

[1] Garcilasso describes the apparition which, according to his story, appeared to the prince who was afterwards Ynca Uira-ccocha, as having had a beard.

[2] Garcilasso gives the same name to the wife of Ynca Uira-ccocha (ii, p. 88). *Runtu* means an egg.

[3] In the valley of the Vilcamayu, near Cuzco.

The Inca was near a river,[1] where his camp was pitched, and when he knew of the victory he felt much joy. Then his captains came down with the spoil and the captives. The Indians who had escaped from the battle, with other captains of Calca and of the neighbourhood, saw that their plans had turned out so badly, and that the only course for them was to try the good faith of the conqueror, and to seek for peace, and a moderate servitude such as many others had agreed to. They came forth to a place on the mountain and said, in a loud voice, "Live for ever! live, O powerful Inca Viracocha, our lord!" At the noise caused by the voices the Cuzco troops flew to arms, but very little time elapsed before the conquered were prostrate on the ground before Viracocha Inca, where without rising, one who was held to be the wisest amongst them, raising his voice began to say: "You ought, O Inca, neither to become proud at the victory which God has given you, nor to despise us for having been defeated; for to you and to the Incas it is permitted to be lords over other tribes, and to us it is given to defend the liberty which we received from our fathers, with all our power, and when we are unable to succeed in this, it is for us to obey and submit with a good grace. Therefore give the order that no more of us are to be killed, and no more harm to be done, and dispose of us according to your will." And when the principal Indian had spoken these words, the rest asked for mercy with loud groans.

The Inca replied that if harm had come, their anger had been the occasion of it, for at first they would not believe his words nor receive his friendship; that now he freely granted them their lands and property as at first, and that, in conformity with the laws, they would pay tribute and do service. He ordered them to build two palaces, one within the city of Cuzco, and the other in Saqui, as a place of recreation. They answered that they would do so, and the Inca ordered the captives to be released and their property to be restored. In

1 The river Vilcamayu.

order that they might understand what they had to do, and that no dissensions might arise among them, he ordered a delegate with great power to remain among them, without depriving the native lord of his jurisdiction.

These events having passed, the Inca Viracocha sent a messenger to summon those of Caitomarca, who had made strong places on the other side of a river, without ever having shown a desire of friendship with the Incas who were lords of Cuzco. When the messenger of the Inca Viracocha arrived, they reviled him, calling the Inca a mad man, for believing that they would easily submit to his rule.

CHAPTER XXXIX.

*How Viracocha Inca threw a stone of fire with a sling at Caito-
marca, and how they made reverence.*

As soon as Viracocha Inca had despatched the messenger, he
ordered the camp to be raised, and a march to be undertaken
in the direction of Caitomarca. Advancing by the road, they
arrived at a river, where the Inca ordered a halt for rest.
Being in this place, the messenger arrived, who reported how
those of Caitomarca had mocked at him, and how they had
said that they felt no fear of the Incas. When this message
was understood by the Inca Viracocha, he rose up on the
litter with great anger, ordering the troops to advance with
all speed. This was done, until they came to a large and
rapid river, which I believe must have been the river of
Yucay.[1] Here the Inca ordered his tents to be pitched, in-
tending to attack the enemy's town on the other side; but the
current was so strong that this was not possible. Those of
Caitomarca came to the river side, whence they hurled many
stones from their slings at the Inca's camp, and began to
utter cries and great shouts. For it is a strange custom with
these people, when they fight with each other, how little they
allow their mouths to rest.

For two days the Inca was on the banks of that river
without being able to cross it, for there was no bridge; nor
is it clear whether they had those which are now in use
before the time of the Incas: some say that they had them,
while others maintain the contrary. They relate that Viracocha Inca ordered a small stone to be put into a strong flame,
and when it was very hot he applied a certain preparation to

---

[1] Or Vilcamayu.

it which would make it set fire to anything it touched. He then ordered it to be put into a sling made of gold wire, with which, when he was inclined, he was accustomed to hurl stones, and with great force he threw the heated missile into the town of Caitomarca. It fell on the eave of a roof which was thatched with very dry straw, and presently the thatch burnt, so that the Indians cried out to know what had happened, and who had set fire to the house. Then an old woman presented herself before them and said, "Listen to what I declare, and to what is certain. Think not that the house has been set on fire by any one here, but believe that the fire came from heaven. For I beheld a burning stone, which, falling from on high, struck the house and destroyed it as you see."

When the principal leaders, and the elders of the town heard this, being such great soothsayers and wizards, they believed that the stone had been sent by the hand of God as a punishment for disobeying the Inca. Presently, without waiting for an answer from the oracle or offering up any sacrifice, they crossed the river in *balsas*, bringing presents to the Inca. When they were brought into his presence, they asked for peace and made great offers of their persons and estates, as their allies had previously done.

The Inca Viracocha, on learning what those of Caitomarca had said, replied with great dissimulation that if they had not quickly come on that day, he had determined to attack them on the following morning, in great *balsas* which he had caused to be prepared. The agreement was then made between those of Caitomarca and the Inca; and that sovereign gave to the captain or lord of Caitomarca one of his own women, a native of Cuzco, which was esteemed a great favor.

The fame of the Inca's deeds was spread abroad in the neighbouring districts, and many, without seeing the arms of the Cuzco army, sent to offer friendship and alliance with the king Inca, who was well pleased, speaking lovingly to one and another, showing great kindness to all, and providing them with what they needed.   Seeing that he was now able to assemble a great army, the Inca determined to call troops together to advance in person into Condesuyo.

CHAPTER XI.

How a tyrant rose up in Cuzco, and of the disturbance he caused. Of the chastisement of certain Mamaconas for having, contrary to their religion, used their bodies uncleanly; and how Viracocha returned to Cuzco.

THE news was received at Cuzco of everything that happened to Viracocha; and when an account was given in the city of the operations against those of Caitomarca, they say that a tyrant rose up in the person of a brother of the late Inca Yupanqui, who, being much annoyed because the lordship and sovereignty had been given to Viracocha and not to him, was watching for an opportunity to seize the supreme power. He entertained this design because he had formed a party among some of the Orejones and principal persons of the lineage of Orin-Cuzcos. On receiving the news of this war which the Inca was engaged in, and it seeming likely that he would find a difficulty in bringing it to a successful end, the conspirator resolved to kill him who had been left as governor of the city, and to take possession.

Capac, for such was his name, eager for the command, assembled his party on a day when all the rest of the Orejones were in the temple of the Sun, and among them Inca Rocca, the governor of the Inca Viracocha, and took up arms. He declared that Viracocha could not retain the sovereignty, and he killed the governor, with many others, whose blood stained the altars and sanctuaries, and the figure of the Sun. The *mamaconas* and priests ran out with much noise, cursing the murderers and declaring that so great a crime deserved a great punishment. A crowd came forth from the city to see what had happened. Some approving of the rebellion, joined with Capac; others, deploring the murders, took up arms, and there was thus a division, many being killed both on one side and on the other. The city resounded with such noise and shouts, that men could not hear their own voices. In this confusion the tyrant got possession, killing many of the women of the Inca. Some fled from the city, and escaped to the camp of Viracocha, who, concealing what he felt, ordered his troops to march towards Cuzco.

To return to the tyrant Capac. When he had got possession of the city, he wanted to appear in public with the fringe, that all might receive him as king. But when the first excitement was over, during which many had lost their judgment and committed great crimes, the very same who had incited the usurper to rise, now upbraided him, went out to meet the Inca, and sought pardon for what they had done.

Capac had no lack of courage to carry through the affair, but he was much disturbed to see how small was the number of those who adhered to him. He cursed those who had deceived and deserted him, and, that he might not behold the return of the Inca, he took poison and died. His women and children, with other relations, imitated his example.

The news of all this came to the royal camp, and the Inca, when he reached the city, went straight to the temple of the Sun to offer up sacrifices. The bodies of Capac and of the others who had died with him, were ordered to be cast forth into the fields, to be devoured by birds of prey ; and those who aided the treason were condemned to death.

The allies and confederates of Viracocha Inca, when they heard what had happened, sent many embassies with presents and offerings of congratulation, and to these embassies he made joyful replies.

At this time, the Orejones say that there were many virgins of rank in the temple of the Sun, who were honored and esteemed, as has been explained in many parts of this history. And they further add that four of them used their bodies uncleanly with certain servants who guarded them, and being discovered they were taken, both the men and the women, and the high priest ordered that they should be judged, and punished.

The Inca had determined to invade Condesuyo, but, feeling tired and old, he gave up the plan. He then ordered that palaces, to be used by him for recreation, should be built in the valley of Xaquixaguana. As he had many sons, and as he knew that the eldest, who was named Inca Urco, to whom the sovereignty would descend, was a man of vicious habits and very cowardly, he desired to deprive him of the inheritance, in order to give it to another who was younger and more worthy, named Inca Yupanqui.

CHAPTER XLI.

*How ambassadors from the tyrants of the Collao came to Cuzco,
and of the departure of Viracocha Inca for the Collao.*

MANY histories and events fell out between the natives of
these provinces in early times; but as I make a rule only to
relate what I hold to be certain, according to the opinions of
the learned natives and to the narrative I took down at
Cuzco, I leave out what I do not clearly understand, and treat
of what I feel sure, as I have already explained several times.

It is well known, among the Orejones, that at this time
ambassadors came to Cuzco from the province of the Collao.
For they relate that, in the reign of Inca Viracocha, a lord
named Zapana ruled over Hatun-colla. In the lake of
Titicaca there are islands inhabited by people with large
balsas, and another lord named Cari went to the islands,
where he fought with the people insomuch that there were
great battles between them, out of which the Cari came forth
a conqueror. But he had no other object than to destroy the
villagers and carry off plunder, without troubling himself to
take prisoners. He returned to Chucuito, where he had established himself, and he had under his sway the towns of
Ylave, Yuli, Zepita, Pomata, and others. With the people he
could collect, after having offered up great sacrifices to his
gods or devils, he determined to march to the province of the
Canas. These men, when they heard of his approach, assembled together, came forth to meet him, and fought a battle in
which they were defeated with much loss. After this victory
Cari determined to continue his advance, and arrived at
Luracachi, where it is said that he fought another battle, and
was equally fortunate.

With these victories Cari became very proud, and the news
spread abroad. When Zapana, the lord of Hatun-colla, heard

of it, he was very sad, and he assembled his friends and vassals to take the field and despoil Cari. But he could not do this so secretly as to prevent Cari from understanding the design of Zapana, and he retired in good order to Chucuito by an unfrequented road, so that Zapana could not molest him. Having arrived in his own country, Cari assembled his principal chiefs, that they might consult touching the designs for Zapana, whose destruction was meditated by Cari, that there might be only one lord in the Collao. Zapana had the same thought in his mind.

And as the valour of the Incas, and the great power of Viracocha was spread abroad over all that region, each of these chiefs, desiring to obtain his friendship, sent ambassadors to Cuzco to secure his alliance and induce him to take part against the rival chief. These messengers set out with great presents, and arrived at Cuzco when the Inca was at the places or *tampus* which, for his diversion, he had ordered to be built in Xaquixaguana. Hearing that they were coming, the Inca ordered that they should be lodged in the city and provided with all they required.

The Inca consulted with the Orejones and venerable councillors touching the course that ought to be adopted in the matter of the embassies that had come from the Collao ; and it was decided that a reply should be sought from the oracles. This is done by the priests in front of the idols. They bow down their shoulders, put their chins into their breasts, and begin to speak in loud voices. Occasionally I myself, with my own ears, have heard the Indians converse with the devil. In the province of Cartagena, in a seaport town called Bahayre,[1] I heard the devil answer in a clear whistle, and so loudly, that a Christian who was in the same town but more than half a league from where I was, heard the same whistle and was dismayed, being rather unwell. On another day the

---

[1] Only Cieza de Leon could have said this. Bahaire is the town in the bay of Cartagena where he was with Heredia in 1533.

Indians made great shoutings, publishing the reply of the devil. In some parts of these lands where they keep the dead in hammocks, the devils occasionally enter into the bodies and give answers. I heard a man named Aranda say that, in the island of Carex,[1] he also saw one of these dead bodies speak, and the lies and nonsense they utter are laughable.

When the Inca determined to seek for an answer from the oracles, he sent for those who were accustomed to manage those things, and they say that the reply was that he should arrange to go to the Collao and seek the alliance of Cari. So he ordered the messengers of Zapana to be brought before him, and told them to say to their lord that he would shortly leave Cuzco and march to the Collao, where he would treat of the question of friendship. To those who came on the part of Cari he said that they were to explain to the lord how he was preparing to come to his aid, and that he would soon be with him.[2] When this was done, the Inca ordered forces to be assembled to march from Cuzco, leaving one of the principal persons of his lineage as governor.

[1] In the bay of Cartagena.

[2] Garcilasso de la Vega places this feud between the two great chiefs of the Collao, Cari and Sapana (or Chipana), in the reign of Ccapac Yupanqui, two generations earlier. He says that the names were those of dynasties, each sovereign becoming Cari or Sapana when he succeeded; adding that, "Cieza de Leon places these events long after the time when they really occurred." His version is that both the chiefs declared that they would abide by the arbitration of the Ynca. They came to the Ynca's camp at Paria, near Oruro, by different roads. The Ynca's decision was that boundary marks should be set up, that peace should be maintained, and that his laws should be observed by both chiefs. Cari and Sapana were, from that time, faithful vassals. Their territories comprised Cochabamba.

It will be seen that the version of Garcilasso is very different from that in the text. See my translation of *Garcilasso de la Vega*, i, pp. 247 to 252.

CHAPTER XLII.

How Viracocha Inca passed by the provinces of the Canches and Canas, and marched until he entered the territory of the Collao, and of what happened between Cari and Zapana.

HAVING determined to march to the Collao, the Inca set out from the city of Cuzco with a large force, passing by Muyna, and by the towns of Urcos and Quiquijana. When the Canches,[1] heard of his approach, they determined to assemble and come forth with their arms, to defend the passage through their land. The Inca, on receiving news of their intention, sent messengers to represent that they should not undertake such an enterprise, for that he did not wish to give them any affront, but rather desired to be their friend, and if their chiefs and captains would come to him, he would give them to drink from his own cup. The Canches replied to the messengers that the Inca should not pass by reason of what they said, and that they were there to defend their country which had been invaded. Returning with this answer, the messengers found the Inca Viracocha in Cangalla, full of anger at the small account in which the Canches held his embassy. He made a rapid march, arriving at a town which is called Compata. Near a river which flows close by, he found the Canches drawn up in order of battle, and here the combat between the two forces took place. Many died on both sides, and the Canches were defeated. Those who were able to do so, fled, and were followed by the conquerors, killing and taking prisoners. After a long time the pursuers returned with the spoils, bringing with them many prisoners, both men and women.

After this had happened, the Canches, throughout the

---

[1] The territory of the Canches was in the upper part of the Vilcamayu valley.

province, sent messengers to the Inca, beseeching him to pardon them, and to receive them into his service. As the Inca desired nothing else, he granted the usual conditions, which were that they should receive those of Cuzco as sovereign lord, and submit their laws and customs, offering tribute of what they produced, in accordance with what was done by other subjects. After passing some days in arranging these affairs, and in making the Canches understand that they must live together in towns, and must not engage in quarrels or wars amongst themselves, he passed onwards.

The Canas[1] had assembled together in large numbers, at a place called Luracachi; and as they had news of what had befallen the Canches, and that the Ynca did not injure those who wished to be his allies, nor allow others to do so, they resolved to make friends with him. The Inca advanced and, when he approached Luracachi and heard of the good will of the Canas, he was much pleased. As there was a temple of Aconcagua in that district, he sent great presents to the idols and priests.

When the ambassadors from the Canas arrived, they were well received by the Inca Viracocha, who replied to them that the principal and most venerable of the Canas should be near, where they would see him; and when he had been some days at the temple of Vilcañota he would hasten to be with them. He gave some fine cloth and ornaments to the messengers, and ordered his own soldiers not to enter the houses of the Canas, nor to take anything that belonged to them, that their good will might not be disturbed nor give place to any other thought.

The Canas, when they heard the message, caused plenty of provisions to be placed along the road, and came down from their villages to serve the Inca, who, with much regard to justice, took care that they should not be injured in any way.

---

[1] The Canas inhabited one side of the valley of Vilcamayu, and the Canches the other—the river dividing them.

They were supplied with flocks and ———[1] which is their wine. On arriving at their vain temple, they made sacrifices in accordance with their heathen practices, killing many lambs. Thence the army advanced to Ayavire, where the Canas had brought more provisions. The Inca spoke to them lovingly, and arranged his peaceful pact, as was his custom with other tribes. The Canas, holding it to be an advantage to them to be governed by such wise and just laws, did not object to the payment of tribute, and the duty of going to Cuzco.

This being done, Viracocha Inca determined to set out for the Collao, where by this time it was known what had happened with the Canches and Canas. They were waiting in Chucuito, and in Hatun Colla. Zapana was aware that Cari had been received well by Viracocha, and that he was expecting the Inca. He, therefore, determined to attack him before he became more powerful by a junction with the forces of the Inca. Cari was equally spirited, and came out with his followers to a town called Paucar-colla. Near this place the armies of the two most powerful tyrants of the district faced each other, in such numbers that it was said they amounted to one hundred and fifty *huarancas*.[2] They joined in battle, and it is related that it was fiercely contested, and that the dead numbered more than 30,000. After it had lasted for a long time, Cari remained the victor, while Zapana and his people were defeated, with the death of many. Zapana himself was killed in this battle.

[1] This word is almost illegible in the Escurial manuscript. Señor Jimenez de la Espada, the Spanish editor, has *surica*. The learned Peruvian, Dr. de la Rosa, has *sinica*. The words for intoxicating liquors in Quichua are *acca*, *azúa*, *huiñapu*, *sora*. The Spaniards also use the word *chicha*. But it is not like any of these, unless it be *sora*.

[2] Thousands.

CHAPTER XLIII.

*How Cari returned to Chucuito; of the arrival of the Inca Vira-
cocha; and of the peace that was agreed to between them.*

As soon as Zapana was dead, Cari took possession of his
camp, and seized upon everything that was in it, with which
he quickly returned to Chucuito.   There he waited for Viracocha Inca, and ordered lodgings to be got ready and provisions to be supplied.   The Inca, while he was on the road,
heard of the victory gained by Cari and of the end of the war.
Although he gave out that he was pleased, in secret he felt
regret at the course things had taken, because he thought that, .
while there were differences between the two chiefs, he would
easily make himself lord of the Collao; and he intended to
return quickly to Cuzco, that no untoward event might
happen.

When he approached Chucuito, Cari came forth with his
principal men to receive him, and he was lodged and attentively served.   As he wished to return to Cuzco, he spoke
with Cari, telling him how much he had rejoiced at his good
success, and that he was coming to his assistance.   In order
to make sure that they should always be good friends, he expressed a desire to give him a daughter of his own for a wife.
Cari answered that he was very old and very weary, and he
prayed the Inca to marry his daughter to a youth, seeing that
there were many to choose from, and that he would have him as
his lord and friend, and consent that he should rule, and that
in this way he would help him in wars and other affairs of
moment.   Then, in presence of the principal men who were
assembled, the Inca Viracocha ordered a large cup of gold
to be brought, and the plighted homage between the two was
taken in this way.   They drank a draught of the wine which
the women had, and the Inca took the cup, and put it on

the top of a very loose stone, saying:—"The sign is this, that the cup shall be here, and I do not move it nor you touch it, in token that that which is agreed upon shall be observed." Then kissing, they made a reverence to the sun, and they had a great *taqui*, with much noise. Then the priests, having uttered certain words, carried the cup to one of their vain temples, where they deposit similar tokens of oaths made by their kings and lords. Having passed some days in Chucuito, Viracocha Inca returned to Cuzco, being attentively waited upon and well received in all parts.

And now many provinces were organized, and the people wore better clothes and had better customs than before, being ruled according the laws of Cuzco. Inca Urco, the son of Viracocha Inca had remained there as governor, of whom they relate that he was very cowardly, remiss, full of vices, and with few virtues. As he was the eldest he had to succeed his father in the kingdom. His father knew his character, and desired much to deprive him of the lordship, and to give it to Inca Yupanqui, his second son, a youth of great valour and of good conduct, resolute and fearless, and endowed with grand and lofty aspirations. But the *Orejones* and principal men of the city did not wish the laws to be broken, which were observed as having been ordained by their ancestors. Although they knew how evil were the inclinations of Inca Urco, still they desired that he, and not another should be the king after the death of his father. I relate this so fully because those who told me, also say that Viracocha Inca sent from Urcos, his messengers to the city, to treat on this matter, but that he could not obtain what he wanted. When he entered Cuzco, he had a grand reception. But he was now very old and weary, so he determined to leave the government of his kingdom to his son, to deliver up the fringe, and to retire to the valley of Yucay and to that of Xaquixaguana to amuse himself and enjoy the rest of his life. He announced his intention to the people of the city, but he was not able to secure the succession for Inca Yupanqui.

CHAPTER XLIV.

How Inca Urco was received as supreme ruler of the whole empire, and assumed the crown at Cuzco, and how the Chancas determined to come forth and make war on those of Cuzco.

THE Orejones, and even all the other natives of these provinces, laughed at the proceedings of the Inca Urco.[1] Owing to his trivialities, they prefer that he should not be looked upon as having enjoyed the dignity of the kingdom. Thus we see that in the narrative derived from the *quipus* and traditions, which they have of the kings who reigned at Cuzco, they are silent as to this one. This I will not be; for in fact, well or ill, with vices or virtues, he governed and reigned over the kingdom for several days. When Viracocha Inca departed for the valley of Xaquixaguana, he sent the fringe or crown to Cuzco, that the elders of the city might deliver it to Inca Urco, having said that what he had done for the city of Cuzco must suffice, and that he wished to pass what remained of life in the enjoyment of rest, for that he was old and unfit for war. His wishes being understood, presently Inca Urco began the fasts and other observances in conformity with their customs and, having finished, he came forth with the crown, and went to the temple of the Sun to perform sacrifices, and there were the usual feasts and drinking bouts at Cuzco.

Inca Urco had married his sister, that he might have a son by her, to succeed to the lordship. He was so vicious, and so given to evil courses that, without caring for her, he went after common women, and after the girls he fancied, and it is even said that he seduced some of the *mamaconas* in the temple; and he had so little honour that he did not even

---

[1] This Ynca is not mentioned by Garcilasso de la Vega.

desire to be respected. He went about the city drinking, and when he had an *arroba* or more of liquor in his body, he conducted himself indecently. And he used to say to the *Orejones* who had beautiful wives, "How are my children?" as much as to say that the children were his and not the children of the husbands. He never built any house or edifice, he disliked arms, and in short they relate no good thing of him except that he was very liberal.

As soon as he had assumed the fringe, after some days had passed, he determined to go and enjoy himself in the houses of pleasure which were built for the recreation of the Incas, leaving as his lieutenant Inca Yupanqui, who was father of Tupac Inca, as we shall presently relate.

Such being the state of affairs at Cuzco, the Chancas, as I have already stated, had conquered the Quichuas and occupied the greater part of the province of Andabailes. As they were victorious, and hearing what was said of the grandeur of Cuzco and of its riches, and of the majesty of the Incas, they did not desire to abandon their conquests, but wished to acquire all they could with their arms. So they made a grand appeal to their gods, and set out from Andabailes, which is the place called by the Spaniards Andaguaylas,[1] and is now an encomienda of Diego Maldonado[2] the rich, leaving a suffi-

---

[1] This is a curious blunder of Cieza de Leon, for the Spanish form of *Andaguaylas* is much more nearly correct than *Andabailes*. The Quichua word is *Anta-huaylla*.

[2] Diego Maldonado, a native of Salamanca, was one of the first conquerors of Peru, and one of the richest. He had a house in the great square of Cuzco. When the hospital was founded there, he, as senior *Regidor*, placed a plaque of silver with his arms engraved on it, under the first stone. He was put in prison by Almagro, with many others; and fought on the side of Vaca de Castro, at the battle of Chupas, when Almagro the lad was defeated; and he fled from the army of Gonzalo Pizarro, to keep himself and his riches on the loyal side. But he found it safer to feign submission and follow Gonzalo's camp. Then news came that his life was forfeited, so he fled from his tent near Lima in the dead of night; though over sixty-eight years of age, ran all night on

cient force there to protect it. Hastu-Huaraca, and a very brave brother of his named Omoguara, with the forces ready for war, set out proudly from their own territory on the road to Cuzco, marching until they arrived at Curampa,[1] where they encamped, doing much injury to the people of the district. But as in those days many of the settlements were on the heights and peaks of the mountains, with strong defences called *pucaras*, they could not kill any great number or make many prisoners, but only ravage the fields.

They departed from Curampa, and arrived at the resting place of Cocha-cassa, and at the river Abancay, destroying everything they found. Thus they approached Cuzco, where the news of their coming had preceded them. When it was known to the aged Viracocha, he left the valley of Xaquixaguana, and went with his women and servants to the valley of Yucay. They also relate that Inca Urco merely laughed, making light of what was really a very serious matter. But the fate of Cuzco was guarded by Inca Yupanqui and his sons, who were destined to save the city from all its danger by their virtues. For not only did he vanquish the Chancas, but he subjugated the greater part of the nations who inhabit those kingdoms, as I shall relate further on.

foot, and hid himself in a cane brake. Next day an Indian took pity on him, made up a bundle of reeds and pushed out to sea, the two sitting across the bundle as on a horse. They were just able to reach one of the ships of Lorenzo de Aldana in Callao bay, which were on the loyal side. He eventually returned to Cuzco and once more became a leading citizen there, taking a part in making the peace between the authorities and Francisco Hernandez Giron. He was with Alonzo de Alvarado in his campaign against Giron, and strongly dissuaded him from giving battle at Chuquinga, where he was defeated. Maldonado was wounded at Pucara, in the last fight with Giron, but survived for twelve years afterwards, living at Cuzco and on his Andahuaylas estates.

[1] On a lofty plateau between Andahulayas and Abancay. The fortress consists of three wide terraces, with a sloping ramp from the ground to the highest one. Near it are the ruins of a town. The nearest modern town is Huancarama, about a league to the east.

CHAPTER XLV.

How the Chancas arrived at the city of Cuzco and pitched their camp there, and of the terror of the inhabitants, and the great valour of Inca Yupanqui.

AFTER the Chancas had offered up sacrifices on the banks of the Apurimac and had arrived near the city of Cuzco, the Captain-General or lord who led them, named Hastu-Huaraca said that they should reflect on the great undertaking they had entered upon, that they should show themselves. to be strong, and that they should feel no fear nor terror whatever of men who thought they could frighten people by making their ears such a size as these enemies did. He also told his followers that they would capture much spoil, and beautiful women with whom they could enjoy themselves. They replied cheerfully that they would do their duty.

As it was known in the city of Cuzco that the enemy was marching against it, and that neither Viracocha Inca nor his son Inca Urco had made any preparation to oppose them, the Orejones and principal people were much disturbed, and offered up great sacrifices according to their custom. They then agreed to ask Inca Yupanqui to take charge of the war, for the common safety. One of the most venerable took the matter in hand, and spoke in the name of the others. He replied that when his father wished to confer the fringe upon him, they would not consent, but insisted that his cowardly brother should be Inca. He himself had never pretended to the royal dignity through usurpation and contrary to the will of the people ; and they should now do what was necessary for the public good, as they had seen that the Inca Urco was unfit for the post. The Orejones replied that, when the war was over, they would adopt such measures as were best for the government of the kingdom. It is said that they then sent messengers through the province, declaring that all who wished to come and be citizens of Cuzco, would be given lands in the valley, and would receive privileges; and so they came from many parts. This being done, the captain, Inca Yupanqui, came forth to the great square where was the stone of war, with the skin of a lion on his head, as a sign that he must be strong as is that animal.

At this time the Chancas had reached Vilca-cunga, and the Inca Yupanqui ordered all the men of war that were in Cuzco to be assembled, with the determination of marching out on the road. Those who appeared most resolute were appointed captains; but, on further consideration, he determined to wait in the city.

The Chancas continued to advance until they pitched their camp on the hill of Carmenca, which overlooks the city, and presently set up their tents. The people of Cuzco had made deep holes full of stones at the approaches to the city, and subtly covered them over on the top, so that those who walked that way might fall in. When the women and children of Cuzco saw the enemy, they were much afraid, and made a great noise. Inca Yupanqui sent messengers to Hastu Huaraca, proposing that there should be an agreement between them, to avoid the slaughter of the people. Hastu Huaraca was proud, and thought little of the embassy. He wanted simply to abide by the decision of battle; but to the importunate prayers of his relations and others, he yielded so far as to agree to a conference with the Inca, and in that sense he replied. The city is situated between hills, in a naturally strong position. The slopes and ridges were scarped, and in many parts sharp stakes of palm were fixed, which are as hard as iron, and more hurtful. The Inca and Hastu Huaraca had an interview, but, as both were ready to fight, it availed little, for being further excited by the words which they spoke to each other, at last they came to blows, at the same time shouting and making a great noise. For the men in that country make an exceeding great noise when they fight. They fought with each other for a long time and the night coming on, the Chancas remained in their tents, and those of the city were all round, watching in every direction, that the enemy might not enter. For neither Cuzco, nor the other towns in those parts, are surrounded by walls.

When the surprise was over, Hastu Huaraca encouraged his followers to be valorous in the fight, and the Inca Yupanqui did the same with the Orejones and the people who were in the city. The Chancas resolutely came forth from their camp with the intention of forcing an entry, and those of Cuzco were determined to defend the city. The battle was renewed, and many fell on either side; but such was the valour of Inca Yupanqui that he gained the victory, and nearly all the Chancas were killed. They say that very few more than five hundred escaped, and among them their captain Hastu Huaraca, who arrived with them at their own province but not without difficulty.[1] The Inca enjoyed the spoil, and got many captives, as well men as women.

[1] According to Garcilasso de la Vega, the Chancas encamped on the plain of Sacsahuana (Xaquixaguana), on the spot where the battle was afterwards fought between Gonzalo Pizarro and the President Gasca. The plain is described by Cieza de Leon in his first Part (p. 320 of my Translation). It is now called the plain of Surite. Here Garcilasso says that the great battle was fought between the Ynca Huira-ccocha and the Chancas (ii, p. 34). The fight raged with desperate fury from dawn until noon; when five thousand Quichuas, who until then had been in ambush, attacked the Chancas on their right flank. More reinforcements arrived, until the Chancas began to think that the very stones were turning into men. At length they broke and fled. It was called the battle of Yahuar-pampa (plain of blood).

CHAPTER XLVI.

How Inca Yupanqui was received as King, the name of Inca being taken from Inca Urco, and how the new Sovereign made a peace with Hastu Huaraca.

As soon as the Chancas were defeated, Inca Yupanqui entered Cuzco in great triumph, and addressed the principal Orejones on their agreement. He said that he had worked for them in the way they had seen, while his brother and his father had done little in opposing the enemy, and that, therefore, they should give him the sovereignty and government of the empire. The people of Cuzco, one with another, discussed the matter, comparing the merits of Inca Yupanqui and Inca Urco, and, by consent of the city, they agreed that Inca Urco should not enter Cuzco again, and that the fringe should be taken from him and given to Inca Yupanqui. Although Inca Urco, when he knew what had been done, wanted to come to Cuzco to justify himself, and was much moved, complaining of his brother and of those who had deprived him of the government; yet they did not yield, nor turn aside from accomplishing what they had resolved to do. There are some who say that the Coya, wife of Inca Urco, left him without having borne him any children, and went to Cuzco, where her second brother Inca Yupanqui received her as his wife. Having performed the fast and the other ceremonies, he came forth with the fringe, and there were great festivals at Cuzco, people flocking thither from all parts. The new Inca ordered all those who had fallen in the battle on his side to be buried with the customary funeral rites. For the Chancas he caused a large house to be erected on the battle field, like a tomb, where all the bodies of the dead were put as a memorial, and the skins were filled with cinders or straw, so that the human form was made to appear in many attitudes. Some of them appearing like men, had drums issuing from their bellies, on which they appeared to be playing. Others were set up with flutes in their mouths. After this fashion they were left until the Spaniards entered Cuzco. Alonzo Carrasco[1] and Juan de Pancorvo,[2] ancient conquerors, related to me how they had seen these skins full of cinders, as did many others of those who came to Cuzco with Pizarro and Almagro.

The Orejones say that in those days there was a large population in Cuzco, and that it was always increasing. Messengers arrived from many parts to congratulate the new king, who answered them all with gracious words. He wished to set out and make war in the region they call Condesuyo, and as he knew by experience how brave and enterprising was Hastu Huaraca, the Lord of Andahuaylas, he thought of inducing him to enter his service. They relate that he sent messengers, asking the chief to come to Cuzco with his brothers and friends, and to enjoy the society of the Inca. Considering that it would be profitable to secure the friendship of Inca Yupanqui, the Lord of Andahuaylas came to Cuzco, and was well received.[3] And as the Inca had sum-

---

[1] I do not find any other mention of Alonzo Carrasco. His name does not appear in the list of conquerors who received shares of the spoils at Caxamarca, nor in Garcilasso de la Vega.

[2] Juan de Pancorvo was a citizen of Cuzco, and had a house on the western side of the great square, which he shared with Alonso de Marchana; for Juan de Pancorvo did not wish him to live in another house, because of the warm and long-continued friendship they always felt for each other. So says Garcilasso de la Vega. Pancorvo had, in his grant, one of the great halls in which the Yncas held their festivals. This he bestowed upon the Franciscan convent. He seems to have been a peaceable man.

[3] Hanco-huallu is the name which Garcilasso de la Vega gives to the warlike chief of the Chancas. He could not endure dependence, even under the mild rule of the Ynca, and, ten years after his defeat, he emigrated with many followers to the forests of Moyobamba. In the First Part, Cieza de Leon says the same thing, calling him Ancoallu (p. 280). Also see further on, at page 157.

moned his army for war, he determined to proceed to Condesuyo.

At this time, they relate that Viracocha Inca died, and they gave him sepulture with less pomp and honor than his ancestors, because he had deserted the city in his old age and had no wish to return when the Chancas made war. I say no more concerning Inca Urco, because the Indians only refer to his history as a thing to laugh at, and putting him on one side, I consider Inca Yupanqui as the ninth king that reigned in Cuzco.

———————

CHAPTER XLVII.

How Inca Yupanqui set out from Cuzco, leaving Lloque Yupanqui as Governor, and of what happened.

As now, by order of Inca Yupanqui, more than 40,000 men had been assembled round the stone of war, the army was passed in review, captains were appointed, and there were feasts and drinking bouts. ·All being ready, the Inca set out from Cuzco in a litter enriched with gold and precious stones, which was surrounded by his guards with halberds, axes, and other arms. Next to him marched the lords, and this king displayed more valour and authority than any of his ancestors. He left in Cuzco, according to what they relate, his brother Lloque Yupanqui as governor. The Coya and the other women travelled in hammocks, and it is said that they carried a great quantity of jewels and of stores. In front, men were sent forward to clear the road, so that neither grass nor stone, large or small, might remain on it.

Arrived at the river Apurimac, they crossed it by the bridge that had been made, and advanced as far as the buildings of Cura-huasi. Many men and women, and some lords and principal men, came forth from the neighbouring places, and when they saw the army they were amazed and cried out, " Great Lord, Child of the Sun", " Monarch of all things", and many other grand names. At this place, they say that a captain of the Chancas, named Tupac Uasco,·was given a *Palla* of Cuzco as his wife, and he highly prized her.

Advancing by the Apurimac and Cocha-cassa, the Inca found that the inhabitants of those parts were in strong *pucaras*, and that they did not live together in villages. So he ordered that they should live in an orderly way, abandoning evil customs, and abstaining from killing each other.

They rejoiced at these orders, and willingly obeyed his commandment. But those of Curampa derided it. This being told to Inca Yupanqui, he defeated them in battle, killing many, and taking others prisoners. As the land was fertile, he ordered one of his officers to remain and organise the district, and to build lodgings and a temple of the Sun.

These arrangements having been made with great care, the King set out from thence, and marched to the province of Andahuaylas, where there was a solemn reception. He remained several days to decide whether he would go to conquer the inhabitants of Guamanga or Xauxa, or the Soras and Lucanas. Having considered the matter in council with his officers, he decided upon going to the Soras.[1] Setting out, he marched over an uninhabited region which leads to the Soras, who were apprised of his approach, and assembled to defend their country.

The Inca Yupanqui had sent captains with parties in many other directions, to induce men to join his service by kind treatment; and he sent messengers to the Soras, admonishing them not to take up arms against him, and promising to make much of them, and to do them no injury. But they did not wish for peace with servitude; but rather to fight for their liberty. So when the two armies came together, there was a battle, concerning which those who can preserve the memory of it, say that it was fiercely contested, and that many fell on both sides. But the victory remained with those of Cuzco. The fugitives who escaped death or capture, fled to their town with much lamentation, where

---

[1] The Soras and Rucanas were tribes of hardy mountaineers, inhabiting the wild region of the maritime cordillera, to the south-west of the Chancas. The Rucauas (the modern province of Lucanas) were described as a handsome and well-disposed people, who were expert bearers of burdens, and had the privilege of carrying the Ynca's litter. The Soras, closely allied to the Rucauas, lived on the left bank of the River Pampas, near its source.

they collected as much of their property as they could, and, taking their women, they abandoned the place, and fled to a strong rock, near the river of Vilcas, where there are many caves and a supply of water. In this fastness many men assembled with their women, with as much provisions as they could get together, for fear of the Inca. Not only the Soras took refuge on the rock, but many from the district of Guamanga, and from the banks of the Vilcas, also fled there, terrified at the news that the Inca wished to be sole lord over the people.

The battle being won, the conquerors enjoyed the spoils; but the Inca ordered that no harm should be done to the captives. They were all released. A captain was ordered to march towards Condesuyo by way of Pumatampu; and when the Inca entered the country of the Soras, and heard that the people had gone to the rocky fastness, he was much incensed, and determined to go and besiege the place. So he commanded his captains to march against it, with the army.

CHAPTER XLVIII.

How the Inca returned to Vilcas, and besieged the Rocky Fastness where the Enemy had taken Refuge.

THE Orejones relate very great things touching this Inca Yupanqui, and Tupac Inca his son, and Huayna Capac his grandson, for these were the sovereigns who displayed most valour. Those who may read of their actions, should believe that I rather detract from, than add to what I have been told; and I simply write what I have received from the Indians. For myself, I believe this and more, from the testimony borne by the remains and signs that these kings have left behind them, and from their great power, which shows that what I write concerning them is only a part of what really happened. Their memory will endure in Peru so long as any men of the native race survive.

Returning to the narrative, as the Inca strongly desired to have those who had taken refuge in the rocks in his power, he marched with his troops until he came to the river of Vilcas.[1] The inhabitants, when they knew that he was there, came in great numbers to see him and to perform services, and they established friendship with the Inca. By his order they began to build great edifices, in the place which we now call Vilcas. Masters were sent from Cuzco to trace the plans, and teach the method of laying the stones and tiles in the edifices. Arriving at the rocky fastness, the Inca used all reasonable means to induce those who had taken refuge there to submit to his alliance, sending messengers to them. But the enemy laughed at his words, and hurled many stones at the camp. The Inca, seeing their disposition, resolved not to depart until he had punished

---

[1] The great River Pampas.

them. He knew that the captains whom he sent to the province of Condesuyo, had fought some battles with the people of that region, had conquered them and brought most of the province under his sway. In order that the people of the Collao might not think that they were safe, and knowing that Hastu Huaraca, the Lord of Andahuaylas, and his brother, Tupac Vasco, were valiant chiefs, he sent them to the Collao to keep the people in obedience. They replied that they would obey his order, and they set out for their own land, to proceed thence to Cuzco, and join the army which was to be assembled there.

The garrison of the rocky fastness still had the intention of defending it, and the Inca surrounded the place with his troops. The siege was long, and several great deeds were performed. At last the provisions failed, and the besieged were obliged to submit, and to serve the Inca like the rest of his subjects, paying tribute and furnishing men for the wars. With this servitude, they remained in favour with the Inca, who was no longer enraged, but ordered provisions and other things to be given to them, and that they should return to their homes. But others affirm that he killed them all, insomuch that not one escaped. I believe the first account, though as regards one or the other, I only know what these Indians relate.

This affair being ended, they say that people came from many parts to submit and offer their services, and that the Inca received them all graciously. He then returned to Cuzco. On the road, he found that many edifices had been built, and that, in most parts, the forts of the natives had been razed, and that they had formed regular towns in the lower country, as he had commanded and ordained.

He was received at Cuzco with the customary pomp, and there were great festivities. The captains who, in obedience to his orders had gone to the war in the Collao, advanced as

far as Chucuito, and were victorious in several battles, bringing all under the dominion of the Inca.   The same was done
in Condesuyo.   The Inca was very powerful; lords and captains arrived from all parts with the leading men of the
districts, paying tribute with regularity, and performing personal services; but all was done with great regularity and
justice.   When they came for an audience with the Inca,
they carried a light burden; they looked but little at his
face; when he spoke, those who heard him trembled from
fear or some other reason.   He seldom appeared in public,
but in war he was always to the front.   He did not allow
any one, without his permission, to possess jewels, nor to be
seated, nor to be carried in a litter.   In short, this was the
sovereign who opened the way for the excellent government
which was established by the Incas.

CHAPTER XLIX.

*How Inca Yupanqui ordered Lloque Yupanqui to proceed to
the Valley of Xauxa, and to bring under his dominion
the Huancas and the Yauyos their neighbours, with other
Nations in that direction.*

THAT which has already been written having taken place, the
Orejones relate that the Inca, finding himself so powerful,
determined to make another call to war, because he wished
to achieve another conquest more important than those that
had gone before. In compliance with his orders, many
chiefs assembled, with a great number of armed men, supplied with the arms they use, which are slings, axes, clubs,
bolas, darts, and some lances. When they assembled, he
ordered that there should be entertainments and feasts; and
to delight them, he came forth each day in a new dress, such
as that which was the special costume of the nation that he
wished to honour on that day. Next day he put on another,
always wearing that of the tribe which was invited to the
entertainment and drinking bout. By this means he pleased
them, and as much as it was possible, he endeared himself
to them. When the great dances were performed, the square
of Cuzco was encircled by a chain of gold, which was ordered
to be made out of the quantity coming as tribute from the
districts. It was as large as I have before described, and
there was further grandeur in the matter of images and
ancient relics.

When they had enjoyed themselves for as many days as
the Inca Yupanqui thought proper, he spoke his wishes to
them, that they should go to the country of the Huancas, and
their neighbours the Yauyos, and induce them to embrace his
friendship and service, without making war; but that if they

refused, then they must be conquered and forced to obey.
They all replied that they would obey his orders with good
will. Captains belonging to each nation were appointed, and
Lloque Yupanqui was general of the whole army. With
him, for counsel, was Capac Yupanqui.[1] Having received
their instructions, they set out from Cuzco and marched to
the province of Andahuaylas, where they were well received
by the Chancas. There set out from that province with
them a captain named Ancoallo, with a large force, to serve
in the war of the Inca.

From Andahuaylas they went to Vilcas, where were the
edifices and temple which Inca Yupanqui had ordered to be
erected, and they spoke with all friendship to those who
were engaged on the works. From Vilcas they marched by
the towns of Guananga, Camgaron,[2] Parcos, Picoy, and Arcos,
which had already submitted to the Inca, and supplied all
the provisions they had, besides making the royal road, large
and very wide, according to orders.

The people of the valley of Xauxa, when they knew that
the enemy was approaching, showed great alarm, and sought
help from their relations and friends, and in their own
temple of Huarivilca they offered up great sacrifices to the
demon which there gave replies. When the succours arrived
there was a great multitude, for they say that more than
40,000 men assembled where now I do not know that there
are 12,000. The Inca captains took up a position overlooking the valley, and wished to gain the goodwill of the
Huancas, and to induce them to come to Cuzco and recognise
the king as their lord, without fighting. With this purpose

---

[1] The Spanish editor suggests that this should be Tupac Yupanqui
the Inca's son. He would be going on his first campaign, to acquire
experience. But Garcilasso has Ccapac Yupanqui, a brother of the Inca,
as the General in this campaign. (See ii, p. 127.)

[2] This is wrongly written in the manuscript. Garcilasso de la Vega
has Asancaru (ii, p. 76).

they sent messengers, but without success. Then there was
a great battle, in which they say that many were killed on
both sides, those of Cuzco remaining conquerors. Lloque
Yupanqui was a very circumspect leader. He would allow
no harm to be done in the valley, prohibited all robbery, and
he released the captives. Seeing the clemency with which conquered people were treated, the Huancas came to speak with
the Incas, and promised to live in accordance with the ordinances of the kings of Cuzco, and to pay tribute of such
produce as they had in the valley. Leaving their villages
on the hill-sides, they sowed the land without dividing it,
until the time of the king Huayna Capac, who marked out
the land which was to belong to each lineage,[1] and they sent
messengers.

[1] Garcilasso de la Vega (ii, p. 129) says that the country of the
Huancas was divided into three provinces, called Sausa, Marcavilca, and
Llacsapalauca.

CHAPTER L.

How the Captains of the Inca left Xauxa, and what happened; and how Ancoallo departed from among them.

THE inhabitants of Bonbon, according to what they relate, had heard of the events of Xauxa, and how the Huancas had been defeated, and, suspecting that the conquerors intended to continue their march, they determined to be prepared, so that they might not be taken unawares. Putting their women and children, with the property they could collect, on a lake[1] which is near their abode, they waited for what might happen. The Inca Captains, when they had arranged the affairs at Xauxa, set out and advanced as far as Bonbon, but as the people had taken refuge on the lake, they were unable to do other harm than eat their provisions. They then passed onwards and came to Tarama, where they found the people in arms. There was a battle, in which many of the people of Tarama were killed and taken prisoners, and those of Cuzco remained victors. As it was the will of the king that those of Tarama should pay tribute and serve like the people of other provinces, in return for which they would be favoured and well treated, they agreed to all that was demanded from them. An account was then sent to Cuzco of all that had been done in this province of Tarama.

The Chancas relate that, as the Indians who came forth from the province of Andahuaylas with the chief Ancoallo had performed great deeds in these wars the Inca captains were jealous. They also bore a grudge against him for what had happened before during the seige of Cuzco. So they determined to kill him. They ordered him to be sent for; but as they came in large numbers with their captain, the Chancas

---

[1] The lake called Pumpu (Bombon) or Chinchay-cocha.

understood their intention and, taking up arms, they defended themselves against those of Cuzco. Although some were killed, others were able, owing to the stoutness and bravery of Ancoallo, to get away. They complained to their gods of the bad faith of the Orejones, and of their ingratitude, declaring that, to see them no more, they would go into voluntary exile. Taking their women with them, they marched through the provinces of Huanuco and Chachapoyas, and, passing the forests of the Andes, they arrived at a very large lake which, I believe, must be that described in the story of El Dorado. Here they established their settlement, and multiplied. The Indians relate great things of that land and of the chief Ancoallo.[1]

The Inca captains, after what has been written had come to pass, returned to the valley of Xauxa, where already great presents and many women had been got together to be sent to Cuzco, and the people of Tarama did the same. The news of all this arrived at Cuzco, and when the Inca heard it, he rejoiced at the success of his captains, although it showed that he was displeased at what had happened respecting Ancoallo. But this was, as it is believed, a kind of dissimulation, for some declared that what was done by the captains was in accordance with his orders. As Tupac Uasco and the other Chancas had gone to make war in the Collao, and had been victorious, the Inca reflected that, when they knew what had happened to Ancoallo, they would turn against their sovereign and commit treason. So he sent messengers with orders to desire that they would come to him, and he commanded, on pain of death, that no one should tell the Chancas what had happened.

The Chancas, as soon as they received the command of the Inca, came to Cuzco ; and when they arrived the Inca spoke to

---

[1] Garcillasso de la Vega calls him Hanco-Huallu, chief of the Chancas (see Book v, cap. xxvi, ii, p. 82), and describes his flight.

them lovingly but with much dissimulation, concealing his evil dealings with Ancoallo, and making it appear, by his words, that he had been himself displeased. The Chancas, when they understood, did not fail to feel the affront, but seeing how little satisfaction could be obtained, they asked permission to return to their province. Having been granted leave, they set out, the Inca giving their principal lord the privilege of sitting in a chair enriched with gold; and other favours.

The Inca took care to adorn the temple of Curi-cancha with great riches, as has already been mentioned. And as Cuzco possessed many provinces in all directions, he gave several to the temple, and he ordered posts to be stationed, that all his subjects should speak one language, and that the royal road should be constructed. Other things are related of this king. It is said that he had great knowledge of the stars, and that he had some acquaintance with the movements of the sun. Hence he took the name of Inca Yupanqui, which means a name of counting[1] and of much understanding. Finding himself so powerful, and notwithstanding that he had great edifices and royal houses in Cuzco, he ordered three walls of most excellent masonry to be built, that it might be a memorial work. And so it appears to this day, no one seeing it without praising it, and recognizing the genius of the masters who conceived it. Each wall has a length of 300 paces.[2] They call one Pucamarca, another Hatun-cancha, and the third Cassana.[3] The walls are of excellent stones, so well adjusted that there is no disproportion, and so admirably laid and fitted that the joining between them cannot be dis-

---

[1] See back, note at page 102.

[2] By my measurement the length is 400 yards.

[3] These three names, according to Garcillasso de la Vega, are not connected with the fortress, but belong to different parts of the city (ii, p. 246).

cerned. The great part of these edifices is so strong and solid that, if they are not demolished, they will endure for many ages.

Within these walls there were buildings like the others they use, where there were a number of mamaconas and other women and damsels of the king, who worked and wove the fine cloth, and there were many pieces of gold and silver, and vases of those metals. I saw many of these stones in the walls, and I was amazed how, being so enormous, they could have been so admirably set in position.

When they had their dances and great festivals in Cuzco much chicha was made by these women; and as people came to Cuzco from so many parts, there was an order that overseers should be placed to watch that none of the gold and silver that was brought in should be taken out again. And governors were placed over different parts of the kingdom, who ruled with great justice and order.

As at this time the Inca ordered the fortress of Cuzco to be built, I will say something concerning it, it being so worthy of notice.

CHAPTER LI.

How the Royal House of the Sun was founded on a hill over-looking Cuzco towards the north, which the Spaniards usually call the fortress; and its wonderful Construction, and the size of the stones that are to be seen there.

THE city of Cuzco is built in a valley, and on the slopes of hills, as I explained in the first part of this history[1] and from the edifices themselves run broad terraces on which they sow their crops, and they rise one above the other like walls, so that the whole slopes were formed in these *andenes*, which made the city stronger, although its position is naturally strong.   For this reason the lords selected it, out of so many other sites.   The dominion of the kings was now become extensive and powerful, and Inca Yupanqui entertained far-reaching thoughts.   Notwithstanding that the temple of the Sun, called *Curi-cancha*, had been enriched and beautified by himself, and that he had erected other great edifices, he resolved to build another house of the Sun which should surpass all existing temples, and to enrich it with all the things that could be obtained, as well gold and silver as precious stones, fine cloth, arms of all the different kinds they used, munitions of war, shoes, plumes of feathers, skins of animals and birds, *coca*, sacks of wool, and valuables of a thousand kinds, in short, all things of which they had any knowledge.   This work was begun with such lofty aspirations, that if their monarchy had endured until to-day it would not yet have been completed.

The Inca ordered that the provinces should provide 20,000 men and that the villages should send the necessary pro-visions.   If any fell sick, another labourer was to supply his

---

[1] See chapter xcii.

place, and he was to return to his home. But these Indians were not kept constantly at a work in progress. They laboured for a limited time, and were then relieved by others, so that they did not feel the demand on their services. There were 4,000 labourers whose duty it was to quarry and get out the stones; 6,000 conveyed them by means of great cables of leather and of *cabuya*[1] to the works. The rest opened the ground and prepared the foundations, some being told off to cut the posts and beams for the wood-work. For their greater convenience, these labourers made their dwelling-huts, each lineage apart, near the place where the works were progressing. To this day most of the walls of these lodgings may be seen. Overseers were stationed to superintend, and there were great masters of the art of building who had been well instructed. Thus on the highest part of a hill to the north of the city, and little more than an arquebus-shot from it, this fortress was built which the natives called the House of the Sun, but which we named the Fortress.

The living rock was excavated for the foundation, which was prepared with such solidity that it will endure as long as the world itself. The work had, according to my estimate, a length of 330 paces,[2] and a width of 200. Its walls were so strong that there is no artillery which could breach them. The principal entrance was a thing worthy of contemplation, to see how well it was built, and how the walls were arranged so that one commanded the other. And in these walls there were stones so large and mighty that it tired the judgment to conceive how they could have been conveyed and placed, and who could have had sufficient power to shape them, seeing that among these people there are so few tools. Some of these stones are of a width of twelve feet and more than twenty

---

[1] Fibre of *Agava tuberosa*.

[2] Four hundred yards according to the Editor's measurement.

long, others are thicker than a bullock.[1]   All the stones are laid and joined with such delicacy that a rial could not be put in between two of them.

I went to see this edifice twice.   On one occasioñ I was accompanied by Tomas Vasquez,[2] a conqueror, and on the the other I found Hernando de Guzman there, he who was present at the siege,[3] and Juan de la Haya.[4]   Those who read this should believe that I relate nothing that I did not see.   As I walked about, observing what was to be seen, I beheld, near the fortress, a stone which measured 260 of my *palmos* in circuit, and so high that it looked as if it was in its original position.   All the Indians say that the stone got tired at this point, and that they were unable to move it further.[5]   Assuredly if I had not myself seen that the stone had been

---

[1] The largest stones are, by my measurements :—First, 10 feet high, by 6 broad ; second, 16½ feet high, by 6 broad ; third, 14 feet high, by 8 broad ; fourth, 14 feet high, by 12 broad.

[2] Tomas Vasquez, one of the first conquerors, had a house in Cuzco, and an estate in Ayaviri.   (See chapter iv.)   He distinguished himself in the battle of Las Salinas, fighting against Almagro.   He joined Giron in his insurrection, and commanded the rebel cavalry.   At Pucara he deserted Giron, went over to the royal camp, and obtained a pardon.   He retired to his estates, but was afterwards put to death by order of the Viceroy Marquis of Cañete in 1557.

[3] The siege of Cuzco by Manco Ynca, in 1526.

[4] This name is not clear in the manuscript.   It may be La Rea. The Peruvian editor has Juan de la Plaza.

[5] There are several versions of the native tradition relating to this monolith, which is called *piedra cansada*, or the "tired stone", in Quichua, *saycusca rumi*.   The Spanish editor gives the least known and most curious of these versions, which he found in the manuscript history of the Yncas by Padre Morúa.   He says that an Ynca of the blood royal, named Urco or Urcon, a great engineer and architect, was the official who directed the moving of the tired stone from the quarry, and that on reaching this spot where it stopped, the Indians who were dragging it, killed him.   This Urcon designed and traced out the fortress of Cuzco. He also conceived and carried out the idea of transporting from Quito the best soil for potatoes, with the object of raising them in it for the sovereign's table.   With this soil he made the hill called *Allpa Suntu*, to the east of the fortress.

hewn and shaped I should not have believed, however much it might have been asserted, that the force of man would have sufficed to bring it to where it now is. There it remains, as a testimony of what manner of men those were who conceived so good a work. The Spaniards have so pillaged and ruined it, that I should be sorry to have been guilty of the fault of those in power who have permitted so magnificent a work to be so ruined. They have not considered the time to come, for it would have been better to have preserved the edifice and to have put a guard over it.[1]

There were many buildings within the fortress, some small, one over the other, and others, which were large, were underground. They made two blocks of buildings, one larger than the other, wide and so well-built, that I know not how I can exaggerate the art with which the stones are laid and worked; and they say that the subterranean edifices are even better. Other things were told me, which I do not repeat, because I am not certain of their accuracy. This fortress was commenced in the time of Ynca Yupanqui. His son, Tupac Inca, as well as Huayna Ccapac and Huascar,

---

[1] The Spanish editor here has the following note. He says that the fault did not lie with the Spaniards, but in the very natural want of archæological knowledge in Cieza himself, and in his extreme credulity, believing all the stories of the Orejones and descendants of the Yncas, for whom everything that was worthy of notice in the country was the exclusive work of those sovereigns. It is now a generally received opinion that the very ancient cyclopean work at Cuzco was due to a people who lived long before Ynca Yupanqui, and even before Manco Ccapac, if it be true that the latter appeared in the beginning of the eleventh century. Moreover, the Yncas themselves destroyed some, and left others, without completing what had been begun by their predecessors. Not all the ruins in Peru were due to Spanish vandalism. On the contrary, the Viceroy Don Francisco de Toledo and others, far from contributing to the destruction of the fortress of Cuzco, took measures to preserve it, and, on more than one occasion, prevented the stones from being used for modern buildings. This was especially the case in the year 1577, when the Jesuits of Cuzco applied for leave to take stones from the fortress for their monastery and church, and were refused.

worked much at it, and although it is still worthy of admiration, it was formerly without comparison grander. When the Spaniards entered Cuzco, the Indians of Quizquiz had already collected great treasure ; but some was still found, and it is believed that there is a great quantity in the vicinity. It would be well to give orders for the preservation of what is left of this fortress, and of that of Huarcu,[1] as memorials of the grandeur of this people, and even for utility, as they could be made serviceable at so little cost. With this I will return to the narrative.

[1] The Viceroy Don Andres Hurtado de Mendoza, Marquis of Cañete, ordered the fortress at Huarcu (valley of Cañete on the coast) to be repaired and garrisoned, a few years after this was written by Cieza de Leon. It is called the fortress of Hervay, and there are still considerable remains of it at the mouth of the Cañete river, overlooking the Pacific.

CHAPTER LII.

*How Inca Yupanqui set out from Cuzco and marched to the
Collao, and of what happened there.*

THESE Indians have no letters, and can only preserve their
history by the memory of events handed down from generation to generation, and by their songs and *quipus*. I say
this, because their narratives vary in many particulars, some
saying one thing, and others giving a different version.
Human judgment would not suffice to decide what is truest,
without taking, from these various stories, what the people
themselves consider to be most accurate, for record. I write
this for the benefit of the Spaniards who are in Peru, and who
pretend to a knowledge of many native secrets. They are
aware that I knew and understood what they think that
they know and understand, and a good deal more; and that
from all this, I have decided upon writing what they will see,
having worked hard at collecting the materials, as they
themselves well know.

The Orejones relate that, the affairs of Inca Yupanqui
being in this state, he determined to set out from Cuzco with
a large force, to march to the region they call Collao.
Leaving a governor in the city, he set out and marched until
he arrived at the great town of Ayaviri. The people did not
wish to come to him in due form. The Inca, therefore, took
them by surprise, and killed all the inhabitants, both men
and women, doing the same to the people of Copacopa.
The destruction of Ayaviri was such, that nearly all perished.
There only remained a few who were horrified to see so great
a calamity, and wandered, like mad creatures, in the fields,
calling on their ancestors with great moanings and words of
fear.[1] The Inca hit upon the useful idea of planting a

---

[1] See chapter xlviii of the First Part.

colony in the beautiful meadows and fields of Ayaviri, near which the bright river flows; and he ordered that sufficient *mitimaes* should come, with their women, to people the district. So it was done, and large buildings with a temple of the Sun were erected for them, with a storehouse and provisions. Thus Ayaviri, peopled by *mitimaes*, continued to be more prosperous than it was before; and the Indians who survived from the wars and the cruelty of the Spaniards, are all descended from *mitimaes*, and not from natives, as has been written.

Besides this, they relate that certain captains having gone, by order of the Inca, with a sufficient force to make war on those of Anti-suyu, comprising the tribes in the forests to the eastward, they came upon snakes as large as thick beams, which killed all they could, insomuch that, without seeing any other enemy, these creatures made war on them in such sort, that very few returned out of the great number that set out. The Inca was much incensed when he received this news. Being with his followers, a sorceress said to him that she would go and charm the snakes, so that they should be gentle and foolish, and do no harm to any one, even though they themselves should feel the desire. Approving of the plan, if it should be equal to the promise, the Inca ordered it to be put in execution, which was done accordingly in the belief of the people, but not of mine, because it seems nonsense. The snakes having been enchanted, the enemies were attacked, many were made to submit by force, and others by persuasion and kind words.

The Inca set out from Ayaviri, and they say that he marched by the road of Omasayo, which was, for the convenience of his royal person, made broad as we now see it. He went by Asillo and Azangaro, where he had some encounters with the natives. But he spoke such words, and gave them such presents, that he brought them to his friendship and service. Thenceforward they adopted the policy which all other tribes use who have friendship and alliance with the Incas, and they arranged their habitations in towns on the open plain.

Passing forward, they relate that the Inca Yupanqui visited the other tribes bordering on the great lake of Titicaca ; and, by his wise dealings, he brought them all into his service. In each town he wore the dress used by the natives, a thing which gave great pleasure to them. He entered upon the lake of Titicaca, and beheld the islands which are surrounded by it, ordering a temple of the Sun and palaces to be erected on the largest, for the use of himself and his descendants. Having brought the whole region of the Collao under his sway, he returned in great triumph to Cuzco, where, as soon as he entered, he ordered that there should be the customary festivals, and people came from the other provinces with valuable presents, and the governors and delegates were very careful to comply with all that the Inca commanded.

CHAPTER LIII.

How Inca Yupanqui set out from Cuzco, and what he did.

THE fame of Inca Yupanqui flew over the land in such wise that his great deeds were discussed in all parts. Many, without seeing either banner or captain of his, came to know more and to offer vassalage, affirming that his ancestors must have fallen from heaven, seeing that they knew how to live in such concert and honour. Inca Yupanqui, without losing his gravity, answered them kindly, that he did not wish to injure any nation whatever, but that they should obey him, seeing that the Sun wished and commanded it. When he had again assembled an army, he set out towards the region called Condesuyo (Cunti-suyu), and subjugated the Yanahuaras and Chumbivilicas, and with some other tribes of Condesuyo he had sharp encounters. Yet, although they offered much opposition, his power and ability were such that, after much loss to themselves, they accepted him as lord, as the rest had done. Having arranged the affairs of these districts, and appointed rulers over the people, ordering that they should do no injury to his subjects, he returned to Cuzco. First, however, he placed governors in the principal places, whose duty it was to regulate the affairs of the provinces, both as regards the mode of living of the people, including the assembling into regular towns, and the prevention of any wrong being done, even to the most humble.

After this, they further relate that the Inca rested for some days at Cuzco, for he wished to proceed in person to the Andes (Antis), whither he had sent his spies and harbingers to examine the country and report upon the condition of the people. As the whole country was, by his order, full of deposits of provisions, he arranged that the road he had to take should be well supplied, and it was so. He then set out from

Cuzco with the captains and men of war, leaving a governor for the administration of justice. Traversing the mountains and snowy passes, he received reports from his scouts, touching the density of the forests, and how that, although they found the great snakes which are engendered in these thickets, yet they did no harm; yet the scouts were astounded to see how fierce and monstrous they were.

When the natives of these parts knew that the Inca had entered their country, as many of them had already been engaged in his service by the captains who preceded him, they came to do *mucha*[1], bringing presents of plumes of feathers, coca, and other products of their land, and he received them all kindly. As regards the rest of the Indians in the forests, those who wished to be his vassals sent messengers, and those who did not, abandoned their habitations and retired with their women into the densest parts of the forests.

Inca Yupanqui received important information that, after a few days' journey to the eastward, there was a rich and well-peopled country. He became very anxious to discover it, and would have passed onward. But tidings came of some disturbance at Cuzco, when he had arrived at a place called Marcapata. So he returned in great haste to Cuzco, where he remained for some days.

The Indians say that the province of the Collao was very large, and in those days it contained a great number of people and of lordships among the natives, which were very powerful. When they knew that Inca Yupanqui had entered the forests of the Antis, believing that he would either be killed there or return defeated, they agreed as one man, from Vilcañota onwards, but in great secrecy, to rebel and not to continue under the dominion of the Incas. They declared that united they were great, that their fathers had been free, and they would not remain captive, with so many lands subject to one sole lord. They all detested the rule which the Inca

[1] Worship.

had placed over them, although they had received no injury
or ill treatment, nor had the governors or delegates been
tyrannical or exacting.   But they assembled in Hatun-
colla and in Chucuito, where there met together Cari, and
Zapana, and Humalla, and the lord of Azangaro, and many
others.   They made their vow, in accordance with their blindness, to proceed with their design and resolve; and for
greater assurance, they all drank from one cup, and ordered
that it should be placed in a temple amongst sacred things,
as a testimony of what they had done.   Throughout the empire this rebellion in the Collao, and the deaths that had been
inflicted on the Orejones, became known.   The tidings led to
other disturbances in several parts, and in many places there
were insurrections.   This disturbed the arrangements respecting the *mitimaes*.   The governors were warned ; and
above all, the great valour of Tupac Inca Yupanqui was displayed, who reigned from that time, as I shall explain.

CHAPTER LIV.

How the Inca Yupanqui, having grown very old, resigned the Government of the Kingdom to Tupac Inca, his Son.

INCA YUPANQUI did not betray any anxiety in public when he received news of the insurrection in the Collao, but, with great resolution, he ordered an army to be assembled that he might go in person to punish the rebels. He sent his messengers to the Canas and Canchis, exhorting them to remain firm in their allegiance without allowing the inconstancy of the Collao to affect them. When the Inca was on the point of setting out from Cuzco, being very old, he felt tired of the wars he had waged, and of the long journeys he had made, and so bowed down and broken, that he considered himself unfit, either for this campaign, or for the continued government of so great an empire. So he sent for the High Priest and Orejones, and the principal men of the city, and said that he was now so old that his proper place was by the fireside, and not conducting a campaign.[1] He gave them to understand that this was said in all sincerity, and that they should take his son Tupac Inca Yupanqui for their Inca, a resolute

[1] The reign of this Ynca Yupanqui appears to include two reigns according to Garcilasso de la Vega. Cieza de Leon makes one generation where Garcilasso makes two, namely Pachacutec and Ynca Yupanqui. Pachacutec means " he who changes the world", and Garcilasso says that the name should have been given to Viracocha, the father, who changed the course of events by his victory over the Chancas, but that it was given to his son. Cieza de Leon attributes the victory over the Chancas to this very son, whom he calls Yupanqui, and to whom the surname Pachacutec rightly belongs. It seems likely, therefore, that Cieza's version of the genealogy is the more correct of the two.

Garcilasso, however, makes two long reigns where Cieza has only one. To Pachacutec he attributes the conquest of the Huancas, Caxamarca, and the coast valleys, and he records several of his laws and wise sayings (ii, p. 208). To Yupanqui he assigns the expedition into the eastern forests, and the conquest of Chile.

youth, as they had seen in the former war in which he had served. He told them to deliver the fringe to him, that he might be venerated and acknowledged by all as their lord. He would then take steps for the punishment of the rebels in the Collao who had risen and put to death the Orejones and delegates who had been left amongst them.

Those for whom he had sent, replied that all should be done as he desired, and that they would obey in all things as they always had done. In the provinces of the Canchis and Canas they made great receptions with rich presents, and they had constructed, in the place they called Cacha, some edifices very worthy to behold, after the fashion which is usual with them.

The Collas, when they knew that Tupac Inca was marching against them in great power, sought help from their neighbours, and assembled most of them with the determination to await his approach, and to give him battle. They relate that Tupac Inca had news of all this, and that, as his disposition was merciful, and although he well knew the advantage he had over his enemies, he sent from among his neighbours, the Canas, some messengers to declare that his desire was not to be an enemy, and to punish in proportion to the crime that had been committed, when the governors and delegates of his father were killed without having done any wrong whatever. His wish was that they should lay down their arms and submit, that they might be well governed, and recognise one sovereign, rather than many lords.

With this message an Orejon was sent, carrying some presents for the principal people among the Collas. But it availed nothing, nor did they desire to swear allegiance, but rather to maintain the confederation they had formed. With the lords of their villages as captains, they advanced towards the position where Tupac Inca was encamped. All accounts agree that, in the town called Pucara they took up a position in a fortress which they had made there, and when the Inca arrived they prepared to fight with their accustomed shouts. There was a battle between the opposing forces, in which many were killed on both sides, but the Collas were defeated. Great numbers were taken prisoners, both men and women, and there would have been more if the Inca had caused the pursuit to be more hotly continued. The Inca spoke sharply to Cari, the lord of Chucuito, asking him how he had answered to the peace which his grandfather Viracocha Inca had established with him. He said he would not kill him, but would send him to Cuzco, where he would be punished. Accordingly, he and the other prisoners were sent to Cuzco under guard; and, in memory of the victory over the Collas in that place, the Inca ordered great images of stone to be set up, and a huge piece of the hill to be broken up, as well as other things, which he will see and note who travels that way. I did myself, and I remained there two days to see and understand everything thoroughly.[1]

[1] See chapter cii of the First Part.

CHAPTER LV.

How the Collas asked for peace, and how the Inca granted it
and returned to Cuzco.

THE Collas who escaped from the battle were much astonished at the result, and made haste to get away, believing that those of Cuzco were closely following. So they fled
in terror, turning their heads from time to time to see what
was not there, for the Inca had stopped the pursuit. Having
crossed the Desaguadero, all the principal chiefs assembled
and took counsel together. They determined to send to the
Inca and ask for peace, and, if he received them into his service, that they would pay the tribute that was due up to the
time they rebelled, and that hereafter they would always be
loyal. The most important among them were chosen to treat
on this matter, and they met Tupac Inca advancing in pursuit. He listened to the embassy with complacency, and answered with the words of a human conqueror, saying that
he grieved for what had happened owing to their conduct,
and that they might safely come to Chucuito, where he would
arrange the terms of peace in such a way as would be profitable to them. When they heard this, they put the matter in
train.

The Inca ordered large supplies to be brought, and the lord
Humalla came to receive him. The Inca spoke favourably
both to him and the other lords and captains. Before the
peace was arranged, they relate that great dancing and drinking festivals were celebrated. When they were concluded,
and all the chiefs being assembled, the Inca said that he
should not require the arrears of tribute to be paid, as they
amounted to a large quantity. But as they had rebelled
without cause or reason, it would be necessary to station gar-

risons of men of war, and that they must supply the soldiers with provisions and women. They said that they would do this; and he also ordered that *mitimaes* should come from other lands, and that a large number of emigrants from the Collas should be removed from their own districts to others. Governors and delegates were left amongst them, to collect the tribute. This being done, the Inca said that they must abide by a law which he should ordain, that their conduct might always be had in memory. The law was that only one thousand natives of their province should ever enter Cuzco, including women, on pain of death if more should enter. They were grieved at this order, but they agreed to comply with it, as with the rest of his commands. It is certain that if there was the fixed number of Collas in Cuzco, no others could enter after the number was complete, until some went out, and, if they wished to do so, they could not, because the gate-keepers, collectors of tolls, and guards who were stationed to see who went in and out, would not permit or consent to it. Among these people they did not resort to bribery to gain their ends, nor did they ever tell a lie to their kings on any account, nor betray a secret. This is a thing worthy of all praise.

Having settled the affairs of the province of Collao, put things in order, and given the chiefs their instructions, the Inca returned to Cuzco, first sending his messengers to Condesuyos and to the Antis, to report what had taken place there, whether the governor had committed any fault, or the natives had made any disturbance. Accompanied by a great company and many principal chiefs, he entered Cuzco, and was received with much honor. They offered up great sacrifices to the Sun, and there were festivities for those who were engaged in the work of building the fortress by order of Inca Yupanqui. The Coya, wife and sister of the Inca, named Mama Ocllo, also made great rejoicings with festivity and dancing.

Tupac Inca now determined to set out on the road of
Chincha-suyu, to subjugate the provinces beyond Tarama
and Bonbon. He, therefore, ordered a general summons
to be issued for soldiers to assemble throughout the provinces.

CHAPTER LVI.

How Tupac Inca Yupanqui set out from Cuzco, and how he conquered all the country from thence to Quito, and touching his great deeds.

I COULD well give a longer account of this conquest of Quito by Tupac Inca Yupanqui, but I have so much to write touching other events that I cannot spare the space, nor can I relate what he did, except summarily. On the departure of the king from the city of Cuzco, it was not known in what direction he was going to make war, because he did not make known his intention, except to his councillors. More than 200,000 men assembled, with so much baggage and stores that the plain was covered with them. He sent orders, by the posts, to the governors of provinces that all should bring provisions, munitions, and arms to the royal road of Chinchasuyu. This road was made without deviating from the line traced by order of his father, nor so near it as that both could be joined into one. It was grand and very handsomely constructed, with the order and industry touching which I have already written, and in all parts there were preparations for the great multitude that was to pass along it, without anything being wanting. None of the king's soldiers were allowed to pick so much as a cob of maize, and, if any man did, it did not cost him less than his life. The natives carried the loads, and performed the other personal services, but it may be held for certain that they did not go beyond the appointed places ; and as they worked willingly, and faith and justice were observed towards them, they did not feel the work.

A garrison, with *mitimaes*, and a governor selected from among the most faithful of his friends, were left in Cuzco. The Inca then set out, taking, as his captain-general and chief councillor, his uncle, Ccapac Yupanqui, not he who made the war against those of Xauxa, for that chief had been put to death owing to some offence he had given. The Inca advanced to Vilcas, where he stopped for some days, enjoying the sight of the temple and other edifices that had been built. He ordered that there should always be silversmiths making vases and other ornaments for the temple and palace of Vilcas.

The Inca arrived at Xauxa, where the Huancas prepared a solemn reception. Thence he sent messengers in all directions, announcing to the people that he desired to win their friendship, without giving them offence or making war. He said that they must have heard how the Incas of Cuzco exercised no tyranny and imposed no exactions on those who were their allies and vassals, and that, in exchange for the service and homage they gave, they received much good from their sovereign. In Bonbon they knew the great power with which the Inca came, and, as they expected great things from his clemency, they came to do him homage. Those of Yauyo did the same, as well as those of Apurima and many others. He received them all very well, giving women to some, to others coca, and to others mantles and shirts. He himself wore the dress of the people among whom he was, which was the way in which they received most satisfaction.

In the provinces which lie between Xauxa and Caxamalca, they relate that there were some wars, and he ordered forts and strongholds to be made for defence against the natives. But, generally, he subdued them by his policy, and without shedding much blood, as well the intermediate tribes, as those of Caxamalca. In all parts he left governors and delegates, and established posts to keep open his communications. He did not leave any great province without ordering houses and a Temple of the Sun to be built, and establishing *mitimacs*. They also relate that he entered Huanuco, and ordered

that fine palace to be built, which we behold to this day.[1]
Being among those of Chachapoyas, he waged such war that
they were defeated at all points. In Caxamalca the Inca
left people of Cuzco, that they might instruct the natives
touching what they should wear, and the tribute they should
contribute, and, above all, how they should worship and reverence the Sun as their god.

In all parts they called the Inca their father, and he took
care that no one should do any damage in the fields by which
they passed, nor ill-treat any man or woman. He who committed any such offence was presently punished with death.
He arranged that those who submitted should build their
towns in due order, that they should not wage war upon
each other, nor eat human flesh, nor commit any other
crimes against the law of nature.

He entered the country of the Bracamoras, but returned
flying, for it is an evil region covered with forest. In the
country of the Paltas, in Huancabamba, Caxas, and Ayavaca,
he had great trouble in subjugating the people, who were
strong and warlike. They maintained the contest against him
during more than five moons. At length they asked for
peace, which was granted with the usual conditions. On one
day the peace was established, and on the next, the country
was full of *mitimaes* with governors, without depriving the

---

[1] The ruins are 18 leagues west of the present town of Huanuco, in
the province of Huamalies, 12,156 feet above the sea. They are of
great extent, covering more than half a mile in length. They show work
of the same character as the palaces at Cuzco. The work includes a re-
servoir 250 feet long by 130, a bath of cut stone, and a stone aqueduct.
A doorway of cut stone, with a long rectangular room on each side, opens
to another at a distance of 240 feet, and further on there is another doorway. Squier says,— " The perspective through this series of portals is
the finest to be found in the ancient works of Peru." Above the
second portal are rudely-cut animal figures. There are many other
ruined buildings, and what is called the castle, 180 feet long by 80, with
a fine cut-stone wall 13 feet high. An inclined plane leads up to the
terre-plein, which is entered by two portals.

native chiefs. Store-houses were built, provisions were collected in them, and the royal road was constructed, with a series of forts throughout.

From these districts, Tupac Inca Yupanqui advanced until he came to the country of the Cañaris, with whom he also had quarrels and disputes; but the same happened with them as with others, they remained his vassals, and he ordered them to proceed to Cuzco and settle in that city—more than 15,000 men, with their women, and the principal chief to govern them. It was done as he commanded. Some pretend that the sending of the Cañaris to Cuzco happened in the time of Huayna Ccapac. At Tumebamba, the Inca ordered great edifices to be built, respecting which I treated in ·the First Part.[1] From this place he sent .embassies in various directions, inviting the people to come and see him, and many, without making war, offered their services. Those who took another course were obliged, by an advance of captains and troops, to do by force what others did of their own free will.

The affairs of the country of the Cañaris having been settled, the Inca marched by Tiquizambi, Cayambi, and the Purnaes, and many other districts, where they recount great things that he did; and the knowledge he must have possessed to make himself monarch of such great kingdoms, seems almost incredible. In Tacunga, he waged fierce war with the natives, and, after they were subdued, he made peace. Here he ordered such grand edifices to be erected as to exceed those of Cuzco in perfection. He rested at Tacunga for some days; and nearly every day a messenger arrived from Cuzco, reporting the state of affairs there, while, from other parts, the runners constantly arrived with reports on the administration of the different provinces by the governors. And tidings arrived of a disturbance at Cuzco among the Orejones themselves, which caused some anxiety. But

[1] Chapter xliv.

another report quickly followed that all was settled again, and that the governor of the city had severely punished the authors of the uproar.

From Tacunga the Inca advanced until he came to the place we call Quito, where the city of San Francisco del Quito is founded. As the country seemed inviting, and as good as Cuzco, the Inca here founded a place which he called Quito, peopling it with *mitimaes*. Here he made edifices and store-houses, saying, " Cuzco must be the capital of one part of my great empire and Quito of the other." He gave important powers to the Governor of Quito, and placed his own governors and delegates in all the surrounding districts. He ordered that there should be a garrison of men, both for peace and war, at Caranguri ; and he removed the inhabitants from one village to another, making them exchange their abodes. In all parts they worshipped the Sun, and adopted the customs of the Incas, insomuch that it appeared as if they had all been born in Cuzco. They loved the Inca so much that they called him Father of all, the good Lord, the just, the judge. In the province of the Cañaris, they assert that Huayna Ccapac was born, and that great festivities took place at his birth. All the inhabitants of those provinces which had been brought under the orderly rule of the great Tupac Inca, arranged their towns with regularity, and made rest-houses on the royal roads. They were diligent to learn the general language of Cuzco and the laws which it was their duty to observe. Masters who came from Cuzco superintended the building of the edifices, and instructed others in the art ; and in like manner the rest of the things which the king ordered were completed.

CHAPTER LVII.

How the Inca sent from Quito to know whether his commands had been obeyed, and how, leaving that province in good order, he set out to go to the valleys of the Yuncas.

WHEN Tupac Inca Yupanqui had become lord of the country as far as Quito, in the manner already described, and being himself still at Quito, he resolved to take steps to ensure that his orders were complied with and carried out. He, therefore, directed those who among his followers were most expert to be carried by the natives in hammocks, some to one part, some to another, overlooking and examining the condition of the new provinces, taking account of the governors and collectors of tribute, and judging of their dealings with the natives.

The Inca sent his Orejones to the provinces which we call Puerto Viejo,[1] to induce the inhabitants to submit, as the others had done, and to instruct them how they were to sow, to work, to dress, and to worship the Sun, and to make them understand the orderly system of living, and of policy. They relate that these Orejones were killed, as a reward for the good they came to do; and that Tupac Inca sent certain captains, with troops, to punish the murderers. But when the barbarians knew of their approach, they assembled in such numbers that they conquered and killed the Inca's troops, at which he showed anger. But as he had important affairs on his hands, and had occasion to proceed in person to Cuzco, he was not in a position to chastise them for what they had done.

At Quito, the Inca received news that his orders had been well attended to in the provinces, and that his delegates had

---

[1] Puerto Viejo was a seaport in 1° 2′ S. latitude. It was founded by Francisco Pacheco on March 12th, 1535, by order of Almagro.

instructed the people over whom they were placed, and had treated them well; while the people were happy, and did what was required of them. From many lords there arrived ambassadors every day, with valuable presents, and the Inca's court was full of great men, and his palaces of vases of gold and silver, and other precious things. In the morning the Inca had a meal, and from noon until rather late he gave public audiences to those who desired to speak with him, accompanied by his guard. From that time until the night he passed in drinking, and then supper was served by the light of torches. For these people did not use tallow or wax, although they had plenty of both.

The Inca left a venerable Orejon in Quito, as the captain-general and lieutenant, who, according to all accounts, was intelligent, brave, and of noble presence. His name was Chalco Mayta, and he was given permission to travel in a litter and to be served in gold, and other privileges which he highly appreciated. Above all things, he was ordered to send a messenger to the Inca every month, with a full report of all that had happened, of the condition of the country, the yield of the harvests, increase of flocks, as well as the usual reports of the annual deaths and births, according to the system already described. The great road from Quito to Cuzco, which is a greater distance than from Seville to Rome, was as much used as the road from Seville to Triana, and I cannot say more.

The great Tupac Inca had long heard of the fertility of the coast valleys and of their beauty, and of the great esteem in which their lords were held. He now determined to send messengers with presents for the principal men, and a request that they would receive him as a friend and comrade, as he, in like manner, desired to be with them. He said that when he passed through their valleys, he would not make war if they desired peace, that he would give them some of his women and cloths, and would take theirs in exchange,

with other things of a like nature. Throughout the coast
the tidings of the great conquests of Tupac Inca Yupanqui
had spread, and that he was not cruel nor bloodthirsty, nor
did harm to any except those who were troublesome and opposed themselves to him. Those who brought the news also
praised the customs and religion of the people of Cuzco, holding the Orejones to be sacred persons, and that the Incas
were either children of the Sun or had some deity within
themselves. Considering these and other reports, many resolved to seek the Inca's friendship before they had even seen
his banners, and they sent their ambassadors with messages
to that effect, and bearing many presents. They requested
him to be pleased to come to their valleys to enjoy the
delights of them and to be served by the inhabitants. Approving of their wish, and giving fresh instructions to the
Governor of Quito, the Inca left that city to assume dominion
over the Yuncas of the coast.

CHAPTER LVIII.

How Tupac Inca Yupanqui marched by the coast valleys, and how all the Yuncas came under his dominion.

As the King Tupac Inca had determined to go to the coast valleys, to bring the inhabitants under his sway, he descended to that of Tumbez, and was respectfully received by the people; to whom he showed much kindness, and put on the dress which they usually wore, to give them more contentment. He commended the principal men for wishing to receive him as their lord without going to war, and promised to look upon them as his own children. They, being well satisfied to hear his good words and to see the way in which he treated them, gave their obedience in good faith, allowing governors to remain with them, and buildings to be erected. But some Indians affirm that Tupac Inca passed on without making any settlement in this district, and that there was none until the reign of Huayna Ccapac. If we attend to everything they say, we shall never come to any conclusion.

Leaving this valley, the Inca visited the others on the sea coast, making a royal road as he travelled, very large and grand, as may be seen from what now remains of it. In most parts he was served, and the people came to him with presents, but occasionally there was resistance to his advance. However, there was no part where the people did not eventually submit and become his vassals. In these valleys he rested for some days, drinking and enjoying his pleasures, while he rejoiced to look upon the beauty of the country. Great edifices and temples were built by his order. They say that in the valley of Chimu there was a fierce war with the lord, and that, in one battle, the Incas were very nearly being defeated at all points. But his soldiers were at last able to prevail and to conquer their enemies. Tupac Inca, by his clemency, pardoned them, ordering that those who remained alive should continue the sowing of their lands, and should not again take up arms. The Inca's delegate remained in Chimu, and the rest of the valley sent their tribute to Caxamalca. As the natives were expert in the working of metals, many were sent to Cuzco, and to the capitals of provinces, where they worked gold and silver ornaments and vases, and any other things that were ordered.[1] From Chimu the Inca passed on to Parmunquilla[2] where he ordered a fortress to be built. It may still be seen, though abandoned and in ruins.

These Yuncas were very refined, and the lords were luxurious and fond of festivities. They travelled on the shoulders of vassals, had many women, were rich in gold and silver, cloth, precious stones, and flocks. In those times they were served with much pomp. Heralds and buffoons went before them, porters attended on them, and they observed religious ceremonies. Some voluntarily submitted to the Inca, while others took up arms against him ; but finally he remained sovereign and lord over the whole of them. He did not deprive them of their liberties, nor prohibit their ancient customs, so that they might adopt others. He left expert men who could instruct them in all that the Inca desired they should understand ; and great care was taken that they should learn the general language. He caused *mitimaes* to be established, and posts along the roads. A moderate tribute

[1] Garcilasso de la Vega gives a fuller account of the war with Chimu. (ii, pp. 193 to 201.)

[2] Parmunca. In his First Part (p. 247) Cieza de Leon calls these ruins Pormonga. They are near the coast, south of Guarmay. The outer walls are 300 yards long by 200. The interior is divided into small houses, separated by lanes. The walls are partly covered with a kind of plaster, on which were painted representations of birds and beasts. The ruined fortress stands at the extremity of a plain, close to the foot of some rugged mountains, about a league from the sea.

was imposed, and that which was given as tribute was to be the produce of their own land, so that the people need not seek it from afar; justice was maintained, but what was promised by the people must be fulfilled. If not, the loss was their own, and the Inca recovered his full revenue. No native lord received a lordship; but many men were taken out of the valleys and removed to others, or were removed to other parts to perform the duties they understood.

The Inca marched through the remaining valleys in the best order possible, not permitting any injury whatever to be done, either in the towns or in the fields that he passed. The natives had plenty of provisions collected in the store-houses that had been built along the road. In this way the Inca advanced until he arrived at the valley of Pachacamac, where was the very ancient and sacred temple of the Yuncas, which he wished very much to see. When he arrived at that valley, they say that he only wished that there should be a Temple of the Sun ; but as he found that the existing temple was so revered and esteemed by the natives, he did not venture to alter anything. He contented himself with causing a great house of the Sun to be made, with mama-conas and priests, that sacrifices might be offered up in accordance with his religion.[1] Many Indians say that the Inca himself spoke with the devil who was in the idol of Pachacamac, and that he heard how the idol was the creator of the world and other nonsense, which I do not put down, because it is not worth while. It is also said that the Inca besought the idol to tell him with what service he would be most pleased and honoured, and that the devil

---

[1] The original Yunca temple, called by the Yncas Pachacamac, was on a terraced height overlooking the sea, and about 500 feet above its level. The Temple of the Sun was about a mile and a half distant, the ruin now being called *Mamaconas*. This latter ruin is certainly of Ynca origin.

replied that they should sacrifice to him much blood of human beings and of sheep.

After this they say that great sacrifices were offered up in Pachacamac by Tupac Inca Yupanqui, and great festivals were celebrated. The Inca then returned to Cuzco by a road which he made, crossing the snowy range of Pariacaca,[1] and coming out in the valley of Xauxa. It is no small sight to behold the grandeur of that range, and what great terraces it has, and to this day men pass by that snow-covered region. Visiting the mountainous provinces, and ordering and providing what was most conducive to good government, the Inca arrived at Cuzco, where he was received with great festivities and dances, while many sacrifices were offered up in the temple, to commemorate his victories.

[1] The pass of Pariacaca is in the province of Huarochiri. The terraces or " stairs" mentioned in the text are near the summit. Acosta describes his great sufferings while crossing this formidable pass (i, p. 130). Father Avila has recorded the strange traditions of the natives touching Pariacaca. (See my Translation.)

CHAPTER LIX.

How Tupac Inca again set out from Cuzco, and of the fierce war he waged with those of Huarco; and how, after he had conquered them, he returned to Cuzco.

THE province of Chincha was, in former days, an important part of this kingdom of Peru, and very populous, insomuch that, before the time of Tupac Inca, the Chinchas, with their captains, had made incursions as far as the Collao, whence they returned to their province with great spoils.[1] Hence they had always been respected and feared by their neighbours. It is said that the Inca, father of Tupac Inca, had sent from the country of the Soras a captain named Ccapac Inca, to persuade the Chinchas to come under his dominion. Although he went and induced some of them to agree, it was but a small part, for the rest rose up in arms, and prepared to defend their country in such sort that the Orejon made the best of his way back again.[2] They had not again seen a captain of the Incas, as they themselves declare, until they were subjugated by Tupac Inca. In this matter, I know no more than what the people themselves relate.

Returning to the narrative, after the Inca had gone back to Cuzco, as has been mentioned, and had devoted as many days as he pleased to enjoying himself and to amusements, he gave orders for the assembly of another army, to complete the conquest of the coast region. His commands were obeyed; and soon the captains of the provinces with their contingents of troops arrived at Cuzco. After having made

---

[1] See also Garcilasso de la Vega on the alleged ancient conquests of the Yuncas (ii, p. 153). He declares that the assertions of the coast people as to their former incursions into the Collao are false.

[2] On the other hand, Garcilasso attributes the conquest of the Chinchas to this Ccapac Yupanqui, in the time of the Inca Pachacutec.

arrangements for the government of the city, he set out from Cuzco, and came down to the coast by the road of Huatara.[1] His approach being known, many waited with the intention of accepting him as their lord, and many others were resolved to make war, and, if possible, to maintain their liberties. In the valley of Nasca there were many people and preparations for war.

Tupac Inca, when he arrived at Nasca, on the coast, received and despatched embassies, and there were some encounters and skirmishes; but they consented to what the Inca required of them, that they should build strong forts, receive *mitimaes*, and pay the tribute imposed on them. From thence the Inca went to the valley of Yca, where he met with more resistance than at Nasca; but his prudence enabled him, without fighting, to turn enemies into friends, and these were conciliated like the others. In Chincha, the people were waiting for the arrival of the Inca in their valley, with more than 30,000 armed men, and they expected support from their neighbours. Tupac Inca, when he knew it, sent messengers, with great presents, to the chiefs and principal captains, instructing the ambassador to make great offers in his name, to assure them that he did not desire war, but rather peace and brotherhood, and other messages of that kind. The Chinchas heard what the Inca said, and received his presents. Some of their principal men then visited him, and treated of peace with such success, that it was concluded. The Chinchas laid down their arms and received Tupac Inca, who presently proceeded to Chincha. This account is given both by the Chinchas themselves, and by the Orejones of Cuzco. Other Indians of other provinces, whom I have heard, tell the story in a

---

[1] This road leads to the valley of Pisco. The subsequent narrative seems to show that the author here makes a mistake, and that the Inca descended to the coast at Nasca, much further south.

different manner, for they say that there was a great war. But I believe that Tupac Inca became Lord of Chincha without fighting.[1]

When the Inca arrived in that valley, he found it to be so beautiful and so extensive, that he rejoiced greatly. He praised the customs of the natives, and with loving words he asked them to adopt such of the customs of Cuzco as fitted with their own. They were well content, and obeyed him in all things. Having made all suitable arrangements, he went back to Yca, whence he marched to the valley called Huarco,[2] because he heard that the people were waiting for him in warlike guise. This, indeed, was the truth, for the natives of that valley, despising their neighbours for having submitted to a strange king without reason, and given up possession of their lands to him, had assembled with great resolution, and had erected strong forts or *pucaras* within their boundaries, near the sea shore. Here they put their women and children. The Inca, marching with his army in battle array, came in sight of the enemy, and sent ambassadors with menaces and threats. They, however, would not adopt the rule of their neighbours, which was to submit to strangers, but prepared for war. As the summer was approaching, and the heat was great, the soldiers of the Inca fell sick, which induced him to retire as cautiously as possible. The Huarcos came forth from their valley, collected their harvests, and sowed their fields. They also got their arms ready, that they might be ready to receive the people of Cuzco, if they again came to attack them.

Tupac Inca returned to Cuzco; and as men have little constancy, when they saw that the Huarcos remained in possession of their liberties, there began to be changes

[1] Garcilasso de la Vega says that the Chinchas carried on a long war before they were subdued (ii, p. 150).

[2] Now called Cañete.

among them, while some rebelled and threw off the yoke of
the Inca. These were natives of the valleys on the sea
coast.   All this came to the knowledge of the king, and
during the remainder of that summer he was engaged in
assembling troops, and sending Orejones to visit the provinces
in all parts of the empire. He was resolved to gain the
lordship of Huarco, even if it should cost very dear. When
autumn was come, and the heats of summer were passed,
he descended to the coast with the largest army that he
could collect. He sent ambassadors into the valleys, up-
braiding the people for their weakness of purpose in pre-
suming to rise against him, urging them to be firm in their
friendship henceforward, for that if not, they would be
visited by cruel war. When he reached the borders of the
valley of Huarco, on the skirts of a mountain, he ordered a
city to be founded, to which he gave the name of Cuzco, in-
tending it to be his principal residence. The streets, and
hills, and open square received the same names as those of
the real city. He said that until Huarco was conquered,
and the people had become his subjects, he would remain in
that place, and that a garrison should always be maintained
there. When his directions had been carried out, he advanced with his troops in the direction of the enemy, and
surrounded their position. He was so firm in his purpose,
that he never sent any one to treat with them ; but carried
on the war, which was so obstinate, that, they say, it lasted
for three years. In the summers the Inca went to Cuzco,
leaving a garrison in the new Cuzco that he had built, so
that there might always be troops opposed to the enemy.

Thus it was that one side maintained their resolve to be
lords, and the other side was equally determined not to be
slaves. But at last, at the end of three years, the Huarcos
became weak ; and the Inca, knowing their condition, sent
new ambassadors, proposing that they should be his friends
and comrades, and saying that he had no wish but that their

children should intermarry, and that thus their alliance should be one of perfect equality. Other things were said with intent to deceive, for in reality Tupac Inca considered that these people deserved severe punishment for having caused so much trouble. The Huarcos, feeling that they could not hold out for many days longer, and that, with the conditions offered by the Inca, it would be better to enjoy tranquillity and repose, agreed to what the Inca proposed. Evacuating the fortress, their principal men went to make reverence to the Inca, who, without more ado, ordered his people to kill them all. This was done with great cruelty. All the principal and most honoured chiefs who came were put to death, and the sentence was also executed on those who had remained away. They killed a great number, as their descendants relate to this day, and the great heaps of bones testify to the truth of what they say. We believe that what is related by the people on this subject, is what you see written down.

This being done, the Inca ordered an important fortress to be erected, in such manner as I have related in my First Part.[1] The valley having been subdued, and governors established in it, with *mitimaes*, the Inca received embassies, who came from the Yuncas, as well as from many tribes in the mountains. He then ordered the new Cuzco which he had built to be pulled down, and returned with his army to the city of Cuzco, where he was received with great demonstration of joy. They offered up sacrifices in his honour, both in the temple and where the oracles spoke, afterwards making the people joyful with feasts, drinking-bouts, and solemn recitations.

---

[1] Chapter lxxiii. This is the fortress called Hervay, at the mouth of the river of Cañete, the well-preserved ruins of which may still be seen. I examined them carefully in 1853. See an account of them in a note to my translation of the First Part of *Cieza de Leon*, p. 259.

CHAPTER LX.

How Tupac Inca once more set out from Cuzco, and how he went to the Collao, and from thence to Chile, subjugating the nations in that direction, and of his death.

TUPAC INCA, having returned to Cuzco after having gained the great victories which have been described, was enjoying himself at banquets and drinking-bouts, with his wives, damsels, and children, for several days. Among his children was Huayna Ccapac, he who was to succeed as king, and who was growing up very vigorous and brave. After the festivities, Tupac Inca thought of visiting the Collao and subduing the region beyond. With this object, he ordered the soldiers to be summoned from all parts, and many tents to be prepared for passing the night in the desert places. The troops began to arrive with their captains, and were lodged round the city, those whom the law prohibited not entering Cuzco. Both one and the other were provided with all that was necessary, the governors and purveyors of the city keeping a full account. When all who had .to go to the war were assembled, sacrifices were offered up to their gods in conformity with their blindness, making the soothsayers seek an answer touching the war from the oracles. After a general and very splendid feast, Tupac Inca set out from Cuzco, leaving his eldest son Huayna Ccapac as his lieutenant; and with great splendour and state, he travelled to Colla-suyu, visiting his garrisons and royal *tampus*, and being entertained in the villages of the Canas and Canchis.

Entering the Collao, he advanced as far as Chucuito, where the chiefs of the land assembled to make a festival. Owing to the good order that was established, they had sufficient provisions ready for the 300,000 men who composed the

army. Some chiefs of the Collao offered to go in person with
the Inca. He went on the lake of Titicaca, with some lords
whom he selected, and approved of the edifices which his
father had ordered to be built, and of the excellence of the work.
He offered up great sacrifices in the temple, and presented
rich gifts to the priests and to the idol, worthy of so great a
lord as he was. He then returned to the army, and marched
through the whole province of the Collao until he came to
the end of it. He sent his messengers to all the nations of
the Charcas, Carangas, and other inhabitants of that region.
Of these, some consented to submit, while others resisted;
but the Inca's power was such that the latter were easily subdued. The conquered were treated with great clemency, and
those who submitted with much affection. In Paria, the
Inca ordered edifices to be built, and also in other parts.
Certainly great events must have taken place in connection
with Tupac Inca, many of which have been forgotten, owing
to the want of letters; and I set down briefly some few out
of many that we know, having been heard by us who are in
those parts.

Having been victorious in the country beyond Charcas, the
Inca traversed many provinces, and vast snow-covered deserts, until he arrived in the country we call Chile. He conquered, and became lord over all that land; and they say
that he advanced as far as the river Maule. In Chile he
built some edifices, and received, as tribute from those parts,
much gold. He left governors and *mitimaes*, put the conquered country in good order, and returned to Cuzco.

Towards the eastern limits he sent instructed Orejones, in
the dress of merchants, to see what lands there were in that
direction, and what kind of people dwelt there. Having
arranged these things, he returned to Cuzco, whence they
affirm that he set out again at the end of a few days. With
the troops he had ordered to assemble he then entered the
region of the Antis, and suffered great hardships in forcing

his way through the dense forests. He conquered some of
the tribes, and ordered large plantations of coca to be cultivated for the supply of Cuzco, to which place he returned.

They affirm that after a few days the Inca was attacked by
an illness, of which he died, leaving to his son the government of his kingdom, his wives and children ; and, after saying a few other things, he expired. There was great lamentation, and such strong feeling, from Quito to Chile, that it is
wonderful to listen to the Indians who relate the events of
that time.

Where or in what place he was interred they do not say.
They relate that a great number of women, servants, and
pages were killed, to be buried with him, with so much treasure that it must have amounted to more than a million : for
ordinary lords have been buried with upwards of 100,000
castellanos. Besides the people who were put into his tomb,
they put to death and buried many men and women in divers
parts of the kingdom ; and in all parts they mourned for an
entire year. Most of the women shaved their heads, putting
on ropes of grass ; and at the end of the year they came to
do him honour. The other things which they used to do, I
prefer not to repeat, because they savour of heathenism. But
the Christians who were in Cuzco in 1550 will remember
what they saw of the honours done at the end of the year
of mourning for Paullu Inca,[1] who had himself become a
Christian. So that they can imagine what it must have
been in the days when the departed kings were reigning, and
before they lost their empire.

---

[1] Paullu was a son of Huayna Ccapac, and a younger brother of
Huascar and of the Ynca Manco. He accompanied Almagro in his
expedition to Chile, and was with Almagro the lad at the battle of
Chupas. In 1543 he was baptised under the name of Don Cristobal,
and he lived at Cuzco, respected by the Spaniards and beloved by the
native population. He died in May 1549. His son Carlos Ynca was a
schoolfellow of Garcilasso de la Vega, and had a son Melchor Carlos
Ynca, a knight of Santiago, who went to Spain in 1602, and died at
Alcala de Henares in 1610.

CHAPTER LXI.

How Huayna Ccapac reigned in Cuzco, who was the twelfth King Inca.

WHEN the great King Tupac Inca Yupanqui died, they prepared to perform the obsequies and ceremonies of his interment after the manner of his ancestors, and with great pomp. The Orejones relate that some provinces conspired to recover their liberty, and shake off the yoke of the Incas, but the good management of the Inca governors, assisted by the captains and *mitimaes*, kept order during a trying time. Huayna Capac was not careless, nor did he fail to understand that it would be necessary for him to display valour in order to preserve that which his father had gained with so much labour. Shortly he entered upon the fast, and he who governed the city proved loyal and faithful. There did not fail to be some disturbance among the Incas themselves, for some sons of Tupac Inca, begotten on other women than the Coya, wished to set up a claim to the royal dignity. The people, however, were loyal to Huayna Capac, and not only would not consent, but applauded the punishment inflicted on them. When the fast was ended, Huayna Capac came forth with the fringe, very richly adorned, and performed the ceremonies according to the custom of his ancestors, at the end of which his name was declared with great acclamations: "*Huayna Capac*," "*Inca zapalla tucuillacta uya*," which is as much as to say—"Huayna Capac alone is king; let all the city hear him."[1]

Huayna Capac, according to the account of many Indians who had seen and knew him, was not of any great stature, but well-built, with good features and much gravity. He

---

[1] *Huayna*, youth; *ccapac*, rich; *inca*, king; *zapalla*, sole; *tucui*, ruler; *llacta*, city; *uya*, hear.

was a man of few words but many deeds, a severe judge, who punished without mercy. He wished to be so feared that the Indians should dream of him at night. He ate according to the custom of his people. He listened to those who spoke well to him, and believed very easily. Parasites and flatterers, who are not wanting among those people, had much influence. He gave ear to lies, which was the reason that many died without fault. The youths who, tempted by the flesh, slept with his wives or damsels, or with those who lived in the temple of the Sun, were ordered to be put to death, and the women suffered the same punishment. The penalties for making disturbances and for insubordination were deprivation of property, and the bestowal on another. For other offences there was merely corporal chastisement. His father looked over many of these crimes, especially with regard to women; for when any one was detected with them, he said that he was only a boy.

The mother of Huayna Capac, principal queen, wife, and sister of Tupac Inca Yupanqui, was named Mama Ocllo. They say that she was a very prudent lady, and that she informed her son respecting many things that she had seen Tupac Inca do. She was so fond of her son that she entreated him not to go to Quito or Chile, until she was dead. They relate, that to please her and to comply with her request, he was in Cuzco, without leaving it, until she died and was interred with great pomp. Much treasure and fine clothes, with women and servants were put into her tomb. All the treasures of the deceased Incas, and the fields which they call *chacaras*, were kept entire from the first, without being used or touched; for among these people there were neither wars nor other needs for which money would be of any use. For this reason we believe that there are vast treasures in the bowels of the earth which are lost for ever, unless peradventure some one building, or doing some other work, should hit upon some out of the great quantity that must exist.

CHAPTER LXII.

How Huayna Capac departed from Cuzco, and what he did.

HUAYNA CAPAC had ordered the principal lords of the natives of the provinces to appear before him, and, his court being full of them, he took for his wife his sister Chimbo Ocllo, and on this occasion there were great festivities, which ended the mourning for Tupac Inca. These being concluded, he ordered that 50,000 soldiers should accompany him to visit the provinces of his kingdom. As he ordered, so it was done, and he set out from Cuzco with greater pomp and authority than his father. For the litter was so rich, according to the statement of those who carried the king on their shoulders, that the great and numerous ornaments were priceless, besides the gold of which they were made. He travelled by the way of Xaquixaguana and Andahuaylas, and arrived at the country of the Soras and Lucanas, whence he sent embassies to many parts of the coast region, and of the mountains, and received replies, with great offerings and presents.

From these places he returned to Cuzco, where he ordered the offering up of great sacrifices to the Sun and to the most venerated among their gods, that they might be favourable to him in the enterprise he wished to undertake. He also gave presents to the idols of the Huacas. He ascertained from the soothsayers, through the utterances of the devils, or else through their own invention, that he would be successful and prosperous in his undertakings, and that he would return to Cuzco with great honour and profit. These ceremonies being completed, the armed men and their captains arrived from many directions and were lodged outside, receiving provisions from the city.

Those who were employed on the building of the fortress

continued to work without the cessation of a single day. The great chain of gold was brought out into the square of Cuzco, and there were dances and drinking-bouts. The captains received their appointments near the Stone of War, according to their custom. Huayna Capac then ordered that there should be a conference, where he addressed the people in a vehement speech, urging those who accompanied him to be loyal, as well as those who remained behind. They answered that they would be faithful to his service; of which speech he approved, and he held out hopes of great rewards. All things necessary having been prepared, the Inca set out from Cuzco with the whole army, and journeyed along a road as grand and wide as we now behold it; for all of us who have been in those parts have seen it, and travelled over it. He marched to the Collao, receiving the services proffered by the provinces through which he passed, as a matter of course. For they say that the Inca considered that it was merely their duty. He investigated what tribute they paid, and what were the capabilities of each province. He collected many women. The most beautiful he could find were reserved for himself, and others were given to his captains and favourites. The others were placed in the temple of the Sun and there detained.

On entering the Collao, he had an account taken of the great flocks and of how many thousand loads of fine wool they yielded every year to those who made the cloth for his house and service. He went to the island of Titicaca and ordered great sacrifices to be offered up. At Chuqui-apu,[1] he ordered that Indians should be collected, with overseers, to obtain gold, in conformity with the order and regulations that have been explained. Advancing onwards, he gave orders that the Charcas and other nations as far as the Chichas, should get out a great quantity of ingots of silver to be sent to Cuzco, without fail. He removed some *mitimaes* from one

---

[1] The modern La Paz.

part to another, although much time had passed since they were established. He ordered that they should work without any holidays, because in the land where there were holidays, the men thought of nothing but how to create scandals and seduce women. Wherever he passed, he ordered *tampus* and other buildings to be erected; the plans of which he traced out himself. His soldiers, although numerous, were so well disciplined that they did not move a step from the camp, and the natives along their line of march supplied them with all they required, so amply that what remained over was more than what was used. In some places they built baths, at others they raised land marks, and in the deserts they made large houses. Along every road that the Inca traversed, they left works of this kind, insomuch that the account of them excites admiration. He who did wrong was punished without fail, while those who served well were rewarded.

Having arranged these and other matters, he advanced to the provinces now subject to the town of La Plata,[1] and to those of Tucuman. He sent captains with an army against the Chiriguanos, but they were not successful, returning after having been put to flight. In another direction, towards the South Sea, he sent more captains with troops, to subdue those valleys and towns which had not submitted to his father. He himself proceeded, with the rest of his army, towards Chile, completing the subjugation of the tribes along the road. He traversed the uninhabited region with great difficulty, and heavy were the snow storms which broke over his people. They carried tents for their protection at night, with many *yana-conas*[2] and female servants. Over all the snowy wilds they made the royal road, with post houses placed by the Inca.

---

[1] Chuquisaca. Now called Sucre, the capital of the republic of Bolivia.

[2] Domestic servants.

He arrived at the province they call Chile,[1] where he remained for more than a year, bringing the people under subjection, and arranging the administration. He ordered that the quantity of ingots of gold which he had indicated should be obtained. *Mitimaes* were established, and many Chilian communities were removed from one place to another. In some places he constructed forts which they call *pucaras*, for the wars that were waged with some of the tribes. The Inca marched much more over the land than his father, until he said that he had seen the end of it, and he ordered memorials to be set up in many places, that in future his greatness might be known.[2] The affairs of Chile having been put in order, he appointed his delegates and governors, and instructed them always to report what happened in that province to the court of Cuzco. He charged them to execute

[1] The name Chile did not belong to the whole country included in the present Republic of Chile, nor even to any large part of it. The north part of modern Chile was known to the Yncas as Copayapu (Copiapu); further south was the province of Coquimpu (Coquimbo); and the central part of modern Chile was called Canconicagua, and also Chilli, the latter name being probably that of a chief. Valdivia adopted the name of Canconicagua, while Almagro called it the valley of Chilli. The followers of Almagro and assassins of Pizarro were always known as "los de Chile". The name of Chile was long applied only to the valley of Aconcagua, including Quillota ; and that was no doubt the sense in which it was used by the natives and by their Ynca conquerors. Afterwards, the Spaniards gave the name of Chile to the whole country on the Pacific coast, from Copiapo to Valdivia. The native form of the word was Chilli, which the Spaniards softened into Chile. In the north of Peru, in the provinces of Chachapoyas and Pataz, there are three villages called Chilia ; and the word occurs in several names of places in southern Peru, such as Pacon-chile, Chilihua, and the river Chile at Arequipa. The word *Chiri* means cold in Quichua. But Vicuña Mackenna maintains (*Relaciones Historicas*: art. "Origen del Nombre de Chile", p. 92) that the name is indigenous to the country, and was used before the Ynca conquest; that originally it was local, and was applied only to the valley of Aconcagua, but that it had no special meaning.

[2] "*Y formas de hombres crecidos.*" The meaning is not clear. The Spanish editor suggests "*Y fuera mas de hombres creida.*"

justice and to allow no disturbance or tumult, but to execute the promoters, without sparing any.

The Inca returned to Cuzco, where he was received with great honour by the city, and the priests of the temple of Curi-cancha gave him many blessings. He made the people rejoice at the great festivals he ordered. Many children were born to him, who were brought up by their mothers. Among others Atahualpa was born, according to the opinion of all the Indians of Cuzco, who say that it was so. His mother was called Tuta Palla, a native of Quillaco, although others say that she was of the lineage of the Urin-Cuzco. From his childhood Atahualpa always accompanied his father, and he was older than Huascar.

CHAPTER LXIII.

How Huayna Capac again ordered that an army should be assembled, and how he set out for Quito.

HUAYNA CAPAC enjoyed a rest of some months at Cuzco, during which he assembled the priests of the temples and diviners of the oracles. He ordered sacrifices to be made, and the offering of the capacocha[1] was celebrated with grandeur and great outlay, the mouth-pieces of the oracles returning very full of gold. Each one gave a reply such as was most likely to please the king. This, with other things, having been done, Huayna Capac ordered that there should be made a road more royal, grander and wider than that of his father, to extend to Quito, whither he intended to go. The ordinary post and store-houses were to be established along it. That it might be known throughout all the land that this was his will, messengers went forth to announce it, and afterwards Orejones went to see that the orders were complied with. Accordingly the grandest road was constructed that there is in the world, as well as the longest, for it extended from Cuzco to Quito, and was connected with that from Cuzco to Chile. I believe that, since the history of man has been recorded, there has been no account of such grandeur as is to be seen in this road, which passes over deep valleys and lofty mountains, by snowy heights, over falls of water, through live rocks, and along the edges of furious torrents. In all these places it is level and paved, along mountain slopes well excavated, by the mountains well terraced, through the living rock cut, along the river banks supported by walls, in the snowy heights with steps and resting places, in all parts clean swept, clear of stones, with

---

[1] See p. 91.

post and store-houses, and temples of the Sun at intervals. Oh! what greater things can be said of Alexander, or of any of the powerful kings who have ruled in the world, than that they had made such a road as this, and conceived the works which were required for it! The road constructed by the Romans in Spain, and any others of which we read, are not to be compared with it. And it was finished in less time than it is possible to imagine, for the Incas were no longer in ordering it than were their subjects in executing the work.[1]

The king called a general assembly of his forces throughout all the provinces of his government, and such numbers came from all parts that they covered the plains. After there had been festivities and drinking-bouts, and the affairs of Cuzco had been regulated, the Inca Huayna Capac set out with *yscay-pacha-huaranca-runa cuna*, which means 200,000 men of war ;[2] besides the *yana-conas* and women, of whose number no account was taken. The Inca took with him two thousand women, and left in Cuzco more than four thousand. The delegates and governors who were in charge at the capitals of the provinces, had arranged that stores and arms should be collected from all parts, and everything else that was required for a warlike expedition. Thus all the great store-houses were filled, so that at every four leagues, which was the length of a day's journey, there were provisions for the whole of this great multitude of people, and not only was there no fault, but there was a surplus, after the soldiers and all the women and servant lads, and porters, had been satisfied.

When Huayna Capac set out along the road which had

---

[1] Cieza de Leon also gives an account of the roads of the Yncas in his First Part (chapter xlii), p. 153, which is quoted *in extenso* by Garcilasso de la Vega (i, lib. ix, cap. 13). See also Zarate (*Historia del Peru*, lib. i, cap. 10), and, for a modern account, Velasco (*Historia de Quito*, i, p. 59).

[2] *Yscay*, "two"; *pacha*, "hundred"; *huaranca*, "thousand"; *runa*, "men"; *cuna*, the plural particle.

been made by his order, he marched until he arrived at
Vilcas, where he rested for a few days in the lodgings which
had been made near those of his father. He rejoiced to see
that the temple of the Sun was finished, and he left a quantity
of gold and silver ingots to make ornaments and vases. He
ordered that great care should be taken with regard to the
due maintenance of the priests and *mamaconas*. He ascended
to a beautiful terrace which had been prepared for him.
They then offered sacrifice, in accordance with their blindness,
and killed many birds and animals, with some men and children, to propitiate their gods.

This being done, the king set out from this place with his
army, and did not stop until he arrived at the valley of
Xauxa, where there was some dispute respecting the division
of land among the local chiefs. When Huayna Capac understood the controversy, after he had performed sacrifices
as in Vilcas, he ordered the chiefs Alaya, Cusi-chuca, and
Huacaropa to assemble, and equitably divided the land in
the way which is adopted to this day. He sent embassies
to the Yauyos and Yuncas, and some gifts to the chiefs of
Bonbon, for, as they had a force in the lake, in parts where
they swam, they spoke loosely, and he did not wish to converse with them until he saw their intentions. The lords of
Xauxa did great services, and some of the captains and
soldiers joined the army. Marching by Bonbon, they only
halted a short time, because the Inca wished to go on to
Caxamarca, a place more suitable for resting, surrounded by
great and very lofty districts. Along the road, people were
constantly arriving with embassies and presents.

The Inca arrived at Caxamarca and rested there for some
days, ordering that his soldiers should be lodged in the
neighbourhood, and should be fed with the provisions in the
store-houses. With a selected force he entered the country of
the Huancachupachos, and waged a fierce war, for the natives
had not been reduced to entire submission by the Inca's

father.   The Inca was able to complete the work, appointing governors and captains, and selecting chiefs from among the natives to administer the land.   Formerly these people had not known chiefs other than those who, being most powerful, led them to war, and arranged peace when they desired it. Among the Chachapoyas the Inca met with great resistance; insomuch that he was twice defeated by the defenders of their country and put to flight.   Receiving some succour, the Inca again attacked the Chachapoyas, and routed them so completely that they sued for peace, desisting, on their parts, from all acts of war.   The Inca granted peace on conditions very favourable to himself, and many of the natives were ordered to go and live in Cuzco, where their descendants still reside.   He took many women, for they are beautiful and graceful, and very white.   He established garrisons of military *mitimaes* to guard the frontier.   A governor was appointed to live at the principal place in the district.   He made other arangements, punished several of the principal chiefs for having made war, and then returned to Caxamarca. The Inca continued his journey, and put in order the affairs of the provinces of Caxas, Ayavaca, Huancabamba, and the others which border on them.

CHAPTER LXIV.

How Huayna Capac entered the country of Bracamoros, and returned flying, and of the other events that happened until he arrived at Quito.

IT is well known to many natives of these parts that Huayna Capac entered the country which we call Bracamoros, and that he returned flying before the fury of the men who dwell there. They had chosen leaders, and assembled to defend themselves against any one who should attack them. This is stated, not only by the Orejones, but also by the Lord of Chincha, and some principal men of the Collao and of Xauxa. They all say that, while Huayna Capac was engaged in settling the districts which had been traversed and subjugated by his father, it came to his knowledge how that, in the Bracamoros, there were many men and women who possessed fertile lands; that far in the interior of that land, there were many rivers and a lake; and that this region was well peopled. Desirous of discovery, and anxious to extend his dominion, he ordered a chosen band, with little baggage, to march with him into that country, leaving the camp under command of a Captain-General. Entering the country, they advanced, opening the road with great labour, for, after passing the snowy cordillera, they found themselves in the forests of the Andes. They came to great rivers which they had to cross, and heavy rains fell from the heavens. The Inca came to where the natives were watching in their strongholds, whence they insolently defied him. The war began, and so many of the savages came forth, most of them naked, that the Inca determined to retire, which he did without gaining anything in that land. The natives harassed his retreat in such sort that his soldiers, sometimes flying, at others facing their pursuers, at others sending them presents, returned flying to their own territory, saying that they had avenged themselves on the long-tailed ones. They said this because some of them had brought away the long strips of cloth which the natives wore between their legs.

From these lands they also affirm that the Inca sent captains, with a sufficient force, to explore the sea-coast in a northerly direction, and to bring under the Inca's dominion the natives of Guayaquil and Puerto Viejo. The captains marched into these districts, where they waged war and fought some battles, sometimes being victorious and at others sustaining reverses. Thus, they advanced as far as Collique, where they met with people who went about naked and fed on human flesh, having the customs which are now practised and used by the dwellers on the river of San Juan. From this point they returned, not wishing to penetrate further, but to report what they had done to the king. Meanwhile, he had arrived at the country of the Cañaris, where he enjoyed himself exceedingly. For they say that this was the place of his birth, and that he found that great lodgings and store-houses had been built, and abundant supplies collected. He sent embassies to inspect the districts, and ambassadors came to him from many provinces, with presents.

I am given to understand that, owing to a tumult which took place in certain towns of the district of Cuzco, the Inca was so incensed that, after having caused the leaders to be beheaded, he gave express orders that the Indians of those places should bring the quantity he should specify of the stones of Cuzco, to make edifices of the first importance in Tumebamba, and that they should drag them with cables; and his orders were obeyed. Huayna Capac often said that to keep the people of those kingdoms well under subjection, it was a good thing, when they had no other work to do, to make them remove a hill from one place to another. He even ordered stones and slabs to be brought from Cuzco, for

the edifices of Quito, and to this day they remain in the
buildings where they were placed.

Huayna Capac set out from Tumebamba, and went by
Purnaes, resting for some days at Riobamba, in Mocha and
Tacunga, and his people were allowed to drink of the
beverages that had been prepared for them in all parts. The
Inca was visited and saluted by many captains and lords of
those parts. He sent Orejones of his own lineage to the provinces of the coast and of the mountains, to inspect the
accounts of the *quipu-camayos*, who are their accountants, to
see what was stored in the government houses, to ascertain
how the governors treated the natives, and whether the
temples of the Sun, the oracles, and *huacas* were properly
maintained. He also sent messengers to Cuzco to see that
all his orders were duly attended to. There was not a day
that runners did not arrive, not a few but many, from Cuzco,
the Collao, Chile, and all parts of the empire.

From Tacunga the Inca continued his journey to Quito,
where he was received, according to the mode and usage,
with great festivities. His father's governor delivered up the
treasures to him, which were numerous, with the fine cloth
and other things that he had charge of. The Inca honoured
him, praising his fidelity, calling him father, and assuring
him that he would always esteem him for the great services
he performed for his father and himself. The towns in the
neighbourhood of Quito sent many presents and provisions
for the king, and he ordered that more and stronger edifices
should be built there than there were before. The works
were at once commenced, and those were finished which we
found when our people conquered that land.

CHAPTER LXV.

How Huayna Capac marched through the coast valleys, and what he did.

SOME of the Orejones relate that Huayna Capac returned to Cuzco from Quito, by the coast valleys to Pachacamac; while others deny this and maintain that he remained at Quito until his death. In this matter, seeking out the version which is most accurate, I adopt what I heard from some principal chiefs who served in that war, in person. They say that, while the Inca was at Quito, ambassadors came from many parts to congratulate him in the name of their respective countries. Feeling that all was peacefully settled in the mountainous provinces, he thought it would be well to undertake a journey to the province of Puerto Viejo, to that which we call Guayaquil, and to the valleys of the Yuncas. The captains and principal men of his council approved the thought, and advised that it should be put into execution. Many troops remained in Quito. The Inca set forth with a suitable force, and entered those lands, where he had some skirmishes with the natives. But, eventually, one after another submitted, and governors, with *mitimaes*, were established.

Puná[1] waged a fierce war with Tumbez, and the Inca commanded them to desist, and that the people of Puná should submit to him. This was deeply felt by Tumbalá, because he was Lord of Puná. But he did not venture to resist the Inca; on the contrary, he submitted, and offered presents to secure a treacherous peace. When the Inca departed, he plotted with the people of the mainland to kill many Orejones, with their captains, who were to set out from a river to cross to the opposite shore. But Huayna Capac re-

[1] The island in the bay of Guayaquil.

ceived the tidings, and did what I have written in chapter liii of my First Part.[1]   He inflicted severe punishment, and ordered the paved road to be made which is called the Pass of Huayna Capac.[2]   He then returned to Tumbez, where edifices and a temple of the Sun had been erected.   People came from the surrounding districts to do him reverence with much humility.   The Inca proceeded to visit the coast valleys, ordering the government, fixing the limits of land, and rules for distributing water, commanding that the people should not go to war, and doing what has been described in other places. They say of him that, being in the beautiful valley of Chay- anta, near Chimu, which is where the city of Truxillo now stands, there was an old man working in a field.   When he heard that the king was passing near, he gathered two or three "*pepinos*",[3] which, with the earth attached, he brought with him, and said : "Hucha Hatun apu micucampa", which means, " *Very great Lord, eat thou.*"[4]   Before the lords and other people, the Inca took the "*pepinos*", and, eating one of them, he said before all present, to please the old man, " Suylluy ancha mizqui cay", or, in our language, "*Of a truth this is very sweet.*"   From this incident every one derived much gratification.

[1] This is chapter liv of the edition of 1554.   See my Translation, p. 192.   In this chapter Cieza de Leon gives a full account of the treacherous murder of the Orejones by the people of Puná.   Garcilasso de la Vega, in his version of the affair, copies largely from Cieza de Leon (i, lib. ix, caps. 1, 2, 3).

[2] Where now stands the city of Guayaquil.   In the 17th century the place still retained the name of the " Pass of Huayna Capac".

[3] *Pepino* is a cucurbitaceous plant, and grown in great abundance on the coast of Peru.   The plant is only a foot and a half high, and creeps along the ground.   The fruit is from four to five inches long, cylin- drical, and somewhat pointed at both ends.   The husk is of a yellowish- green colour, with long rose-coloured stripes.   The edible part is solid, juicy, and well flavoured, but very indigestible.

[4] *Ancha*, "very"; *hatun*, "great"; *Apu*, "Lord"; *micu*, "eat"; *campa*, "thou".

Passing onwards, he did in Chimu, in Guañapa, Guarmay, Huaura, Rimac, and the other valleys, what appeared good for his service; and when he arrived at Pachacamac there were great festivals, and many dances and drinking-bouts. The priests, with their lies, said the evil things that were invented by their cunning, according to custom, and some even spake by the mouth of the same demon, for in those times it is publicly known that he spoke to certain persons. Huayna Capac, it is said, give this demon over 100 *arrobas* of gold and 1000 of silver, besides other treasure, stones and emeralds, so that he adorned the new temple more than the temple of the Sun and the ancient shrine at Pachacamac.

Some Indians say that the Inca ascended thence to Cuzco, others that he retired to Quito. He certainly visited all the coast valleys, and made the great road through them which we now see, and we know that he built great storehouses and temples of the Sun in other parts of the valleys. Having seen that all things were arranged, as well in the mountains as on the coast, and the whole empire being at peace, he returned to Quito. He made war on the fathers of those whom they now call Huambracunas, and discovered as far as the river of Ancasmayu.

CHAPTER LXVI.

*How, when Huayna Capac was about to march from Quito, he
sent forward certain of his captains, who returned flying
before the enemy, and what he did in consequence.*

HUAYNA CAPAC being in Quito, with all his captains and
veteran soldiers, they relate as certainly true that he ordered
certain of them to go forth and conquer some countries whose
inhabitants had never desired to obtain his friendship. These
people, when they knew what was intended at Cuzco, sought
aid from their neighbours to resist any invaders that might
come against them, and they had prepared forts and strong
places, with plenty of arms of the kind used by them.
Huayna Capac marched past their county to reach another
land which bordered upon it, all being within the district
we now call Quito. As the captains and troops were marching along, despising those of whom they were in search,
and thinking they could easily possess themselves of their
lands and farms, they found that things were different from
what they supposed. For suddenly the natives came out
with great clamour, and attacked the invaders with such
resolution, that they killed and made captive a great number, entirely defeating the rest, who turned their backs and
fled precipitately, the natives pursuing and killing the fugitives, and taking many prisoners.

Some of the fleetest of foot ran until they came to the
Inca, to whom alone they reported the disaster, which
annoyed him not a little. Considering the matter prudently,
he came to a decision becoming a great man. This was to
order those who had brought the news to keep silence, and
to tell no one what they knew. They were directed to return
along the road, and tell the fugitives to stop at the first hill
they came to, without fear, for that the Inca would attack

the enemy with fresh troops, and avenge the affront. With this message they returned. The Inca felt anxiety, because he reflected that if his soldiers heard the news in the place where they were encamped, all would be in confusion and he would be in greater straits. But he dissimulated, and told them to prepare, as he wished to march against a certain tribe whom they would see when they reached their country. Getting out of his litter, he marched in front of his army for a day and a half, and those who were flying in great numbers, when they saw that the approaching army consisted of their own people, stopped on one side, while the pursuers began to attack them, and killed many. But Huayna Capac surrounded them on three sides, which amazed them not a little, and even those who had been conquered, rallied and fought in such sort that the ground was covered with dead. When the pursuers wished to retreat, they found the pass occupied, and so many were slain that very few remained alive except the prisoners, who were numerous. So that all was altered, the Inca himself having defeated and killed those who came to defeat him. When the result was known the conquerors were very well satisfied.

Huayna Capac recovered those of his people who were still alive, and ordered tombs to be made over those who were dead, and honours to be paid them according to their heathen practices. For they all know that the soul is immortal. They also set up figures and heaps of stones on the battle-field, as a memorial of what had been done. Huayna Capac then sent the news to Cuzco, re-organised his army, and advanced to Caranque.

The people of Otavalo, Cayambi, Cochasqui, Pifo, and other districts had made a league with many other tribes, to resist subjugation by the Inca, preferring death to the loss of their liberty. They made strong forts in their country, and resisted the payment of tribute, or the sending of presents to so distant a place as Cuzco. Having agreed on this between themselves, they awaited the approach of the Inca, who came to make war upon them. The army advanced to their frontier, where the Inca caused forts (called *pucaras*) to be constructed, and sent messages to the people with presents, asking them not to make war, as he only desired peace with fair conditions; that they would always find favour from him, as from his father; that he desired to take nothing from them, but rather to confer benefits. These kind words availed nothing, for their reply was that he should leave their country at once, and if not, they would drive him out by force. They then advanced against the Inca, who was much incensed, and put his army in battle array. They attacked him with such fury, that if it had not been for the fortress he had caused to be built, his troops would have been defeated at all points. But, knowing the danger, they retired into the *pucara*, where all who had not been killed or captured were assembled.

CHAPTER LXVII.

How Huayna Capac assembled all his power, gave battle to his enemies, and defeated them; and of the great cruelty with which he treated them.

WHEN the natives saw how they had shut up the Inca in his fortress, and had killed many of the Orejones, they were very joyful, and they made so great a noise that they could not hear themselves. They brought drums, and drank and sang, sending messengers over all the country, with the news that they had the Inca shut up with all his people. Many believed it and rejoiced, and some even came to help their friends.

Huayna Capac had provisions in the fort, and he had sent to summon the governors of Quito to come with reinforcements, for the enemy would not desist from their attacks. He tried, many times, to pacify them, sending embassies with presents; but it was all of no avail. The Inca increased his army, and the enemy did the same, resolutely determined to attack and defeat him, or die in the attempt. They assaulted the fortress, and broke through two lines of defence. If there had not been others round the hill, without doubt the enemy would have been victorious. But it was the custom of the Incas, in their defensive works, to make a circle with two doorways, and further up another, and so on until there were seven or eight, so that if one was lost, the defenders could retire to the next. Thus the Inca and his army retreated to the strongest part of the hill, whence, at the end of some days, he came forth and attacked the enemy with great courage.

They relate that, when his captains arrived with reinforcements, he took the field, but the battle was long doubtful. At length, those of Cuzco, by a stratagem, killed a great

number of the enemy, and those who remained turned and
fled. The tyrannical king was so enraged against them for
having taken up arms to defend their country from conquest,
that he ordered his soldiers to seek them all out, and with
great diligence they searched for and captured them all.
Very few were able to hide themselves. Near the banks of
a lake, he ordered them all to be beheaded in his presence,
and their bodies to be thrown into the water. The blood of
those who were killed was in such quantity that the water
lost its colour, and nothing could be seen but a thick mass
of blood. Having perpetrated this cruelty, and most evil
deed, Huayna Capac ordered the sons of the dead men to
be brought before him, and, looking at them, he said,
"Campa manan pucula tucuy huambracuna", which means,
" *You will not make war upon me, for you are all boys now.*"[1]
From that time the conquered people were called " Huambracuna (*Huayna-cuna*) to this day, and they were very valiant.
The lake received the name it still bears, which is *Yahuar-
cocha*, or "the lake of blood". In this country governors and
mitimaes were stationed, as in all other parts.[2]

After he had re-organised the country, the Inca passed

---

[1] *Campa*, "you" (dative) ; *manan*, "not"; *pucula* must be a clerical
error, it may be *pucuna* (correctly *poccuna*), from *poccuni*, "to ripen, to
become mature"; *tucuy*, "all"; *huambracuna* is a mistake, it should be
huayna-cuna, "boys". Cieza de Leon translates erroneously. It should
be, " You are not grown up," " You are all boys."

[2] Garcilasso de la Vega also tells the story of this war of the Caranques and of their punishment (II, p. 447). This country is on the
northern frontier of the empire of the Yncas, and of the province of
Quito. Garcilasso gives a violently prejudiced account of the war, and
endeavours to blacken the character of the Caranques, by way of ex-
cusing the Ynca's cruelty. Cieza de Leon alludes to the affair in the
First Part (p. 133 of my Translation). Versions of it are also given
by Balboa (p. 149), Montesinos (p. 221), and Velasco in his *History of
Quito* (I, p. 18). Balboa describes the Caranque war as having continued through three bloody campaigns, and says that a number of
Collas, with their chiefs, whom he names, were serving in the Ynca army.

onwards with great renown from his past victory, and proceeded with his discoveries until he reached the river Ancasmayu, which was the northern limit of the empire. He learnt from the natives that further on there were many tribes who went naked without any shame, and that all fed on human flesh. He made some defensive works in the district of Pasto, and ordered the principal men to pay tribute. They replied that they had nothing to give ; so he issued his command that each house should be obliged to give, every month, a rather large basket full of lice, as tribute. At first they laughed at this order; but afterwards, notwithstanding the quantity of lice they had, they could not fill so many baskets. They bred from the sheep which the Inca ordered to be given to them, and paid tribute from the increase, as well as of the food and roots of that country. For certain reasons which influenced him, Huayna Capac returned to Quito, ordering that there should be a temple of the Sun and a garrison, with a captain-general and governor in Caranque, to guard the frontier.

CHAPTER LXVIII.

How the King Huayna Capac returned to Quito, and how he knew of the arrival of Spaniards on the coast, and of his death.

In this same year[1] Francisco Pizarro was on this coast with thirteen Christians,[2] and the tidings of them was brought to Huayna Capac at Quito. Particulars were reported of the dress they wore, of their ship, and how they were white and bearded, how that they spoke little, were not so fond of drinking as the natives, and other things which the people had observed. Anxious to see such men, they say that the Inca ordered that one of two of these men who had been left behind, should be brought to him, the rest having gone back with their leader to the Isle of Gorgona, where he had left certain Spaniards with their Indians, as we shall explain in its place.[3] Some Indians say that after the others had gone, they killed the two that were left behind, at which Huayna Capac was much displeased. Others relate that they were

---

[1] 1526.

[2] The names of the thirteen companions of Pizarro, as enumerated in the Capitulation for the conquest of Peru, made by Francisco Pizarro with Queen Juana on July 26th, 1529, were:—

Bartolomé Ruiz (Pilot).	Alonzo de Molina.
Cristóbal de Peralta.	Pedro Alcon.
Pedro de Candia.	Garcia de Jaren.
Domingo de Soraluce.	Anton de Carrion.
Nicolás de Ribera.	Alonso Briceño.
Francisco de Cuellar.	Martin de Paz.

Juan de la Torre.

Xeres, Pizarro's secretary, says that the number was 16. See the whole subject discussed in a note at page 8 of my translation of the narrative of Francisco Xeres (Hakluyt Society, 1872).

[3] In the Third Part, still inedited.

sent to the Inca; but that they were put to death on the road when the news came that the Inca was no more. Others, again, declare that the two men died. What we believe to be most probable is, that the Indians killed them shortly after they had been left behind.

Huayna Capac· was in Quito with a great company of people. He was very powerful, his dominion extending from the river of Ancasmayu to the river of Maule, a distance of more than 1,200 leagues. He was so rich, that they relate that he had caused to be brought to Quito over 500 loads of gold, more than 1,000 of silver, many precious stones, and much fine cloth. He was feared by all his subjects, because he was a stern dispenser of justice. In the midst of his power, they say that a great pestilence broke out, which was so contagious, that over 200,000 souls died throughout the provinces, for it prevailed in all parts. The Inca caught the disease, and all that was said to free him from death was of no avail, because the great God was not served by his recovery. When he felt that the pestilence had touched him, he ordered great sacrifices to be offered up for his health throughout the land, and at all the *huacas* and temples of the Sun. And as he became worse, he called his captains and relations, and addressed them on several subjects. Among other things, they relate that he foretold that the people who had been seen in the ship, would return with great power, and would conquer the country. This was probably a fable, and if he said so, it must have been through the mouth of a devil, for who could know that the Spaniards went to arrange their return as conquerors? Others say that, considering the extensive territory of the Quillacingas and Popayan, and that the empire was very extensive for one person to rule, he ordained that from Quito to the north, the dominion should be under his son Atahualpa, whom he loved dearly, because he had always accompanied him in his wars. He desired that the rest of the empire should be ruled by

Huascar, the sole heir of the whole.   Other Indians say that he did not divide the kingdom; but that he said to those who were present, that they well knew how he had wished that his son Huascar, by his sister Chimpu Ocllo,[1] should be lord after his own time, at which all the people of Cuzco were well contented.   He had other sons of great valour, among whom were Nanque Yupanqui, Tupac Inca, Huanca Auqui, Tupac Hualpa, Titu, Huaman Hualpa, Manco Inca, Huascar, Cusi Hualpa, Paullu Tupac Yupanqui, Conono, Atahualpa.   He did not desire to give them anything of the great possessions he left, but that they should receive all from their brother, as he had inherited all from his father. For he trusted much that his son would keep his promise, and that he would fulfil all that his heart desired, although he was still a boy.   He ordered his chiefs to love him and treat him as their sovereign, and that, until he was of full age to govern, Colla Tupac, his uncle, should be his guardian. When he had said this, he died.

As soon as Huayna Capac was dead, the lamentations were so great that the shouting rose up to the clouds, and the noise so stupefied the birds that they fell from a great height to the ground.   The news was carried to all parts, and everywhere the sorrow was deep.   In Quito, as they relate, the people mourned for ten days, while the lamentations of the Cañaris continued for a whole month.   Many principal lords accompanied the body to Cuzco, all the men and women along the road coming out to weep and groan.   In Cuzco there was more lamentation.   Sacrifices were offered up in the temples, and preparations were made for the interment in accordance with custom, the soul being supposed to be in heaven.   They killed, to be buried in the same tomb, more than 4,000 souls, women, pages, and other servants; as well as

---

[1] Ciui Chimpu Runtu, the second legitimate wife of Huayna Ccapac. According to most authors, the name of the mother of Huascar was Rahua Ocllo.

treasure, precious stones, and fine cloth. It was truly a very great sum that was buried with him. They do not say where, nor in what manner he was interred; but they concur in stating that his sepulchre was in Cuzco. Some Indians told me that they buried him in the river Ancasmayu, diverting it from its course to make the tomb. But I do not believe it. My impression is that those are right who say that he was buried in Cuzco.[1]

The Indians relate many things relating to this king, insomuch that what I have written and narrated is nothing. Assuredly, I believe that there are so many things left to write touching this king, his fathers and grandfathers, that it would form another history larger than what has already been recorded.

[1] He was quite right. In 1571 the Viceroy, Don Francisco de Toledo, received information that Huayna Ccapac was buried in Cuzco, where Polo de Ondegardo afterwards found his mummy, with others. (See *G. de la Vega*, I, p. 273 ; and II, p. 91.)

CHAPTER LXIX.

Of the lineage and character of Huascar and Atahualpa.

THE empire of the Incas was in a state of such profound peace when Huayna Capac died, that there was not to be found a man, throughout its vast extent, who would dare to raise his head to foment disturbance, or to refuse obedience, as well from fear of the Inca, as on account of the *mitimaes* who were stationed in all parts, and maintained order. As when Alexander died in Babylon, many of his servants and captains became kings and ruled over extensive dominions; so on the death of Huayna Capac there were wars and differences between his two sons; and in the meantime the Spaniards arrived. Many of the *mitimaes* became lords, because the natural chiefs having been killed in the wars, the colonists had an opportunity of gaining the goodwill of the people.

There would be much to say in relating the history of these powerful lords in detail, but I will not deviate from my plan of telling the story briefly, for the good reasons which I have already explained. Huascar was the son of Huayna Capac; and Atahualpa also. Huascar was the younger, and Atahualpa the elder brother. Huascar was the son of the Coya, his father's sister and principal wife. Atahualpa was the son of a woman of Quilaco, named Tupac Palla. Both were born in Cuzco, and not in Quito, as some have said and even written, but they have done so without understanding the facts. For Huayna Capac was in the conquest of Quito, and in those parts for about twelve years, and when he died his son Atahualpa was already thirty years of age. They say that his mother was the lady of Quito, but there never was any lady of that country, for the Incas themselves were kings and lords of Quito.[1] Huascar was born in Cuzco, and Atahualpa was older by four or five years. This is certain, and is what I believe. Huascar was popular in Cuzco and throughout the kingdom, owing to his being the rightful heir. Atahualpa was a favourite with his father's old captains and with the soldiers, because he accompanied them to the wars in his boyhood, and because his father, when he was alive, loved him so well that he would not let the boy eat anything except what he himself put on his plate. Huascar was merciful and pious. Atahualpa was cruel and vindictive. Both were generous, but the latter was a man of greater spirit and force of character, the former of more valour. The one claimed to be sole lord and to rule without an equal; the other was resolved to reign by breaking the established laws and usages of the Incas. The law was that no one could be king except the eldest son of the sovereign and of his sister, although there might be other older sons by other women. Huascar wished his father's army to be with him. Atahualpa was dismayed because he was not near Cuzco, where he could perform the fast in that city and come forth with the fringe, to be received by all as king.

---

[1] The author alludes to Lopez de Gomara in his chapter entitled "Linaje de Atabaliba". Velasco, who follows Gomara, says that the name of the Queen of Quito was Scyri Paccha.

CHAPTER LXX.

How Huascar was acknowledged as King in Cuzco, after the death of his father.

HUAYNA CAPAC being dead, and the mourning and lamentation having been performed, although he left more than forty sons, none attempted to deviate from their allegiance to Huascar, to whom, as they well knew, the kingdom belonged. Although it was known that the order of Huayna Capac was that the uncle of Huascar should govern, there were not wanting those who advised the young Inca to assume the fringe at once, and with it the government of the whole country as king. As most of the native lords of provinces had come to Cuzco for the obsequies of Huayna Capac, it was represented that the feast of the coronation might be very grand, and thus he resolved to act. Leaving the government of the city in the hands of the officer to whom it had been entrusted by his father, he entered upon the fast with the accustomed observances. He came forth with the fringe, and there were great festivities. The cable of gold was brought out into the square, with the images of the Incas, and, in accordance with their usage, they spent some days in drinking-bouts. At the end of these days of feasting, the news was sent to all parts of the kingdom, with the orders of the new king, and certain Orejones were sent to Quito to bring back his father's women and household.

Atahualpa received the news that Huascar had assumed the fringe, and that he desired that all should yield him obedience. The captains of Huayna Capac had not yet departed from Quito and its neighbourhood, and there were secret communications between them as to the possibility of remaining in those lands of Quito, without going to Cuzco at the call of Huascar, for they had found the land of Quito to be as good as that of Cuzco. Some among them hesitated, saying that it was not lawful to refrain from recognising the great Inca, who was lord of all. But Illa Tupac[1] was not loyal to Huascar, as Huayna Capac had requested, and he had promised; for they say that he engaged in secret negotiations and discussions with Atahualpa. He said that, among the sons of Huayna Capac, this one showed the most spirit and valour, and that his father ordered that he should govern Quito and its territory. He spoke in this way to the captains Chalcuchima, Acla-hualpa, Rumi-ñaui,[2] Quizquiz, Peco-pagua,[3] and many others, urging them to assist in making Atahualpa the Inca of those parts, as his brother was of Cuzco. These, with Illa Tupac who was a traitor to his natural lord Huascar, having been left as governor until the Inca should be of full age, agreed to recognise Atahualpa, who was then declared to be lord. The women of his father were delivered to him, whom he received as his own, and his father's household and house service were handed over to him, to do with them according to his will.

Some say, that some of the sons of Huayna Capac, brothers of Huascar and Atahualpa, with other Orejones, fled to Cuzco, and reported what had happened to the Inca. Huascar, and the other Orejones of Cuzco, felt what had been done by Atahualpa to be an evil act worthy of reprobation, contrary to the will of their gods, and to the laws and ordinances of the departed kings. They said that they would not consent or endure that the bastard should take the name of Inca, and that he must be punished for the favour he had obtained from the captains and soldiers of his father's army. Huascar, therefore, ordered that a summons should be sent to all the provinces, that arms should be made, and the store-houses

---

[1] Before he is called Colla Tupac.

[2] *Rumi*, "a stone"; *ñaui*, "eye". "Stone-eyed."

[3] This is the reading of the Peruvian editor. The Spanish editor has Sepocopagua.

provided with all things necessary, because he had to make war on the traitors, if they would not recognise him as their lord. He sent ambassadors to the Cañaris, inviting their friendship. It is also said that he despatched an Orejon to Atahualpa himself, to persuade him not to persist in his intentions, being so evil. The envoy was also to speak with Colla Tupac, the Inca's uncle, to advise him that he should become loyal. These things being done, Huascar named one of the principal lords of Cuzco, named Atoc,[1] as his Captain-General.

[1] *Atoc* means " a fox" in Quichua.

CHAPTER LXXI.

*How the differences between Huascar and Atahualpa began,
and how great battles were fought between them.*

IT was understood throughout the realm of Peru that
Huascar was Inca, and as such that he gave orders, and sent
Orejones to the chief places in all the provinces to provide
what he required. He was so intelligent, and was so popular,
that he was much beloved by his people. When he began
to reign, his age was about twenty-five, a little more or less.
Having appointed Atoc to be his Captain-General, he ordered
him, after having taken the people he would require from
places along the road, as well *mitimaes* as natives, to march
to Quito and put down the rebellion of the Inca's brother.

The Indians recount the subsequent events in several
ways. I always follow the best version, which is held by
the oldest and best informed among them, who are lords.
For the common people, in all they say, cannot be relied
upon as affirming the truth. Some relate that Atahualpa,
not only resolved to refuse obedience to his brother, who was
king, but even pretended to the sovereignty, seeing that the
captains and soldiers of his father were on his side. He
went to the country of the Cañaris, where he spoke with the
native chiefs and with the *mitimaes*, telling them a plausible
story. He said that his desire was not to injure his brother,
as he wished for his welfare; but to keep friends with all,
and to make another Cuzco at Quito, where all could enjoy
themselves. He said that he had such good affection for
them, that he would cause edifices and lodgings to be made
for himself in Tumebamba. There, as Inca and lord, he
would be able to amuse himself with his women, as did his
father and grandfather. He made other speeches on this
subject, which were not listened to with such pleasure as he

supposed. For the messenger from Huascar had arrived, and spoken to the Cañaris and *mitimaes*, saying that the Inca sought their friendship, and that he implored the favour of the Sun and of his gods for them. He told the Cañaris that they should not consent to such an evil deed as the Inca's brother meditated. They replied by declaring their desire to see Huascar, and raising up their hands, they promised to remain loyal.

This being their wish, Atahualpa was unable to obtain his object, and they say that the Cañaris, with the captain and *mitimaes*, seized him, with the intention of delivering him up to Huascar. But having placed him in a room of the *tampu*, he escaped, and went to Quito, where he gave out that it had been the will of his God to turn him into a serpent, to enable him to escape from his enemies. He told his adherents that all should be got ready to begin a war. Other Indians affirm as a certain fact that the captain Atoc, with his troops, arrived at the country of the Cañaris, where Atahualpa was, and that it was he who took the Inca's brother prisoner, before he escaped in the way that has already been mentioned. For my part, I believe, although I may be wrong, that Atoc found that Atahualpa had escaped from his prison, and, much disturbed at this, he collected all the men he could from the Cañaris, and marched towards Quito, sending to all parts to strengthen the governors and *mitimaes* in their loyalty to Huascar. It is related, as a fact, that Atahualpa escaped by means of a *coa* or tool which a Quella woman gave him. He made a hole with it at a time when those who were in the *tampu* were heated with what they had drunk. By using great haste, he reached Quito before he could be overtaken by his enemies, who wanted very much to get him again into their power.

CHAPTER LXXII.

*How Atahualpa set out from Quito with his army and
captains, and how he gave battle to Atoc in the villages
of Ambato.*

As the posts on the royal roads were so numerous, nothing
happened in any part of the empire that was unknown, and
when it was understood that Atahualpa had escaped by such
good luck, and was in Quito assembling his troops, it was
known that a war was certain. Hence there were divisions
into parties; great disturbances; and thoughts directed to evil
ends. Huascar had no one who would not obey him, and
did not desire that he should come out of the affair with
honour and power. Atahualpa had, on his side, the captains
and men of the army, and many native lords and *mitimaes*
of the Quito provinces. They relate that, being in Quito, he
made haste to prepare his army to march, swearing, in their
manner, that he would inflict great punishment on the
Cañaris for the affront he had received from them. He
knew that Atoc was approaching with his army, which exceeded, according to what they say, forty *huarancas* or
thousands of men, and he made haste to come forth and
meet him.

Atoc advanced because Atahualpa had not been able to
assemble the men in the provinces. He addressed his men,
exhorting them to do honour to the Inca Huascar, and to
exert themselves to chastise the shameless conduct of Atahualpa. To justify his cause, Atoc sent certain Indians as
messengers to Atahualpa, urging him to rest satisfied with
what he had already done, and not to plunge the empire
into civil war; but to submit to the Inca, as the wisest
course for him. Although these messengers were principal
Orejones, they relate that Atahualpa laughed at what they

had to say, and that, after many threats, he ordered them to
be killed. He then pursued his road in a rich litter, carried
on the shoulders of his principal and favourite followers.

They say that Atahualpa entrusted the conduct of the war
to his Captain-General Chalcuchima, and to two other chiefs,
named Quizquiz and Ucumari.[1] As Atoc did not halt with
his army, they encountered him near the town called
Ambato, where the battle began, and was hotly contested.
Chalcuchima, having occupied a hill, came down with 5,000
chosen men, at an opportune moment, and attacked the tired
enemy, killing a great number, while the rest fled in confusion. They were pursued, and many were captured, including Atoc himself. Those who gave me this information say
that he was fastened to a post, where they killed him with
great cruelty. Chalcuchima made a drinking-cup out of his
skull, adorned with gold. The most correct estimate, in my
judgment, is that 15,000 or 16,000 men were killed in this
battle, on both sides. Those who were taken prisoners were
killed without mercy, by order of Atahualpa. I have passed
by this town of Ambato, where they say that the battle was
fought, and, judging from the number of bones, it would
appear that even more people were killed than they state.

With this victory Atahualpa remained in great renown.
The news was divulged in all parts of the kingdom. His
adherents were called together, and hailed him as Inca. He
said that he would assume the fringe at Tumebamba,
though, if this ceremony was not performed at Cuzco, it
was considered absurd and invalid. He ordered his wounded
to be cured, he was served as a king, and he marched to
Tumebamba.

[1] *Ucumari* means " a bear" in Quichua.

CHAPTER LXXIII.

How Huascar sent new captains and troops against his enemy, and how Atahualpa arrived at Tumebamba, where he perpetrated great cruelties; also what happened between him and the captains of Huascar.

FEW days elapsed after the Captain Atoc was defeated at Ambato, before the disaster was known, not only in Cuzco, but throughout the empire. Huascar was much alarmed, and from that time he feared that the end of the trouble might be fatal. His councillors decided that Cuzco should not be abandoned, but that a fresh army with new captains should take the field. But there were great lamentations for the dead, and sacrifices were offered up in the temples and to the oracles, according to custom. Huascar summoned many native chiefs of the Collao, of the Canchis, Canas, Charcas, Cavangas, those of Condesuyo, and many of those of Chincha-suyo. When they had assembled, he spoke to them of what his brother had done, and appealed to them to be good friends and companions. They answered as he desired, because they venerated the religious custom not to receive any one as Inca, except him who had assumed the fringe at Cuzco, which Huascar had done some days before. As it was necessary to arrange for the continuance of the war, the Inca appointed his brother, Huanca Auqui, to be his Captain-General. Some Orejones say that he was not a brother of the Inca, but a son of Ilaquito.[1] With him other principal chiefs were sent as captains, named Ahuapanti,[2] Urco Huaranca,. and Inca Rocca. These captains set out from

---

[1] Ylaquita, according to the Peruvian editor.

[2] Abaute in the manuscript, for which the Spanish editor suggests Ahuapanti.

Cuzco with all the soldiers they could collect, and accompanied by many native lords and *mitimaes*, and Huanca Auqui reinforced his army on the road, as he advanced. He marched in search of Atahualpa, who was at Tumebamba, with his captains and many principal men who had come to gain his favour, seeing that he was a conqueror. The Cañaris were afraid of Atahualpa, because they had imprisoned him and despised his commands, and they knew him to be vindictive and very blood-thirsty. When he came near the principal edifices, I heard from many Indians that, to appease his anger, they sent a great company of children, and another of men of all ages, to go forth to his richly-adorned litter, in which he travelled with great pomp, bearing green branches and palm leaves in their hands, and praying for grace and friendship, and that past injuries might be forgiven. They besought him with such clamour and with such humility, that it would have broken a heart of stone. But it made little impression on the cruel Atahualpa, for they say that he ordered his captains and soldiers to kill all who had come out to him, which was done, only sparing a few children and the women dedicated to the service of the temple, who were kept without shedding any of their blood, to preserve the honour of their deity the Sun.

This being done, he ordered some particular chiefs in the province to be killed, and placed a captain of his own to govern it. Assembling his principal adherents, he then assumed the fringe and took the title of Inca in Tumebamba, although the act was invalid, as has been explained, because it was not performed in Cuzco. However, he had the right of his arms, which he held to be good law. I have also heard from some Indians of position that Atahualpa assumed the fringe in Tumebamba before Atoc was defeated or even set out from Cuzco, and that Huascar knew it and provided accordingly. But on the whole it seems to me that the version I first wrote is the most probable.

Huanca Auqui made rapid marches, wishing to arrive at the country of the Cañaris before Atahualpa could do the harm which he actually did. Some of those who escaped from the battle of Ambato had joined him. All authorities affirm that he had with him more than 80,000 soldiers, and Atahualpa assembled little less at Tumebamba, whence he set out, declaring that he would not stop until he reached Cuzco. The two armies encountered each other in the province of the Paltas, near Caxabamba, and after the captains had addressed their troops, the battle began. They say that Atahualpa was not present; but that he witnessed the conflict from an adjacent hill. God was served in that, notwithstanding that there were many Orejones and captains well instructed in the art of war in the army of Huascar, and that Huanca Auqui did his duty like a loyal and good servant of the king, Atahualpa should be victorious, with the death of many of his adversaries. They declare that in both armies more than 35,000 were killed, besides many wounded.

The victors followed up the fugitives, killing and taking prisoners, and plundering the camp. Atahualpa was so joyful that he declared the gods were fighting for him. The reason he did not advance to Cuzco in person was that the Spaniards had entered the country a few days before, and that he had received the news of their arrival.[1]

We will not give the conclusion of this war between the Indians, because it would not be according to the order of events, and the narrative can wait for insertion in its proper place.

---

[1] The fullest account of the war between the two brothers is to be found in the narrative of Balboa. It is made interesting by a romantic love story, which is developed as the military record unfolds itself. There is another detailed account of the war given by Santa Cruz Pachacuti (see my Translation, pp. 111-119). The chapters devoted to it by Garcilasso de la Vega give less detail and are very prejudiced. On his own showing, he exaggerates the extent of the massacres at Cuzco (I, lib. ix, chapters 32 to 39).

Down to this point is what it has seemed well for me to write concerning the Incas, which is all derived from the account which I took down in Cuzco. If another should undertake to tell it more in detail and with greater accuracy the road is open to him. For I have not attempted what I was unable to perform; although for what I have done, I have worked in a way known to God, who lives and reigns for ever. Most of what I have written was seen by the Doctor Bravo de Saravia,[1] and the Licentiate Hernando de Santillan,[2] Judges of the Royal Audience of the city of the Kings.

[1] Melchor Bravo de Saravia was one of the judges who came out with the President Gasca. He was afterwards President of the Audience of Chile. After the departure of Gasca, he was, as President of the Audience, practically Governor of Peru from 1552, when the Viceroy Mendoza died, until 1556, when his successor, the Marquis of Cañete, arrived.

[2] Hernando de Santillan was a colleague of Bravo de Saravia. He wrote an account of the origin, lineage, and government of the Yncas, which was first printed at Madrid in 1879, edited by Don Marcos Ximénes de Espada.

INDEX.

NAMES OF PLACES AND TRIBES.

QUICHUA WORDS.

NAMES OF INDIANS AND GODS.

NAMES OF SPANIARDS.

GENERAL INDEX.